Hillcrest Edition

THE WRITINGS OF

MARK TWAIN

VOLUME XI

This is the authorized
Uniform Edition of all
my books.

Mark Twain

Laura coquetting with Mr. Buckstone

THE

GILDED AGE

A Tale of To-Day

BY

MARK TWAIN
(Samuel L. Clemens)

AND

CHARLES DUDLEY WARNER

IN TWO VOLUMES

VOL. II

NEW YORK AND LONDON
HARPER & BROTHERS PUBLISHERS
1906

ILLUSTRATIONS

PHOTOGRAVURE

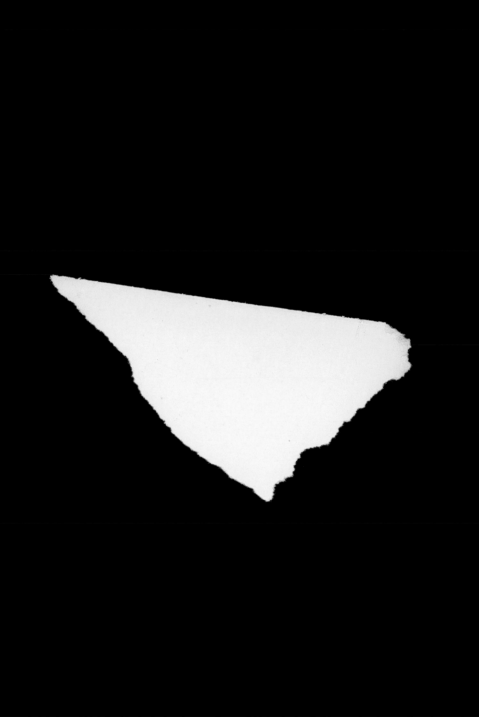

THE GILDED AGE

CHAPTER I.

LAURA'S SUCCESS IN WASHINGTON SOCIETY

Lo, swiche sleightes and subtiltees
In women ben; for ay as besy as bees
Ben they us sely men for to deceive,
And from a sothe wol they ever weive.*

Chaucer.

WASHINGTON'S delight in his beautiful sister was measureless. He said that she had always been the queenliest creature in the land, but that she was only commonplace before, compared to what she was now, so extraordinary was the improvement wrought by rich fashionable attire.

"But your criticisms are too full of brotherly partiality to be depended on, Washington. Other people will judge differently."

"Indeed they won't. You'll see. There will never be a woman in Washington that can compare with you. You'll be famous within a fortnight, Laura. Everybody will want to know you. You wait — you'll see."

Laura wished in her heart that the prophecy might

---

*See publishers' note, Volume I.

come true; and privately she even believed it might — for she had brought all the women whom she had seen since she left home under sharp inspection, and the result had not been unsatisfactory to her.

During a week or two Washington drove about the city every day with her and familiarized her with all of its salient features. She was beginning to feel very much at home with the town itself, and she was also fast acquiring ease with the distinguished people she met at the Dilworthy table, and losing what little of country timidity she had brought with her from Hawkeye. She noticed with secret pleasure the little start of admiration that always manifested itself in the faces of the guests when she entered the drawing-room arrayed in evening costume ; she took comforting note of the fact that these guests directed a very liberal share of their conversation toward her; she observed with surprise, that famous statesmen and soldiers did not talk like gods, as a general thing, but said rather commonplace things for the most part; and she was filled with gratification to discover that she, on the contrary, was making a good many shrewd speeches and now and then a really brilliant one, and, furthermore, that they were beginning to be repeated in social circles about the town.

Congress began its sittings, and every day or two Washington escorted her to the galleries set apart for lady members of the households of Senators and Representatives. Here was a larger field and a wider competition, but still she saw that many eyes were uplifted toward her face, and that first one person and then another called a neighbor's attention to her; she was not too dull to perceive that the speeches of some of the younger statesmen were delivered about as much and perhaps more at her than to the presiding officer; and she was not sorry to see that the dapper young Senator from Iowa came at once and stood in the open space before the president's desk to exhibit his feet as soon as she entered the gallery, whereas she had early learned from common report that his usual custom was to prop them on his desk and enjoy them himself with a selfish disregard of other people's longings.

Invitations began to flow in upon her, and soon she was fairly " in society." " The season " was now in full bloom, and the first select reception was at hand — that is to say, a reception confined to invited guests.

Senator Dilworthy had become well convinced, by this time, that his judgment of the country-bred Missouri girl had not deceived him — it was plain that she was going to be a peerless missionary in the field of labor he designed her for, and therefore it would be perfectly safe and likewise judicious to send her forth well panoplied for her work. So he had added new and still richer costumes to her wardrobe, and assisted their attractions with costly jewelry — loans on the future land sale.

This first select reception took place at a cabinet

minister's — or, rather, a cabinet secretary's — mansion. When Laura and the Senator arrived, about half past nine or ten in the evening, the place was already pretty well crowded, and the white-gloved negro servant at the door was still receiving streams of guests. The drawing-rooms were brilliant with gaslight, and as hot as ovens. The host and hostess stood just within the door of entrance. Laura was presented, and then she passed on into the maelstrom of bejeweled and richly attired low-necked ladies and white-kid-gloved and steel - pen - coated gentlemen; and wherever she moved she was followed by a buzz of admiration that was grateful to all her senses — so grateful, indeed, that her white face was tinged and its beauty heightened by a perceptible suffusion of color. She caught such remarks as, "Who is she?" "Superb woman!" "That is the new beauty from the West," etc., etc.

Whenever she halted, she was presently surrounded by Ministers, Generals, Congressmen, and all manner of aristocratic people. Introductions followed, and then the usual original question, "How do you like Washington, Miss Hawkins?" supplemented by that other usual original question, "Is this your first visit?"

These two exciting topics being exhausted, conversation generally drifted into calmer channels, only to be interrupted at frequent intervals by new introductions and new inquiries as to how Laura liked the capital and whether it was her first visit or not. And thus for an hour or more the Duchess moved through the crush in a rapture of happiness, for her doubts were dead and gone, now — she knew she could conquer here. A familiar face appeared in the midst of the multitude, and Harry Brierly fought his difficult way to her side, his eyes shouting their gratification, so to speak:

"Oh, this *is* a happiness! Tell me, my dear Miss Hawkins——"

"Sh! I know what you are going to ask. I *do* like Washington — I like it ever so much!"

"No, but I was going to ask——"

"Yes, I am coming to it, coming to it as fast as I can. It *is* my first visit. I think you should know that yourself."

And straightway a wave of the crowd swept her beyond his reach.

"Now what can the girl mean? Of course she likes Washington — I'm not such a dummy as to have to ask her that. And as to its being her first visit, why! hang it, she knows that I *knew* it was. Does she think I have turned idiot? Curious girl, anyway. But how they do swarm about her! She is the reigning belle of Washington after this night. She'll know five hundred of the heaviest guns in the town before this night's nonsense is over. And this isn't even the beginning. Just as I used to say — she'll be a card in the matter of — yes, *sir!* She shall turn the men's heads and I'll turn the women's! What a team that will be in politics here. I wouldn't

take a quarter of a million for what I can do in this
present session — no, indeed, I wouldn't. Now,
here — I don't altogether like this. That insignifi-
cant secretary of legation is — why, she's smiling on
him as if he — and now on the Admiral! Now she's
illuminating that stuffy Congressman from Massachusetts — vulgar, ungrammatical shovel-maker —
greasy knave of spades. I don't like this sort of
thing. She doesn't appear to be much distressed
about *me* — she hasn't looked this way once. All
right, my bird of Paradise, if it suits you, go on.
But I think I know your sex. *I'll* go to smiling
around a little, too, and see what effect *that* will have
on you."

And he did "smile around a little," and got as
near to her as he could to watch the effect, but the
scheme was a failure — he could not get her attention. She seemed wholly unconscious of him, and
so he could not flirt with any spirit; he could only
talk disjointedly; he could not keep his eyes on the
charmers he talked to; he grew irritable, jealous,
and very unhappy. He gave up his enterprise,
leaned his shoulder against a fluted pilaster and
pouted while he kept watch upon Laura's every
movement. His other shoulder stole the bloom
from many a lovely cheek that brushed him in the
surging crush, but he noted it not. He was too
busy cursing himself inwardly for being an egotistical
imbecile. An hour ago he had thought to take this
country lass under his protection and show her

" life " and enjoy her wonder and delight — and here she was, immersed in the marvel up to her eyes, and just a trifle more at home in it than he was himself. And now his angry comments ran on again :

" Now she's sweetening old Brother Balaam ; and he — well, he is inviting her to the Congressional prayer-meeting, no doubt — better let old Dilworthy alone to see that she doesn't overlook that. And now its Splurge of New York ; and now its Batters of New Hampshire — and now the Vice-President ! Well, I may as well adjourn. I've got enough."

But he hadn't. He got as far as the door — and then struggled back to take one more look, hating himself all the while for his weakness.

Toward midnight, when supper was announced, the crowd thronged to the supper room, where a long table was decked out with what seemed a rare repast, but which consisted of things better calculated to feast the eye than the appetite. The ladies were soon seated in files along the wall, and in groups here and there, and the colored waiters filled the plates and glasses, and the male guests moved hither and thither conveying them to the privileged sex.

Harry took an ice and stood up by the table with other gentlemen, and listened to the buzz of conversation while he ate.

From these remarks he learned a good deal about Laura that was news to him. For instance, that she

was of a distinguished Western family; that she was
highly educated; that she was very rich and a great
landed heiress; that she was not a professor of
religion, and yet was a Christian in the truest and
best sense of the word, for her whole heart was devoted to the accomplishment of a great and noble
enterprise — none other than the sacrificing of her
landed estates to the uplifting of the down-trodden
negro and the turning of his erring feet into the way
of light and righteousness. Harry observed that as
soon as one listener had absorbed the story, he
turned about and delivered it to his next neighbor,
and the latter individual straightway passed it on.
And thus he saw it travel the round of the gentlemen and overflow rearward among the ladies. He
could not trace it backward to its fountain-head, and
so he could not tell who it was that started it.

One thing annoyed Harry a great deal; and that
was the reflection that he might have been in
Washington days and days ago and thrown his
fascinations about Laura with permanent effect while
she was new and strange to the capital, instead of
dawdling in Philadelphia to no purpose. He feared
he had " missed a trick," as he expressed it.

He only found one little opportunity of speaking
again with Laura before the evening's festivities
ended, and then, for the first time in years, his airy
self-complacency failed him, his tongue's easy confidence forsook it in a great measure, and he was
conscious of an unheroic timidity. He was glad to

get away and find a place where he could despise himself in private and try to grow his clipped plumes again.

When Laura reached home she was tired but exultant, and Senator Dilworthy was pleased and satisfied. He called Laura " my daughter," next morning, and gave her some " pin money," as he termed it, and she sent a hundred and fifty dollars of it to her mother and loaned a trifle to Colonel Sellers. Then the Senator had a long private conference with Laura, and unfolded certain plans of his for the good of the country, and religion, and the poor, and temperance, and showed her how she could assist him in developing these worthy and noble enterprises.

2**

CHAPTER II.

— Itancan Ihduhomni eciyapi, Itancan Tohanokihi-eca eciyapi, Itancan Iapiwaxte eciyapi, he hunkakewicaye cin etanhan otonwe kin caxtonpi; nakun Akicita Wicaxta-ceji-skuya, Akicita Anogite, Akicita Taku-kaxta —

> þe richeste wifmen alle: þat were in londe,
> and þere hehere monnen dohtere. . . .
> þere wes moni pal hende: on faire þā uolke.
> þar was mochel honde: of manicunnes londe,
> for ech wende to beon: betere þan oþer.
>
> *Layamon.*

LAURA soon discovered that there were three distinct aristocracies in Washington. One of these (nicknamed the Antiques), consisted of cultivated, high-bred old families who looked back with pride upon an ancestry that had been always great in the nation's councils and its wars from the birth of the republic downward. Into this select circle it was difficult to gain admission. No. 2 was the aristocracy of the middle ground — of which, more anon. No. 3 lay beyond; of it we will say a word here. We will call it the Aristocracy of the Parvenus — as, indeed, the general public did. Official

(14)

position, no matter how obtained, entitled a man to a place in it, and carried his family with him, no matter whence they sprang. Great wealth gave a man a still higher and nobler place in it than did official position. If this wealth had been acquired by conspicuous ingenuity, with just a pleasant little spice of illegality about it, all the better. This aristocracy was "fast," and not averse to ostentation. The aristocracy of the Antiques ignored the aristocracy of the Parvenus; the Parvenus laughed at the Antiques (and secretly envied them).

There were certain important "society" customs which one in Laura's position needed to understand. For instance, when a lady of any prominence comes to one of our cities and takes up her residence, all the ladies of her grade favor her in turn with an initial call, giving their cards to the servant at the door by way of introduction. They come singly, sometimes; sometimes in couples; — and always in elaborate full dress. They talk two minutes and a quarter and then go. If the lady receiving the call desires a further acquaintance, she must return the visit within two weeks; to neglect it beyond that time means "let the matter drop." But if she does return the visit within two weeks, it then becomes the other party's privilege to continue the acquaintance or drop it. She signifies her willingness to continue it by calling again any time within twelve months; after that, if the parties go on calling upon each other once a year, in our large cities, that is sufficient, and the acquaintanceship holds good. The thing goes along smoothly, now. The annual visits are made and returned with peaceful regularity and bland satisfaction, although it is not necessary that the two ladies shall actually *see* each other oftener than once every few years. Their cards preserve the intimacy and keep the acquaintanceship intact.

For instance, Mrs. A. pays her annual visit, sits in her carriage and sends in her card with the lower right-hand corner turned down, which signifies that she has " called in person;" Mrs. B. sends down word that she is " engaged " or " wishes to be excused "— or if she is a Parvenu and low-bred, she perhaps sends word that she is " not at home." Very good; Mrs. A. drives on happy and content. If Mrs. A.'s daughter marries, or a child is born to the family, Mrs. B. calls, sends in her card with the upper left-hand corner turned down, and then goes along about her affairs — for that inverted corner means " Congratulations." If Mrs. B.'s husband falls down stairs and breaks his neck, Mrs. A. calls, leaves her card with the upper right-hand corner turned down, and then takes her departure; this corner means " Condolence." It is very necessary to get the corners right, else one may unintentionally condole with a friend on a wedding or congratulate her upon a funeral. If either lady is about to leave the city, she goes to the other's house and leaves her card with " P. P. C." engraved under the name — which signifies, " Pay Parting Call." But enough of etiquette. Laura was early instructed in the mysteries of society life by a competent mentor, and thus was preserved from troublesome mistakes.

The first fashionable call she received from a member of the ancient nobility, otherwise the Antiques, was of a pattern with all she received from that limb of the aristocracy afterward. This call was paid by Mrs. Major-General Fulke-Fulkerson and daughter. They drove up at one in the afternoon in a rather antiquated vehicle with a faded coat of arms on the panels, an aged white-wooled negro coachman on the box and a younger darkey beside him — the footman. Both of these servants were dressed in dull brown livery that had seen considerable service.

The ladies entered the drawing-room in full character; that is to say, with Elizabethan stateliness on the part of the dowager, and an easy grace and dignity on the part of the young lady that had a nameless something about it that suggested conscious superiority. The dresses of both ladies were exceedingly rich as to material, but as notably modest as to color and ornament. All parties having seated themselves, the dowager delivered herself of a remark that was not unusual in its form, and yet it came from her lips with the impressiveness of Scripture:

"The weather has been unpropitious of late, Miss Hawkins."

"It has, indeed," said Laura. "The climate seems to be variable."

2

"It is its nature of old, here," said the daughter — stating it apparently as a fact, only, and by her manner waving aside all personal responsibility on account of it. "Is it not so, mamma?"

"Quite so, my child. Do you like winter, Miss Hawkins?" She said "like" as if she had an idea that its dictionary meaning was "approve of."

"Not as well as summer—though I think all seasons have their charms."

"It is a very just remark. The general held similar views. He considered snow in winter proper; sultriness in summer legitimate; frosts in the autumn the same, and rains in spring not objectionable. He was not an exacting man. And I call to mind now that he always admired thunder. You remember, child, your father always admired thunder?"

"He adored it."

"No doubt it reminded him of battle," said Laura.

"Yes, I think perhaps it did. He had a great respect for Nature. He often said there was something striking about the ocean. You remember his saying that, daughter?"

"Yes, often, mother. I remember it very well."

"And hurricanes. He took a great interest in hurricanes. And animals. Dogs, especially — hunting dogs. Also comets. I think we all have our predilections. I think it is this that gives variety to our tastes." Laura coincided with this view. "Do you find it hard and lonely to be so far from your home and friends, Miss Hawkins?"

"I do find it depressing sometimes, but then there is so much about me here that is novel and interesting that my days are made up more of sunshine than shadow."

"Washington is not a dull city in the season," said the young lady. "We have some very good society indeed, and one need not be at a loss for means to pass the time pleasantly. Are you fond of watering places, Miss Hawkins?"

"I have really had no experience of them, but I have always felt a strong desire to see something of fashionable watering-place life."

"We of Washington are unfortunately situated in that respect," said the dowager. "It is a tedious distance to Newport. But there is no help for it."

Laura said to herself, "Long Branch and Cape May are nearer than Newport; doubtless these places are low; I'll feel my way a little and see." Then she said aloud:

"Why, I thought that Long Branch——"

There was no need to "feel" any further — there was that in both faces before her which made that truth apparent. The dowager said:

"Nobody goes *there*, Miss Hawkins — at least, only persons of no position in society. And the President." She added that with tranquillity.

"Newport is damp, and cold, and windy, and excessively disagreeable," said the daughter, "but it is very select. One cannot be fastidious about minor matters when one has no choice."

B

The visit had spun out nearly three minutes, now. Both ladies rose with grave dignity, conferred upon Laura a formal invitation to call, and then retired from the conference. Laura remained in the drawing-room and left them to pilot themselves out of the house — an inhospitable thing, it seemed to her, but then she was following her instructions. She stood, steeped in reverie, a while, and then she said:

"I think I could always enjoy icebergs — as scenery — but not as company."

Still, she knew these two people by reputation, and was aware that they were not icebergs when they were in their own waters and amid their legitimate surroundings, but on the contrary were people to be respected for their stainless characters and esteemed for their social virtues and their benevolent impulses. She thought it a pity that they had to be such changed and dreary creatures on occasions of state.

The first call Laura received from the other extremity of the Washington aristocracy followed close upon the heels of the one we have just been describing. The callers this time were the Hon. Mrs. Oliver Higgins, the Hon. Mrs. Patrique Oreillé (pronounced O-re*lay*), Miss Bridget (pronounced Breezhay) Oreillé, Mrs. Peter Gashly, Miss Gashly, and Miss Emmeline Gashly.

The three carriages arrived at the same moment from different directions. They were new and wonderfully shiny, and the brasses on the harness were

highly polished and bore complicated monograms.
There were showy coats of arms, too, with Latin
mottoes. The coachmen and footmen were clad in
bright new livery, of striking colors, and they had
black rosettes with shaving-brushes projecting above
them, on the sides of their stove-pipe hats.

When the visitors swept into the drawing-room
they filled the place with a suffocating sweetness
procured at the perfumer's. Their costumes, as to
architecture, were the latest fashion intensified; they
were rainbow-hued; they were hung with jewels —
chiefly diamonds. It would have been plain to any
eye that it had cost something to upholster these
women.

The Hon. Mrs. Oliver Higgins was the wife of a
delegate from a distant Territory — a gentleman who
had kept the principal " saloon," and sold the best
whisky in the principal village in his wilderness, and
so, of course, was recognized as the first man of his
commonwealth and its fittest representative. He
was a man of paramount influence at home, for he
was public-spirited, he was chief of the fire department, he had an admirable command of profane
language, and had killed several " parties." His
shirt fronts were always immaculate; his boots
daintily polished, and no man could lift a foot and
fire a dead shot at a stray speck of dirt on it with a
white handkerchief with a finer grace than he; his
watch chain weighed a pound; the gold in his finger
ring was worth forty-five dollars; he wore a dia-

mond cluster-pin, and he parted his hair behind. He had always been regarded as the most elegant gentleman in his Territory, and it was conceded by all that no man thereabouts was anywhere near his equal in the telling of an obscene story, except the venerable white-haired governor himself. The Hon. Higgins had not come to serve his country in Washington for nothing. The appropriation which he had engineered through Congress for the maintenance of the Indians in his Territory would have made all those savages rich if it had ever got to them.

The Hon. Mrs. Higgins was a picturesque woman, and a fluent talker, and she held a tolerably high station among the Parvenus. Her English was fair enough, as a general thing — though, being of New York origin, she had the fashion peculiar to many natives of that city of pronouncing saw and law as if they were spelled sawr and lawr.

Petroleum was the agent that had suddenly transformed the Gashlys from modest hard-working country village folk into "loud" aristocrats and ornaments of the city.

The Hon. Patrique Oreillé was a wealthy Frenchman from Cork. Not that he was wealthy when he first came from Cork, but just the reverse. When he first landed in New York with his wife, he had only halted at Castle Garden for a few minutes to receive and exhibit papers showing that he had resided in this country two years — and then he voted the democratic ticket and went up town to hunt a

house.   He found one, and then went to work as
assistant to an architect and builder, carrying a hod
all day and studying politics evenings.   Industry
and economy soon enabled him to start a low rum
shop in a foul locality, and this gave him political
influence.   In our country it is always our first care
to see that our people have the opportunity of
voting for their choice of men to represent and
govern them — we do not permit our great officials
to appoint the little officials.   We prefer to have so
tremendous a power as that in our own hands.   We
hold it safest to elect our judges and everybody else.
In our cities, the ward meetings elect delegates to
the nominating conventions and instruct them whom
to nominate.   The publicans and their retainers rule
the ward meetings (for everybody else hates the
worry of politics and stays at home) ; the delegates
from the ward meetings organize as a nominating
convention and make up a list of candidates — one
convention offering a democratic and another a
republican list of — incorruptibles; and then the
great meek public come forward at the proper time
and make unhampered choice and bless Heaven that
they live in a free land where no form of despotism
can ever intrude.

Patrick O'Riley (as his name then stood) created
friends and influence very fast, for he was always on
hand at the police courts to give straw bail for his
customers or establish an *alibi* for them in case they
had been beating anybody to death on his premises.

Consequently, he presently became a political leader, and was elected to a petty office under the city government. Out of a meager salary he soon saved money enough to open quite a stylish liquor saloon higher up town, with a faro bank attached and plenty of capital to conduct it with. This gave him fame and great respectability. The position of alderman was forced upon him, and it was just the same as presenting him a gold mine. He had fine horses and carriages, now, and closed up his whisky mill.

By and by he became a large contractor for city work, and was a bosom friend of the great and good Wm. M. Weed himself, who had stolen $20,000,000 from the city and was a man so envied, so honored, so adored, indeed, that when the sheriff went to his office to arrest him as a felon, that sheriff blushed and apologized, and one of the illustrated papers made a picture of the scene and spoke of the matter in such a way as to show that the editor regretted that the offense of an arrest had been offered to so exalted a personage as Mr. Weed.

Mr. O'Riley furnished shingle nails to the new court-house at three thousand dollars a keg, and eighteen gross of 60-cent thermometers at fifteen hundred dollars a dozen; the controller and the board of audit passed the bills, and a mayor, who was simply ignorant but not criminal, signed them. When they were paid, Mr. O'Riley's admirers gave him a solitaire diamond pin of the size of a filbert, in imitation of the liberality of Mr. Weed's friends, and then Mr. O'Riley retired from active service and amused himself with buying real estate at enormous figures and holding it in other people's names. By and by the newspapers came out with exposures and called Weed and O'Riley "thieves" — whereupon the people rose as one man (voting repeatedly) and elected the two gentlemen to their proper theater of action, the New York legislature. The newspapers clamored, and the courts proceeded to try the new legislators for their small irregularities. Our admirable jury system enabled the persecuted ex-officials to secure a jury of nine gentlemen from a neighboring asylum and three graduates from Sing Sing, and presently they walked forth with characters vindicated. The legislature was called upon to spew them forth — a thing which the legislature declined to do. It was like asking children to repudiate their own father. It was a legislature of the modern pattern.

Being now wealthy and distinguished, Mr. O'Reily, still bearing the legislative "Hon." attached to his name (for titles never die in America, although we *do* take a republican pride in poking fun at such trifles), sailed for Europe with his family. They traveled all about, turning their noses up at everything, and not finding it a difficult thing to do, either, because nature had originally given those features a cast in that direction; and finally they established themselves in Paris, that Paradise of

Americans of their sort. They stayed there two years and learned to speak English with a foreign accent — not that it hadn't always had a foreign accent (which was indeed the case), but now the nature of it was changed. Finally they returned home and became ultra-fashionables. They landed here as the Hon. Patrique Oreillé and family, and so are known unto this day.

Laura provided seats for her visitors, and they immediately launched forth into a breezy, sparkling conversation with that easy confidence which is to be found only among persons accustomed to high life.

"I've been intending to call sooner, Miss Hawkins," said the Hon. Mrs. Oreillé, "but the weather's been *so* horrid. How do you like Washington?"

Laura liked it very well, indeed.

Mrs. Gashly — "Is it your first visit?"

Yes, it was her first.

All — "Indeed?"

Mrs. Oreillé — "I'm afraid you'll despise the weather, Miss Hawkins. It's perfectly awful. It always is. I tell Mr. Oreillé I can't and I won't put up with any such a climate. If we were obliged to do it, I wouldn't mind it; but we are *not* obliged to, and so I don't see the use of it. Sometimes it's real pitiful the way the childern pine for Parry — don't look *so* sad, Bridget, *ma chère* — poor child, she can't hear Parry mentioned without getting the blues."

Mrs. Gashly — "Well, I should think so, Mrs.

Oreillé. A body *lives* in Paris, but a body only *stays* here. I dote on Paris; I'd druther scrimp along on ten thousand dollars a year there, than suffer and worry here on a real decent income.''

Miss Gashly —'' Well, then I wish you'd take us back, mother; I'm sure *I* hate this stoopid country enough, even if it *is* our dear native land.''

Miss Emmeline Gashly —'' What, and leave poor Johnny Peterson behind?'' [An airy general laugh applauded this sally.]

Miss Gashly —'' Sister, I should think you'd be ashamed of yourself!''

Miss Emmeline —'' Oh, you needn't ruffle your feathers so. I was only joking. He don't mean anything by coming to the house every evening — only comes to see mother. Of course, that's all!'' [General laughter.]

Miss G., prettily confused —'' Emmeline, how *can* you!''

Mrs. G. — '' Let your sister alone, Emmeline. I never saw such a tease!''

Mrs. Oreillé — '' What lovely corals you have, Miss Hawkins! Just look at them, Bridget, dear. I've a great passion for corals — it's a pity they're getting a little common. I have some elegant ones — not as elegant as yours, though — but of course I don't wear them now.''

Laura —'' I suppose they are rather common, but still I have a great affection for these, because they were given to me by a dear old friend of our family named Murphy. He was a very charming man, but very eccentric. We always supposed he was an Irishman, but after he got rich he went abroad for a year or two, and when he came back you would have been amused to see how interested he was in a potato. He asked what it was! Now you know that when Providence shapes a mouth especially for the accommodation of a potato you can detect that fact at a glance when that mouth is in repose — foreign travel can never remove *that* sign. But he was a very delightful gentleman, and his little foible did not hurt him at all. We all have our shams — I suppose there is a sham somewhere about every individual, if we could manage to ferret it out. I would so like to go to France. I suppose our society here compares very favorably with French society, does it not, Mrs. Oreillé?"

Mrs. O.—"Not by any means, Miss Hawkins! French society is much more elegant — much more so."

Laura—"I am sorry to hear that. I suppose ours has deteriorated of late."

Mrs. O.—"Very much, indeed. There are people in society here that have really no more money to live on than what some of us pay for servant hire. Still, I won't say but what some of them are very good people — and respectable, too."

Laura—"The old families seem to be holding themselves aloof, from what I hear. I suppose you seldom meet in society now the people you used to be familiar with twelve or fifteen years ago?"

Mrs. O.—" Oh, no — hardly ever."

Mr. O'Riley kept his first rum-mill and protected his customers from the law in those days, and this turn of the conversation was rather uncomfortable to madame than otherwise.

Hon. Mrs. Higgins—" Is François' health good now, Mrs. Oreillé?"

Mrs. O. (*Thankful for the intervention*) —" Not very. A body couldn't expect it. He was always delicate — especially his lungs — and this odious climate tells on him strong, now, after Parry, which is so mild."

Mrs. H.—" I should think so. Husband says Percy'll die if he don't have a change; and so I'm going to swap round a little and see what can be done. I saw a lady from Florida last week, and she recommended Key West. I told her Percy couldn't abide winds, as he was threatened with a pulmonary affection, and then she said try St. Augustine. It's an awful distance — ten or twelve hundred mile, they say — but then in a case of this kind a body can't stand back for trouble, you know."

Mrs. O.—" No, of course, that's so. If François don't get better soon we've got to look out for some other place, or else Europe. We've thought some of the Hot Springs, but I don't know. It's a great responsibility and a body wants to go cautious. Is Hildebrand about again, Mrs. Gashly?"

3**

Mrs. G.—"Yes, but that's about all. It was indigestion, you know, and it looks as if it was chronic. And you know I do dread dyspepsia. We've all been worried a good deal about him. The doctor recommended baked apple and spoiled meat, and I think it done him good. It's about the only thing that will stay on his stomach nowadays. We have Dr. Shovel now. Who's your doctor, Mrs. Higgins?"

Mrs. H.—"Well, we had Dr. Spooner a good while, but he runs so much to emetics, which I think are weakening, that we changed off and took Dr. Leathers. We like him very much. He has a fine European reputation, too. The first thing he suggested for Percy was to have him taken out in the back yard for an airing, every afternoon, with nothing at all on."

Mrs. O. and Mrs. G.—"What!"

Mrs. H.—"As true as I'm sitting here. And it actually helped him for two or three days; it did indeed. But after that the doctor said it seemed to be too severe, and so he has fell back on hot foot-baths at night and cold showers in the morning. But I don't think there can be any good sound help for him in such a climate as this. I believe we are going to lose him if we don't make a change."

Mrs. O.—"I suppose you heard of the fright we had two weeks ago last Saturday? No? Why, that is strange — but come to remember, you've all been away to Richmond. François tumbled from the skylight in the second-story hall clean down to the first floor ——"

Everybody —" Mercy ! "

Mrs. O.—" Yes indeed — and broke two of his ribs ——"

Everybody — " What ! "

Mrs. O.—" Just as true as you live. First we though he must be injured internally. It was fifteen minutes past eight in the evening. Of course we were all distracted in a moment — everybody was flying everywhere, and nobody doing anything *worth* anything. By and by I flung out next door and dragged in Dr. Sprague, president of the Medical University — no time to go for our own doctor, of course — and the minute he saw François he said, ' Send for your own physician, madam ' —said it as cross as a bear, too, and turned right on his heel and cleared out without doing a thing ! "

Everybody — " The mean, contemptible brute ! "

Mrs. O.— " Well you may say it. I was nearly out of my wits by this time. But we hurried off the servants after our own doctor and telegraphed mother — she was in New York and rushed down on the first train; and when the doctor got there, lo and behold you he found François had broke one of his legs, too ! "

Everybody —" Goodness ! "

Mrs. O.—" Yes. So he set his leg and bandaged it up, and fixed his ribs and gave him a dose of something to quiet down his excitement and put

him to sleep — poor thing he was trembling and
frightened to death and it was pitiful to see him.
We had him in my bed — Mr. Oreillé slept in the
guest room and I laid down beside François — but
not to sleep — bless you no. Bridget and I set up
all night, and the doctor stayed till two in the
morning, bless his old heart. When mother got
there she was so used up with anxiety that she had
to go to bed and have the doctor; but when she
found that François was not in immediate danger she
rallied, and by night she was able to take a watch
herself. Well, for three days and nights we three
never left that bedside only to take an hour's nap at
a time. And then the doctor said François was out
of danger, and if ever there was a thankful set, in
this world, it was us.''

Laura's respect for these women had augmented
during this conversation, naturally enough; affection
and devotion are qualities that are able to adorn
and render beautiful a character that is otherwise
unattractive, and even repulsive.

Mrs. Gashly —'' I do believe I should a died if I
had been in your place, Mrs. Oreillé. The time
Hildebrand was so low with the pneumonia Emmeline and me were all alone with him most of the time,
and we never took a minute's sleep for as much as
two days and nights. It was at Newport, and we
wouldn't trust hired nurses. One afternoon he had
a fit, and jumped up and run out on the portico of
the hotel with nothing in the world on and the wind

a blowing like ice and we after him scared to death; and when the ladies and gentlemen saw that he had a fit, every lady scattered for her room and not a gentleman lifted his hand to help, the wretches! Well, after that his life hung by a thread for as much as ten days, and the minute he was out of danger Emmeline and me just went to bed sick and worn out. *I* never want to pass through such a time again. Poor dear François — which leg did he break, Mrs. Oreillé?''

Mrs. O.—'' It was his right-hand hind leg. Jump down, François dear, and show the ladies what a cruel limp you've got yet.''

François demurred, but being coaxed and delivered gently upon the floor, he performed very satisfactorily, with his '' right-hand hind leg '' in the air. All were affected — even Laura — but hers was an affection of the stomach. The country-bred girl had not suspected that the little whining ten-ounce black and tan reptile, clad in a red embroidered pigmy blanket and reposing in Mrs. Oreillé's lap all through the visit, was the individual whose sufferings had been stirring the dormant generosities of her nature. She said:

'' Poor little creature! You might have lost him!''

Mrs. O.—'' Oh pray don't mention it, Miss Hawkins — it gives me such a turn!''

Laura —'' And Hildebrand and Percy — are they — are they like this one?''

3

Mrs. G.—"No, Hilly has considerable Skye blood in him, I believe."

Mrs. H.—"Percy's the same, only he is two months and ten days older and has his ears cropped. His father, Martin Farquhar Tupper, was sickly, and died young, but he was the sweetest disposition. His mother had heart disease, but was very gentle and resigned, and a wonderful ratter."*

So carried away had the visitors become by their interest attaching to this discussion of family matters, that their stay had been prolonged to a very improper and unfashionable length; but they suddenly recollected themselves now and took their departure.

Laura's scorn was boundless. The more she thought of these people and their extraordinary talk, the more offensive they seemed to her; and yet she confessed that if one must choose between the two extreme aristocracies it might be best, on the whole, looking at things from a strictly business point of view, to herd with the Parvenus; she was in Washington solely to compass a certain matter and to do it at any cost, and these people might be useful to her, while it was plain that her purposes and her schemes for pushing them would not find favor in the eyes of the Antiques. If it came to choice—

---

* As impossible and exasperating as this conversation may sound to a person who is not an idiot, it is scarcely in any respect an exaggeration of one which one of us actually listened to in an American drawing-room; otherwise we could not venture to put such a chapter into a book which professes to deal with social possibilities.—THE AUTHORS.

and it might come to that, sooner or later — she believed she could come to a decision without much difficulty or many pangs.

But the best aristocracy of the three Washington castes, and really the most powerful, by far, was that of the Middle Ground. It was made up of the families of public men from nearly every state in the Union — men who held positions in both the executive and legislative branches of the government, and whose characters had been for years blemishless, both at home and at the capital. These gentlemen and their households were unostentatious people; they were educated and refined; they troubled themselves but little about the two other orders of nobility, but moved serenely in their wide orbit, confident in their own strength and well aware of the potency of their influence. They had no troublesome appearances to keep up, no rivalries which they cared to distress themselves about, no jealousies to fret over. They could afford to mind their own affairs and leave other combinations to do the same or do otherwise, just as they chose. They were people who were beyond reproach, and that was sufficient.

Senator Dilworthy never came into collision with any of these factions. He labored for them all and with them all. He said that all men were brethren and all were entitled to the honest, unselfish help and countenance of a Christian laborer in the public vineyard.

c

Laura concluded, after reflection, to let circumstances determine the course it might be best for her
to pursue as regarded the several aristocracies.

Now, it might occur to the reader that perhaps
Laura had been somewhat rudely suggestive in her
remarks to Mrs. Oreillé when the subject of corals
was under discussion, but it did not occur to Laura
herself. She was not a person of exaggerated refinement; indeed, the society and the influences that
had formed her character had not been of a nature
calculated to make her so; she thought that "give
and take was fair play," and that to parry an offensive thrust with a sarcasm was a neat and legitimate
thing to do. She sometimes talked to people in a
way which some ladies would consider actually
shocking; but Laura rather prided herself upon
some of her exploits of that character. We are
sorry we cannot make her a faultless heroine; but
we cannot, for the reason that she was human.

She considered herself a superior conversationist.
Long ago, when the possibility had first been brought
before her mind that some day she might move in
Washington society, she had recognized the fact that
practiced conversational powers would be a necessary
weapon in that field; she had also recognized the
fact that since her dealings there must be mainly
with men, and men whom she supposed to be ex-
ceptionally cultivated and able, she would need
heavier shot in her magazine than mere brilliant
"society" nothings; whereupon she had at once

entered upon a tireless and elaborate course of reading, and had never since ceased to devote every unoccupied moment to this sort of preparation. Having now acquired a happy smattering of various information, she used it with good effect — she passed for a singularly well-informed woman in Washington. The quality of her literary tastes had necessarily undergone constant improvement under this regimen, and as necessarily, also, the quality of her language had improved, though it cannot be denied that now and then her former condition of life betrayed itself in just perceptible inelegancies of expression and lapses of grammar.

CHAPTER III.

LAURA IN THE LOBBY

Eet Jomfru Haar drager stærkere end ti Par Öxen.

WHEN Laura had been in Washington three months, she was still the same person, in one respect, that she was when she first arrived there — that is to say, she still bore the name of Laura Hawkins. Otherwise she was perceptibly changed.

She had arrived in a state of grievous uncertainty as to what manner of woman she was, physically and intellectually, as compared with Eastern women; she was well satisfied, now, that her beauty was confessed, her mind a grade above the average, and her powers of fascination rather extraordinary. So she was at ease upon those points. When she arrived, she was possessed of habits of economy and not possessed of money; now she dressed elaborately, gave but little thought to the cost of things, and was very well fortified financially. She kept her mother and Washington freely supplied with money, and did the same by Colonel Sellers — who always insisted upon

(38)

giving his note for loans — with interest: he was
rigid upon that; she *must* take interest; and one of
the Colonel's greatest satisfactions was to go over
his accounts and note what a handsome sum this
accruing interest amounted to, and what a comfortable though modest support it would yield Laura in
case reverses should overtake her.   In truth, he could
not help feeling that he was an efficient shield for
her against poverty; and so, if her expensive ways
ever troubled him for a brief moment, he presently
dismissed the thought and said to himself, " Let her
go on — even if she loses everything she is still safe
— this interest will always afford her a good easy
income."

Laura was on excellent terms with a great many
members of Congress, and there was an undercurrent
of suspicion in some quarters that she was one of
that detested class known as " lobbyists "; but what
belle could escape slander in such a city?   Fair-
minded people declined to condemn her on mere
suspicion, and so the injurious talk made no very
damaging headway.   She was very gay, now, and
very celebrated, and she might well expect to be assailed by many kinds of gossip.   She was growing
used to celebrity, and could already sit calm and
seemingly unconscious, under the fire of fifty lorg-
nettes in a theater, or even overhear the low voice
" That's she !" as she passed along the street without betraying anoyance.

The whole air was full of a vague vast scheme

which was to eventuate in filling Laura's pockets
with millions of money; some had one idea of the
scheme, and some another, but nobody had any
exact knowledge upon the subject. All that any one
felt sure about was, that Laura's landed estates were
princely in value and extent, and that the government was anxious to get hold of them for public
purposes, and that Laura was willing to make the
sale, but not at all anxious about the matter and not
at all in a hurry. It was whispered that Senator
Dilworthy was a stumbling-block in the way of an
immediate sale, because he was resolved that the
government should not have the lands, except with
the understanding that they should be devoted to
the uplifting of the negro race; Laura did not care
what they were devoted to, it was said (a world of
very different gossip to the contrary notwithstanding), but there were several other heirs, and they
would be guided entirely by the Senator's wishes;
and, finally, many people averred that while it would
be easy to sell the lands to the government for the
benefit of the negro, by resorting to the usual
methods of influencing votes, Senator Dilworthy was
unwilling to have so noble a charity sullied by any
taint of corruption — he was resolved that not a vote
should be bought. Nobody could get anything de-
finite from Laura about these matters, and so gossip
had to feed itself chiefly upon guesses. But the
effect of it all was, that Laura was considered to be
very wealthy and likely to be vastly more so in a

little while. Consequently, she was much courted and as much envied. Her wealth attracted many suitors. Perhaps they came to worship her riches, but they remained to worship her. Some of the noblest men of the time succumbed to her fascinations. She frowned upon no lover when he made his first advances, but by and by, when he was hopelessly enthralled, he learned from her own lips that she had formed a resolution never to marry. Then he would go away hating and cursing the whole sex, and she would calmly add his scalp to her string, while she mused upon the bitter day that Colonel Selby trampled her love and her pride in the dust. In time it came to be said that her way was paved with broken hearts.

Poor Washington gradually woke up to the fact that he, too, was an intellectual marvel as well as his gifted sister. He could not conceive how it had come about (it did not occur to him that the gossip about his family's great wealth had anything to do with it). He could not account for it by any process of reasoning, and was simply obliged to accept the fact and give up trying to solve the riddle. He found himself dragged into society and courted, wondered at and envied very much as if he were one of those foreign barbers who flit over here now and then with a self-conferred title of nobility and marry some rich fool's absurd daughter. Sometimes at a dinner party or a reception he would find himself the center of interest, and feel unutterably uncomfortable in the discovery. Being obliged to say something, he would mine his brain and put in a blast, and when the smoke and flying débris had cleared away the result would be what seemed to him but a poor little intellectual clod of dirt or two, and then he would be astonished to see everybody as lost in admiration as if he had brought up a ton or two of virgin gold. Every remark he made delighted his hearers and compelled their applause; he overheard people say he was exceedingly bright — they were chiefly mammas and marriageable young ladies. He found that some of his good things were being repeated about the town. Whenever he heard of an instance of this kind, he would keep that particular remark in mind and analyze it at home in private. At first he could not see that the remark was anything better than a parrot might originate; but by and by he began to feel that perhaps he underrated his powers; and after that he used to analyze his good things with a deal of comfort, and find in them a brilliancy which would have been unapparent to him in earlier days — and then he would make a note of that good thing and say it again the first time he found himself in a new company. Presently he had saved up quite a repertoire of brilliancies; and after that he confined himself to repeating these and ceased to originate any more, lest he might injure his reputation by an unlucky effort.

He was constantly having young ladies thrust upon his notice at receptions, or left upon his hands at

parties, and in time he began to feel that he was being deliberately persecuted in this way; and after
that he could not enjoy society because of his constant dread of these female ambushes and surprises.
He was distressed to find that nearly every time he
showed a young lady a polite attention he was
straightway reported to be engaged to her; and as
some of these reports got into the newspapers occasionally, he had to keep writing to Louise that they
were lies and she must believe in him and not mind
them or allow them to grieve her.

Washington was as much in the dark as anybody
with regard to the great wealth that was hovering in
the air and seemingly on the point of tumbling into
the family pocket. Laura would give him no satisfaction. All she would say, was:

"Wait. Be patient. You will see."

"But will it be soon, Laura?"

"It will not be very long, I think."

"But what makes you think so?"

"I have reasons — and good ones. Just wait, and
be patient."

"But is it going to be as much as people say it
is?"

"What do they say it is?"

"Oh, ever so much. Millions!"

"Yes, it will be a great sum."

"But *how* great, Laura? Will it be millions?"

"Yes, you may call it that. Yes, it *will* be millions. There, now — does that satisfy you?"

"Splendid! I can wait. I can wait patiently —
ever so patiently. Once I was near selling the land
for twenty thousand dollars; once for thirty thousand dollars; once after that for seven thousand dollars; and once for forty thousand dollars — but
something always told me not to do it. What a fool
I would have been to sell it for such a beggarly
trifle! It *is* the land that's to bring the money, isn't
it, Laura? You can tell me that much, can't you?"

"Yes, I don't mind saying that much. It *is* the
land. But mind — don't ever hint that you got it
from me. Don't mention me in the matter at all,
Washington."

"All right — I won't. Millions! Isn't it splendid! I mean to look around for a building lot; a
lot with fine ornamental shrubbery and all that sort
of thing. I will do it to-day. And I might as well
see an architect, too, and get him to go to work at a
plan for a house. I don't intend to spare any expense; I mean to have the noblest house that money
can build." Then after a pause — he did not notice
Laura's smiles —"Laura, would you lay the main
hall in encaustic tiles, or just in fancy patterns of
hard wood?"

Laura laughed a good old-fashioned laugh that had
more of her former natural self about it than any
sound that had issued from her mouth in many
weeks. She said:

" *You* don't change, Washington. You still begin
to squander a fortune right and left the instant you

hear of it in the distance; you never wait till the foremost dollar of it arrives within a hundred miles of you,'' — and she kissed her brother good-bye and left him weltering in his dreams, so to speak.

He got up and walked the floor feverishly during two hours; and when he sat down he had married Louise, built a house, reared a family, married them off, spent upwards of eight hundred thousand dollars on mere luxuries, and died worth twelve millions.

4**

CHAPTER IV.

HOW MAJORITIES ARE SECURED

" Mi-x-in tzakcaamah, x-in tzakcolobch chirech nu zaki caam, nu zaki colo. . . . nu chincu, nu galgab, nu zalmet" . . .
Rabinal-Achi.

Chascus hom a sas palmas deves se meteys viradas.

LAURA went down stairs, knocked at the study door, and entered, scarcely waiting for the response. Senator Dilworthy was alone — with an open Bible in his hand, upside down. Laura smiled, and said, forgetting her acquired correctness of speech:

" It is only me."

" Ah, come in, sit down," and the Senator closed the book and laid it down. "I wanted to see you. Time to report progress from the committee of the whole," and the Senator beamed with his own congressional wit.

" In the committee of the whole things are working very well. We have made ever so much progress in a week. I believe that you and I together could run this government beautifully, uncle."

(46)

The Senator beamed again. He liked to be called "uncle" by this beautiful woman.

"Did you see Hopperson last night after the Congressional prayer meeting?"

"Yes. He came. He's a kind of ——"

"Eh? he is one of my friends, Laura. He's a fine man, a very fine man. I don't know any man in Congress I'd sooner go to for help in any Christian work. What did he say?"

"Oh, he beat around a little. He said he should like to help the negro, his heart went out to the negro, and all that — plenty of them say that — but he was a little afraid of the Tennessee Land bill; if Senator Dilworthy wasn't in it, he should suspect there was a fraud on the government."

"He said that, did he?"

"Yes. And he said he felt he couldn't vote for it. He was shy."

"Not shy, child, cautious. He's a very cautious man. I have been with him a great deal on conference committees. He wants reasons, good ones. Didn't you show him he was in error about the bill?"

"I did. I went over the whole thing. I had to tell him some of the side arrangements, some of the ——"

"You didn't mention me?"

"Oh, no. I told him you were daft about the negro and the philanthropy part of it, as you are."

"Daft is a little strong, Laura. But you know

that I wouldn't touch this bill if it were not for the public good, and for the good of the colored race, much as I am interested in the heirs of this property, and would like to have them succeed."

Laura looked a little incredulous, and the Senator proceeded.

"Don't misunderstand *me*, Laura. I don't deny that it is for the interest of all of us that this bill should go through, and it will. I have no concealments from you. But I have one principle in my public life, which I should like you to keep in mind; it has always been my guide. I never push a private interest if it is not justified and ennobled by some larger public good. I doubt if a Christian would be justified in working for his own salvation if it was not to aid in the salvation of his fellow men."

The Senator spoke with feeling, and then added:

"I hope you showed Hopperson that our motives were pure?"

"Yes, and he seemed to have a new light on the measure. I think he will vote for it."

"I hope so; his name will give tone and strength to it. I knew you would only have to show him that it was just and pure, in order to secure his cordial support."

"I think I convinced him. Yes, I am perfectly sure he will vote right now."

"That's good, that's good," said the Senator, smiling, and rubbing his hands. "Is there anything more?"

"You'll find some changes in that I guess," hand-ing the Senator a printed list of names. "Those checked off are all right."

"Ah — 'm — 'm," running his eye down the list. "That's encouraging. What is the 'C' before some of the names, and the 'B. B.'?"

"Those are my private marks. That 'C' stands for 'convinced,' with argument. The 'B. B.' is a general sign for a relative. You see it stands before three of the Hon. Committee. I expect to see the chairman of the committee to-day, Mr. Buckstone."

"So you must, he ought to be seen without any delay. Buckstone is a worldly sort of a fellow, but he has charitable impulses. If we secure him we shall have a favorable report by the committee, and it will be a great thing to be able to state that fact quietly where it will do good."

"Oh, I saw Senator Balloon."

"He will help us, I suppose? Balloon is a whole-hearted fellow. I can't *help* loving that man, for all his drollery and waggishness. He puts on an air of levity sometimes, but there ain't a man in the Senate knows the Scriptures as he does. He did not make any objections?"

"Not exactly, he said — shall I tell you what he said?" asked Laura, glancing furtively at him.

"Certainly."

"He said he had no doubt it was a good thing; if Senator Dilworthy was in it, it would pay to look into it."

4

The Senator laughed, but rather feebly, and said, "Balloon is always full of his jokes."

"I explained it to him. He said it was all right, he only wanted a word with you," continued Laura. "He is a handsome old gentleman, and he is gallant for an old man."

"My daughter," said the Senator, with a grave look, "I trust there was nothing free in his manner?"

"Free?" repeated Laura, with indignation in her face. "With *me !*"

"There, there, child. I meant nothing, Balloon talks a little freely sometimes, with men. But he is right at heart. His term expires next year and I fear we shall lose him."

"He seemed to be packing the day I was there. His rooms were full of dry goods boxes, into which his servant was crowding all manner of old clothes and stuff. I suppose he will paint 'Pub. Docs' on them and frank them home. That's good economy, isn't it?"

"Yes, yes, but, child, all Congressmen do that. It may not be strictly honest, indeed, it is not unless he had some public documents mixed in with the clothes."

"It's a funny world. Good-bye, uncle. I'm going to see that chairman."

And humming a cheery opera air, she departed to her room to dress for going out. Before she did that, however, she took out her note book and was soon deep in its contents, marking, dashing, erasing, figuring, and talking to herself.

"Free! I wonder what Dilworthy *does* think of me, anyway? One....two....eight....seventeen ....twenty-one,....'m'm....it takes a heap for a majority. Wouldn't Dilworthy open his eyes if he knew some of the things Balloon *did* say to me. There....Hopperson's influence ought to count twenty....the sanctimonious old curmudgeon. Son-in-law....sinecure in the negro institution....That about gauges *him*,...The three committeemen.... sons-in-law. Nothing like a son-in-law here in Washington....or a brother-in-law....And everybody has 'em,...Let's see....sixty-one....with places;....twenty-five....persuaded — it is getting on;....we'll have two-thirds of Congress in time ....Dilworthy must surely know I understand him. Uncle Dilworthy....Uncle Balloon!....Tells very amusing stories....when ladies are not present.... I should think so....'m....'m. Eighty-five.... There. I must find that chairman. Queer.... Buckstone acts....Seemed to be in love....I was *sure* of it. He promised to come here....and he hasn't....Strange. *Very* strange....I must chance to meet him to-day."

Laura dressed and went out, thinking she was perhaps too early for Mr. Buckstone to come from the house, but as he lodged near the bookstore she would drop in there and keep a lookout for him.

While Laura is on her errand to find Mr. Buck-

D

stone, it may not be out of the way to remark that
she knew quite as much of Washington life as Senator Dilworthy gave her credit for, and more than
she thought proper to tell him. She was acquainted
by this time with a good many of the young fellows
of Newspaper Row, and exchanged gossip with
them to their mutual advantage.

They were always talking in the Row, everlastingly
gossiping, bantering, and sarcastically praising things,
and going on in a style which was a curious com-
mingling of earnest and persiflage. Colonel Sellers
liked this talk amazingly, though he was sometimes
a little at sea in it — and perhaps that didn't lessen
the relish of the conversation to the correspondents.

It seems that they had got hold of the dry goods
box packing story about Balloon, one day, and were
talking it over when the Colonel came in. The
Colonel wanted to know all about it, and Hicks told
him. And then Hicks went on, with a serious air:

" Colonel, if you register a letter, it means that it
is of value, doesn't it? And if you pay fifteen cents
for registering it, the government will have to take
extra care of it and even pay you back its full value
if it is lost. Isn't that so?"

" Yes. I suppose it's so."

" Well, Senator Balloon put fifteen cents worth of
stamps on each of those seven huge boxes of old
clothes, and shipped that ton of second-hand rubbish, old boots and pantaloons and what not through
the mails as registered matter! It was an ingenious

thing and it had a genuine touch of humor about it, too.   I think there is more real talent among our public men of to-day than there was among those of old times — a far more fertile fancy, a much happier ingenuity.   Now, Colonel, can you picture Jefferson, or Washington, or John Adams franking their wardrobes through the mails and adding the facetious idea of making the government responsible for the cargo for the sum of one dollar and five cents? Statesmen were dull creatures in those days.   I have a much greater admiration for Senator Balloon.''

'' Yes, Balloon is a man of parts, there is no denying it.''

'' I think so.   He is spoken of for the post of Minister to China, or Austria, and I hope will be appointed.   What we want abroad is good examples of the national character.   John Jay and Benjamin Franklin were well enough in their day, but the nation has made progress since then.   Balloon is a man we know and can depend on to be true to — himself.''

'' Yes, and Balloon has had a good deal of public experience.   He is an old friend of mine.   He was governor of one of the Territories awhile, and was very satisfactory.''

'' Indeed, he was.   He was ex-officio Indian agent, too.   Many a man would have taken the Indian appropriation and devoted the money to feeding and clothing the helpless savages, whose land had been taken from them by the white man in

the interests of civilization; but Balloon knew their
needs better. He built a government sawmill on
the reservation with the money, and the lumber sold
for enormous prices — a relative of his did all the
work free of charge — that is to say, he charged
nothing more than the lumber would bring.''

"But the poor Injuns — not that I care much for
Injuns — what did he do for them?''

"Gave them the outside slabs to fence in the
reservation with. Governor Balloon was nothing
less than a father to the poor Indians. But Balloon
is not alone, we have many truly noble statesmen in
our country's service like Balloon. The Senate is
full of them. Don't you think so, Colonel?''

"Well, I dunno. I honor my country's public
servants as much as any one can. I meet them,
sir, every day, and the more I see of them the more
I esteem them and the more grateful I am that our
institutions give us the opportunity of securing their
services. Few lands are so blest.''

"That is true, Colonel. To be sure you can buy
now and then a Senator or a Representative; but
they do not know it is wrong, and so they are not
ashamed of it. They are gentle, and confiding and
childlike, and, in my opinion, these are qualities that
ennoble them far more than any amount of sinful
sagacity could. I quite agree with you, Colonel
Sellers.''

"Well "— hesitated the Colonel —" I am afraid
some of them do buy their seats — yes, I am afraid

they do — but as Senator Dilworthy himself said to
me, it is sinful, — it is very wrong — it is shameful; Heaven protect *me* from such a charge. That
is what Dilworthy said. And yet when you come
to look at it you cannot deny that we would have to
go without the services of some of our ablest men,
sir, if the country were opposed to — to — bribery.
It is a harsh term. I do not like to use it."

The Colonel interrupted himself at this point to
meet an engagement with the Austrian minister, and
took his leave with his usual courtly bow.

CHAPTER V.

THE BOOK-STORE CLERK

புத்தகங்கள்

"Bataïnadon nin-masinaiganan, kakina gaie onijishinon." — "Missawa onijishining kakina o masinaiganan, kawin gwetch o-wabandansinan."

Baraga.

IN due time Laura alighted at the bookstore, and began to look at the titles of the handsome array of books on the counter. A dapper clerk, of perhaps nineteen or twenty years, with hair accurately parted and surprisingly slick, came bustling up and leaned over with a pretty smile and an affable—

"Can I — was there any particular book you wished to see?"

"Have you Taine's England?"

"Beg pardon?"

"Taine's Notes on England."

The young gentleman scratched the side of his nose with a cedar pencil which he took down from its bracket on the side of his head, and reflected a moment:

"Ah — I see," [with a bright smile]—"Train, you mean — not Taine. George Francis Train. No, ma'm we ——"

"I mean *Taine* — if I may take the liberty."

The clerk reflected again — then:

"Taine....Taine....Is it hymns?"

"No, it isn't hymns. It is a volume that is making a deal of talk just now, and is very widely known — except among parties who sell it."

The clerk glanced at her face to see if a sarcasm might not lurk somewhere in that obscure speech, but the gentle simplicity of the beautiful eyes that met his, banished that suspicion. He went away and conferred with the proprietor. Both appeared to be nonplussed. They thought and talked, and talked and thought by turns. Then both came forward and the proprietor said:

"Is it an American book, ma'm?"

"No, it is an American reprint of an English translation."

"Oh! Yes — yes — I remember, now. We are expecting it every day. It isn't out yet."

"I think you must be mistaken, because you advertised it a week ago."

"Why no — can that be so?"

"Yes, I am sure of it. And besides, here is the book itself, on the counter."

She bought it and the proprietor retired from the field. Then she asked the clerk for the Autocrat of the Breakfast Table — and was pained to see the admiration her beauty had inspired in him fade out of his face. He said with cold dignity, that cook books were somewhat out of their line, but he would order it if she desired it. She said, no, never mind. Then she fell to conning the titles again, finding a delight in the inspection of the Hawthornes, the Long-fellows, the Tennysons, and other favorites of her idle hours. Meantime the clerk's eyes were busy, and no doubt his admiration was returning again — or may be he was only gauging her probable literary tastes by some sagacious system of admeasurement only known to his guild. Now he began to "assist" her in making a selection; but his efforts met with no success — indeed, they only annoyed her and un-pleasantly interrupted her meditations. Presently, while she was holding a copy of "Venetian Life" in her hand and running over a familiar passage here and there, the clerk said, briskly, snatching up a paper-covered volume and striking the counter a smart blow with it to dislodge the dust:

"Now here is a work that we've sold a lot of. Everybody that's read it likes it"— and he intruded it under her nose; "it's a book that I can recom-mend — 'The Pirate's Doom, or the Last of the Buccaneers.' I think it's one of the best things that's come out this season."

Laura pushed it gently aside with her hand and went on filching from "Venetian Life."

"I believe I do not want it," she said.

The clerk hunted around awhile, glancing at one

title and then another, but apparently not finding what he wanted. However, he succeeded at last. Said he:

"Have you ever read this, ma'm? I am sure you'll like it. It's by the author of 'The Hooligans of Hackensack.' It is full of love troubles and mysteries and all sorts of such things. The heroine strangles her own mother. Just glance at the title, please,— 'Gonderil the Vampire, or The Dance of Death.' And here is 'The Jokist's Own Treasury, or, The Phunny Phellow's Bosom Phriend.' The funniest thing! — I've read it four times, ma'm, and I can laugh at the very sight of it yet. And 'Gonderil,'— I assure you it is the most splendid book I ever read. I know you will like these books, ma'm, because I've read them myself and I know what they are."

"Oh, I was perplexed — but I see how it is, now. You must have thought I asked you to tell me what sort of books I wanted — for I am apt to say things which I don't really mean, when I am absent-minded. I suppose I did ask you, didn't I?"

"No, ma'm,— but I ——"

"Yes, I must have done it, else you would not have offered your services, for fear it might be rude. But don't be troubled — it was all my fault. I ought not to have been so heedless — I ought not to have asked you."

"But you didn't ask me, ma'm. We always help customers all we can. You see our experience

— living right among books all the time — that sort
of thing makes us able to help a customer make a
selection, you know."

"Now does it, indeed? It is part of your business, then?"

"Yes'm, we always help."

"How good it is of you. Some people would
think it rather obtrusive, perhaps, but I don't — I
think it is real kindness — even charity. Some people jump to conclusions without any thought — you
have noticed that?"

"Oh, yes," said the clerk, a little perplexed as to
whether to feel comfortable or the reverse; "oh,
yes, indeed, I've often noticed that, ma'm."

"Yes, they jump to conclusions with an absurd
heedlessness. Now some people would think it odd
that because you, with the budding tastes and the
innocent enthusiasms natural to your time of life,
enjoyed the Vampires and the volume of nursery
jokes, you should imagine that an older person
would delight in them, too — but I do not think it
odd at all. I think it natural — perfectly natural —
in you. And kind, too. You look like a person
who not only finds a deep pleasure in any little
thing in the way of literature that strikes you
forcibly, but is willing and glad to share that pleasure with others — and that, I think, is noble and
admirable — very noble and admirable. I think we
ought all to share our pleasures with others, and do
what we can to make each other happy, do not you?"

"Oh, yes. Oh, yes, indeed. Yes, you are quite right, ma'm."

But he was getting unmistakably uncomfortable, now, notwithstanding Laura's confiding sociability and almost affectionate tone.

"Yes, indeed. Many people would think that what a bookseller — or perhaps his clerk — knows about literature *as* literature, in contradistinction to its character as merchandise, would hardly be of much assistance to a person — that is, to an adult, of course — in the selection of food for the mind — except, of course, wrapping paper, or twine, or wafers, or something like that — but I never feel that way. I feel that whatever service you offer me, you offer with a good heart, and I am as grateful for it as if it were the greatest boon to me. And it *is* useful to me — it is bound to be so. It cannot be otherwise. If you show me a book which you have read — not skimmed over or merely glanced at, but *read* — and you tell me that *you* enjoyed it and that *you* could read it three or four times, then I know what book I want——"

"Thank you!— th——"

—"to avoid. Yes, indeed. I think that no information ever comes amiss in this world. Once or twice I have traveled in the cars — and there, you know, the peanut boy always measures you with his eye, and hands you out a book of murders if you are fond of theology; or Tupper or a dictionary or T. S. Arthur if you are fond of poetry; or he

5**

hands you a volume of distressing jokes or a copy
of the American Miscellany if you particularly dis-
like that sort of literary fatty degeneration of the
heart — just for the world like a pleasant-spoken
well-meaning gentleman in any bookstore—. But
here I am running on as if business men had nothing
to do but listen to women talk. You must pardon
me, for I was not thinking. And you must let me
thank you again for helping me. I read a good
deal, and shall be in nearly every day; and I would
be sorry to have you think me a customer who talks
too much and buys too little. Might I ask you to
give me the time? Ah — two — twenty-two. Thank
you very much. I will set mine while I have the
opportunity.''

But she could not get her watch open, apparently.
She tried, and tried again. Then the clerk, trembling at his own audacity, begged to be allowed to
assist. She allowed him. He succeeded, and was
radiant under the sweet influences of her pleased
face and her seductively worded acknowledgments
with gratification. Then he gave her the exact time
again, and anxiously watched her turn the hands
slowly till they reached the precise spot without
accident or loss of life, and then he looked as happy
as a man who had helped a fellow being through a
momentous undertaking, and was grateful to know
that he had not lived in vain. Laura thanked him
once more. The words were music to his ear; but
what were they compared to the ravishing smile with

which she flooded his whole system? When she bowed her adieu and turned away, he was no longer suffering torture in the pillory where she had had him trussed up during so many distressing moments, but he belonged to the list of her conquests and was a flattered and happy thrall, with the dawn-light of love breaking over the eastern elevations of his heart.

It was about the hour, now, for the chairman of the House Committee on Benevolent Appropriations to make his appearance, and Laura stepped to the door to reconnoitre. She glanced up the street, and sure enough——

CHAPTER VI.

LAURA COQUETS WITH BUCKSTONE

𒌷 𒌌 𒌀 𒁹 𒁹 𒁹 𒌝 𒌍

Usa ogn' arte la donna, onde sia cólto
Nella sua rete alcun novello amante;
Nè con tutti, nè sempre un stesso volto
Serba, ma cangia a tempo atti e sembiante.

Tasso.

THAT chairman was nowhere in sight. Such disappointments seldom occur in novels, but are always happening in real life.

She was obliged to make a new plan. She sent him a note, and asked him to call in the evening — which he did.

She received the Hon. Mr. Buckstone with a sunny smile, and said:

"I don't know how I ever dared to send you a note, Mr. Buckstone, for you have the reputation of not being very partial to our sex."

"Why, I am sure my reputation does me wrong, then, Miss Hawkins. I have been married once — is that nothing in my favor?"

(64)

"Oh, yes — that is, it may be and it may not be. If you have known what perfection is in woman, it is fair to argue that inferiority cannot interest you now."

"Even if that were the case it could not affect *you*, Miss Hawkins," said the chairman gallantly. "Fame does not place you in the list of ladies who rank below perfection."

This happy speech delighted Mr. Buckstone as much as it seemed to delight Laura. But it did not confuse him as much as it apparently did her.

"I wish in all sincerity that I could be worthy of such a felicitous compliment as that. But I am a woman, and so I am gratified for it just as it is, and would not have it altered."

"But it is not merely a compliment — that is, an empty compliment — it is the truth. All men will endorse that."

Laura looked pleased, and said:

"It is very kind of you to say it. It is a distinction, indeed, for a country-bred girl like me to be so spoken of by people of brains and culture. You are so kind that I know you will pardon my putting you to the trouble to come this evening."

"Indeed, it was no trouble. It was a pleasure. I am alone in the world since I lost my wife, and I often long for the society of your sex, Miss Hawkins, notwithstanding what people may say to the contrary."

"It is pleasant to hear you say that. I am sure
5

it must be so. If I feel lonely at times, because of my exile from old friends, although surrounded by new ones who are already very dear to me, how much more lonely must you feel, bereft as you are, and with no wholesome relief from the cares of state that weigh you down. For your own sake, as well as for the sake of others, you ought to go into society oftener. I seldom see you at a reception, and when I do you do not usually give me very much of your attention."

"I never imagined that you wished it or I would have been very glad to make myself happy in that way. But one seldom gets an opportunity to say more than a sentence to you in a place like that. You are always the center of a group — a fact which you may have noticed yourself. But if one might come here ——"

"Indeed you would always find a hearty welcome, Mr. Buckstone. I have often wished you would come and tell me more about Cairo and the Pyramids, as you once promised me you would."

"Why, do you remember that yet, Miss Hawkins? I thought ladies' memories were more fickle than that."

"Oh, they are not so fickle as gentlemen's promises. And besides, if I had been inclined to forget, I — did you not give me something by way of a remembrancer?"

"Did I?"

" Think."

" It does seem to me that I did; but I have forgotten what it was now."

" Never, never call a lady's memory fickle again ! Do you recognize this?"

" A little spray of box! I am beaten — I surrender. But have you kept that all this time?"

Laura's confusion was very pretty. She tried to hide it, but the more she tried the more manifest it became and withal the more captivating to look upon. Presently she threw the spray of box from her with an annoyed air, and said :

" I forgot myself. I have been very foolish. I beg that you will forget this absurd thing."

Mr. Buckstone picked up the spray, and sitting down by Laura's side on the sofa, said :

" Please let me keep it, Miss Hawkins. I set a very high value upon it now."

" Give it to me, Mr. Buckstone, and do not speak so. I have been sufficiently punished for my thoughtlessness. You cannot take pleasure in adding to my distress. Please give it to me."

" Indeed I do not wish to distress you. But do not consider the matter so gravely; you have done yourself no wrong. You probably forgot that you had it; but if you had given it to me I would have kept it — and not forgotten it."

" Do not talk so, Mr. Buckstone. Give it to me, please, and forget the matter."

" It would not be kind to refuse, since it troubles

E

you so, and so I restore it. But if you would give me part of it and keep the rest ———''

"So that you might have something to remind you of me when you wished to laugh at my foolishness?"

"Oh, by no means, no! Simply that I might remember that I had once assisted to discomfort you, and be reminded to do so no more."

Laura looked up, and scanned his face a moment. She was about to break the twig, but she hesitated and said:

"If I were sure that you ———" She threw the spray away, and continued: "This is silly! We will change the subject. No, do not insist — I must have my way in this."

Then Mr. Buckstone drew off his forces and proceeded to make a wily advance upon the fortress under cover of carefully-contrived artifices and stratagems of war. But he contended with an alert and suspicious enemy; and so at the end of two hours it was manifest to him that he had made but little progress. Still, he had made some; he was sure of that.

Laura sat alone and communed with herself:

"He is fairly hooked, poor thing. I can play him at my leisure and land him when I choose. He was all ready to be caught, days and days ago — I saw that, very well. He will vote for our bill — no fear about that; and moreover he will work for it, too, before I am done with him. If he had a

woman's eyes he would have noticed that the spray
of box had grown three inches since he first gave it
to me, but a man never sees anything and never
suspects. If I had shown him a whole bush he
would have thought it was the same. Well, it is a
good night's work; the committee is safe. But this
is a desperate game I am playing in these days — a
wearing, sordid, heartless game. If I lose, I lose
everything — even myself. And if I win the game,
will it be worth its cost after all? I do not know.
Sometimes I doubt. Sometimes I half wish I had
not begun. But no matter; I *have* begun, and I
will never turn back; never while I live."

Mr. Buckstone indulged in a reverie as he walked
homeward:

"She is shrewd and deep, and plays her cards
with considerable discretion — but she will lose, for
all that. There is no hurry; I shall come out
winner, all in good time. She *is* the most beautiful
woman in the world; and she surpassed herself to-
night. I suppose I must vote for that bill, in the
end, maybe; but that is not a matter of much consequence — the government can stand it. She is bent
on capturing me, that is plain; but she will find by
and by that what she took for a sleeping garrison
was an ambuscade."

CHAPTER VII.

LAURA SEES COL. SELBY AGAIN

Now this surprising news scaus'd her fall in a trance,
Like as she were dead, no limbs she could advance,
Then her dear brother came, her from the ground he took
And she spake up and said, O my poor heart is broke.

The Barnardcastle Tragedy.

"DON'T you think he is distinguished looking?"

"What! That gawky looking person, with Miss Hawkins?"

"There. He's just speaking to Mrs. Schoonmaker. Such high-bred negligence and unconsciousness. Nothing studied. See his fine eyes."

"Very. They are moving this way now. Maybe he is coming here. But he looks as helpless as a rag baby. Who is he, Blanche?"

"Who is he? And you've been here a week, Grace, and don't know? He's the catch of the season. That's Washington Hawkins — her brother."

"No, is it?"

"Very old family, old Kentucky family, I believe. He's got enormous landed property in Tennessee, I think. The family lost everything, slaves and that sort of thing, you know, in the war. But they have a great deal of land, minerals, mines, and all that. Mr. Hawkins and his sister too are very much interested in the amelioration of the condition of the colored race; they have some plan, with Senator Dilworthy, to convert a large part of their property to something another for the freedmen."

"You don't say so? I thought he was some guy from Pennsylvania. But he *is* different from others. Probably he has lived all his life on his plantation."

It was a day reception of Mrs. Representative Schoonmaker, a sweet woman, of simple and sincere manners. Her house was one of the most popular in Washington. There was less ostentation there than in some others, and people liked to go where the atmosphere reminded them of the peace and purity of home. Mrs. Schoonmaker was as natural and unaffected in Washington society as she was in her own New York house, and kept up the spirit of home-life there, with her husband and children. And that was the reason, probably, why people of refinement liked to go there.

Washington is a microcosm, and one can suit himself with any sort of society within a radius of a mile. To a large portion of the people who frequent Washington or dwell there, the ultra fashion, the shoddy, the jobbery are as utterly distasteful as they would be in a refined New England city. Schoonmaker was not exactly a leader in the House, but he was greatly respected for his fine talents and his honesty. No one would have thought of offering to carry National Improvement Directors Relief stock for him.

These day receptions were attended by more women than men, and those interested in the problem might have studied the costumes of the ladies present, in view of this fact, to discover whether . women dress more for the eyes of women or for effect upon men. It is a very important problem, and has been a good deal discussed, and its solution would form one fixed, philosophical basis, upon which to estimate woman's character. We are inclined to take a medium ground, and aver that woman dresses to please herself, and in obedience to a law of her own nature.

"They are coming this way," said Blanche. People who made way for them to pass, turned to look at them. Washington began to feel that the eyes of the public were on him also, and his eyes rolled about, now towards the ceiling, now towards the floor, in an effort to look unconscious.

"Good morning, Miss Hawkins. Delighted. Mr. Hawkins. My friend, Miss Medlar."

Mr. Hawkins, who was endeavoring to square himself for a bow, put his foot through the train of Mrs. Senator Poplin, who looked round with a scowl, which turned into a smile as she saw who it was. In extricating himself, Mr. Hawkins, who had the care of his hat as well as the introduction on his mind, shambled against Miss Blanche, who said *pardon*, with the prettiest accent, as if the awkwardness were her own. And Mr. Hawkins righted himself.

"Don't you find it very warm to-day, Mr. Hawkins?" said Blanche, by way of a remark.

"It's awful hot," said Washington.

"It's warm for the season," continued Blanche pleasantly. "But I suppose you are accustomed to it," she added, with a general idea that the thermometer always stands at 90 degrees in all parts of the late slave states. "Washington weather generally cannot be very congenial to you?"

"It's congenial," said Washington, brightening up, "when it's not congealed."

"That's very good. Did you hear, Grace? Mr. Hawkins says it's congenial when it's not congealed."

"What is, dear?" said Grace, who was talking with Laura.

The conversation was now finely under way. Washington launched out an observation of his own.

"Did you see those Japs, Miss Leavitt?"

"Oh, yes, aren't they queer? But so high-bred, so picturesque. Do you think that color makes any difference, Mr. Hawkins? I used to be so prejudiced against color."

"Did you? I never was. I used to think my old mammy was handsome."

"How interesting your life must have been! I should like to hear about it."

Washington was about settling himself into his

narrative style, when Mrs. General McFingal caught his eye.

"Have you been at the Capitol to-day, Mr. Hawkins?"

Washington had not. "Is anything uncommon going on?"

"They say it was very exciting. The Alabama business, you know. General Sutler of Massachusetts defied England, and they say he wants war."

"He wants to make himself conspicuous, more like," said Laura. "He always, you have noticed, talks with one eye on the gallery, while the other is on the speaker."

"Well, my husband says, it's nonsense to talk of war, and wicked. *He* knows what war is. If we *do* have war, I hope it will be for the patriots of Cuba. Don't you think we want Cuba, Mr. Hawkins?"

"I think we want it bad," said Washington. "And Santo Domingo. Senator Dilworthy says, we are bound to extend our religion over the isles of the sea. We've got to round out our territory, and ——"

Washington's further observations were broken off by Laura, who whisked him off to another part of the room, and reminded him that they must make their adieux.

"How stupid and tiresome these people are," she said. "Let's go."

They were turning to say good-bye to the hostess, when Laura's attention was arrested by the sight of

a gentleman who was just speaking to Mrs. Schoonmaker. For a second her heart stopped beating.
He was a handsome man of forty and perhaps more,
with grayish hair and whiskers, and he walked with
a cane, as if he were slightly lame. He might be
less than forty, for his face was worn into hard lines,
and he was pale.

No. It could not be, she said to herself. It is
only a resemblance. But as the gentleman turned
and she saw his full face, Laura put out her hand
and clutched Washington's arm to prevent herself
from falling.

Washington, who was not minding anything, as
usual looked 'round in wonder. Laura's eyes were
blazing fire and hatred; he had never seen her look
so before; and her face was livid.

"Why, what is it, sis? Your face is as white as
paper."

"It's he, it's he. Come, come," and she dragged
him away.

"It's who?" asked Washington, when they had
gained the carriage.

"It's nobody, it's nothing. Did I say he? I
was faint with the heat. Don't mention it. Don't
you speak of it," she added earnestly, grasping his
arm.

When she had gained her room she went to the
glass and saw a pallid and haggard face.

"My God," she cried, "this will never do. I
should have killed him, if I could. The scoundrel

still lives, and dares to come here. I ought to kill him. He has no right to live. How I hate him! And yet I loved him. Oh, heavens, how I did love that man! And why didn't he kill me? He might better. He did kill all that was good in me. Oh, but he shall not escape. He shall not escape this time. He may have forgotten. He will find that a woman's hate doesn't forget. The law? What would the law do but protect him and make me an outcast? How all Washington would gather up its virtuous skirts and avoid me, if it knew. I wonder if he hates me as I do him?''

So Laura raved, in tears and in rage by turns, tossed in a tumult of passion, which she gave way to with little effort to control.

A servant came to summon her to dinner. She had a headache. The hour came for the President's reception. She had a raving headache, and the Senator must go without her.

That night of agony was like another night she recalled. How vividly it all came back to her. And at that time she remembered she thought she might be mistaken. He might come back to her. Perhaps he loved her, a little, after all. *Now*, she knew he did not. Now, she knew he was a cold-blooded scoundrel, without pity. Never a word in all these years. She had hoped he was dead. Did his wife live, she wondered. She caught at that, and it gave a new current to her thoughts. Perhaps, after all — she must see him. She could not live without seeing him. Would he smile as in the old days when she loved him so; or would he sneer as when she last saw him? If he looked so, she hated him. If he should call her "Laura, darling," and look *so!* She must find him. She must end her doubts.

Laura kept her room for two days, on one excuse and another — a nervous headache, a cold — to the great anxiety of the Senator's household. Callers, who went away, said she had been too gay — they did not say "fast," though some of them may have thought it. One so conspicuous and successful in society as Laura could not be out of the way two days, without remarks being made, and not all of them complimentary.

When she came down she appeared as usual, a little pale, maybe, but unchanged in manner. If there were any deepened lines about the eyes they had been concealed. Her course of action was quite determined.

At breakfast she asked if any one had heard any unusual noise during the night? Nobody had. Washington never heard any noise of any kind after his eyes were shut. Some people thought he never did when they were open, either.

Senator Dilworthy said he had come in late. He was detained in a little consultation after the Congressional prayer meeting. Perhaps it was his entrance.

No, Laura said. She heard that. It was later. She might have been nervous, but she fancied somebody was trying to get into the house.

6**

Mr. Brierly humorously suggested that it might be, as none of the members were occupied in night session.

The Senator frowned, and said he did not like to hear that kind of newspaper slang. There might be burglars about.

Laura said that very likely it was only her nervousness. But she thought she would feel safer if Washington would let her take one of his pistols. Washington brought her one of his revolvers, and instructed her in the art of loading and firing it.

During the morning Laura drove down to Mrs. Schoonmaker's to pay a friendly call.

"Your receptions are always delightful," she said to that lady, "the pleasant people all seem to come here."

"It's pleasant to hear you say so, Miss Hawkins. I believe my friends like to come here. Though society in Washington is mixed; we have a little of everything."

"I suppose, though, you don't see much of the old rebel element?" said Laura with a smile.

If this seemed to Mrs. Schoonmaker a singular remark for a lady to make, who was meeting "rebels" in society every day, she did not express it in any way, but only said:

"You know we don't say 'rebel' any more. Before we came to Washington I thought rebels would look unlike other people. I find we are very much alike, and that kindness and good nature wear away prejudice. And then you know there are all sorts of common interests. My husband sometimes says that he doesn't see but Confederates are just as eager to get at the treasury as Unionists. You know that Mr. Schoonmaker is on the appropriations."

" Does he know many Southerners?"

" Oh, yes. There were several at my reception the other day. Among others a Confederate colonel — a stranger — handsome man with gray hair — probably you didn't notice him — uses a cane in walking. A very agreeable man. I wondered why he called. When my husband came home and looked over the cards, he said he had a cotton claim. A real Southerner. Perhaps you might know him if I could think of his name. Yes, here's his card — Louisiana."

Laura took the card, looked at it intently till she was sure of the address, and then laid it down, with:

" No, he is no friend of ours."

That afternoon, Laura wrote and dispatched the following note. It was in a round hand, unlike her flowing style, and it was directed to a number and street in Georgetown:

"A Lady at Senator Dilworthy's would like to see Col. George Selby, on business connected with the Cotton Claims. Can he call Wednesday at three o'clock P.M.

On Wednesday at 3 P. M. no one of the family was likely to be in the house except Laura.

CHAPTER VIII.

LAURA AGAIN IN LOVE WITH SELBY

— Belhs amics, tornatz,
Per merce, vas me de cors.

Alphonse II.

Ala khambiatü da zure deseiña?
Hitz eman zenereitan,
Ez behin, bai berritan,
   Enia zinela.
—Ohikua nüzü;
Enüzü khambiatü,
Bihotzian beinin hartü,
   Eta zü maithatü.

Maitia, nun zira?

COLONEL SELBY had just come to Washington, and taken lodgings in Georgetown. His business was to get pay for some cotton that was destroyed during the war. There were many others in Washington on the same errand, some of them with claims as difficult to establish as his. A concert of action was necessary, and he was not, therefore, at all surprised to receive the note from a lady asking him to call at Senator Dilworthy's.

At a little after three on Wednesday he rang the bell of the Senator's residence. It was a handsome mansion on the square opposite the President's house. The owner must be a man of great wealth, the Colonel thought; perhaps, who knows, said he with a smile, he may have got some of my cotton in exchange for salt and quinine after the capture of New Orleans. As this thought passed through his mind he was looking at the remarkable figure of the Hero of New Orleans, holding itself by main strength from sliding off the back of the rearing bronze horse, and lifting its hat in the manner of one who acknowledges the playing of that martial air: " See, the Conquering Hero Comes." " Gad," said the Colonel to himself, " Old Hickory ought to get down and give his seat to General Sutler — but they'd have to tie him on."

Laura was in the drawing-room. She heard the bell, she heard the steps in the hall, and the emphatic thud of the supporting cane. She had risen from her chair and was leaning against the piano, pressing her left hand against the violent beating of her heart. The door opened and the Colonel entered, standing in the full light of the opposite window. Laura was more in the shadow and stood for an instant, long enough for the Colonel to make the inward observation that she was a magnificent woman. She then advanced a step.

" Colonel Selby, is it not?"

The Colonel staggered back, caught himself by a chair, and turned towards her a look of terror.

" Laura? My God!"

6

"Yes, your wife!"

"Oh, no, it can't be. How came you here? I thought you were ——"

"You thought I was dead? You thought you were rid of me? Not so long as you live, Colonel Selby, not so long as you live," Laura in her passion was hurried on to say.

No man had ever accused Colonel Selby of cowardice. But he was a coward before this woman. Maybe he was not the man he once was. Where was his coolness? Where was his sneering, imperturbable manner, with which he could have met, and would have met, any woman he had wronged, if he had only been forewarned. He felt now that he must temporize, that he must gain time. There was danger in Laura's tone. There was something frightful in her calmness. Her steady eyes seemed to devour him.

"You have ruined my life," she said; "and I was so young, so ignorant, and loved you so. You betrayed me, and left me, mocking me and trampling me into the dust, a soiled cast-off. You might better have killed me then. Then I should not have hated you."

"Laura," said the Colonel, nerving himself, but still pale, and speaking appealingly, "don't say that. Reproach me. I deserve it. I was a scoundrel. I was everything monstrous. But your beauty made me crazy. You are right. I was a brute in leaving you as I did. But what could I do? I was married, and ——"

"And your wife still lives?" asked Laura, bending a little forward in her eagerness.

The Colonel noticed the action, and he almost said "No," but he thought of the folly of attempting concealment.

"Yes. She is here."

What little color had wandered back into Laura's face forsook it again. Her heart stood still, her strength seemed going from her limbs. Her last hope was gone. The room swam before her for a moment, and the Colonel stepped toward her, but she waved him back, as hot anger again coursed through her veins, and said:

"And you dare come with her, *here*, and tell me of it, here, and mock me with it! And you think I will have it, George? You think I will let you live with that woman? You think I am as powerless as that day I fell dead at your feet?"

She raged now. She was in a tempest of excitement. And she advanced toward him with a threatening mien. She would kill me if she could, thought the Colonel; but he thought at the same moment, how beautiful she is. He had recovered his head now. She was lovely when he knew her, then a simple country girl. Now she was dazzling, in the fullness of ripe womanhood, a superb creature, with all the fascination that a woman of the world has for such a man as Colonel Selby. Nothing of this was lost on him. He stepped quickly to her, grasped both her hands in his, and said:

F

"Laura, stop! think! Suppose I loved you yet! Suppose I hated my fate! What can I do? I am broken by the war. I have lost everything almost. I had as lief be dead and done with it."

The Colonel spoke with a low remembered voice that thrilled through Laura. He was looking into her eyes as he had looked in those old days, when no birds of all those that sang in the groves where they walked sang a note of warning. He was wounded. He had been punished. Her strength forsook her with her rage, and she sank upon a chair, sobbing:

"Oh! my God, I thought I hated him!"

The Colonel knelt beside her. He took her hand and she let him keep it. She looked down into his face, with a pitiable tenderness, and said in a weak voice:

"And you do love me a little?"

The Colonel vowed and protested. He kissed her hand and her lips. He swore his false soul into perdition.

She wanted love, this woman. Was not her love for George Selby deeper than any other woman's could be? Had she not a right to him? Did he not belong to her by virtue of her overmastering passion? His wife — she was not his wife, except by the law. She could not be. Even with the law she could have no right to stand between two souls that were one. It was an infamous condition in society that George should be tied to *her*.

Laura thought this, believed it, because she desired to believe it. She came to it as an original proposition, founded on the requirements of her own nature. She may have heard, doubtless she had, similar theories that were prevalent at that day, theories of the tyranny of marriage and of the freedom of marriage. She had even heard women lecturers say that marriage should only continue so long as it pleased either party to it — for a year, or a month, or a day. She had not given much heed to this. But she saw its justice now in a flash of revealing desire. It must be right. God would not have permitted her to love George Selby as she did, and him to love her, if it was right for society to raise up a barrier between them. He belonged to her. Had he not confessed it himself?

Not even the religious atmosphere of Senator Dilworthy's house had been sufficient to instill into Laura that deep Christian principle which had been somehow omitted in her training. Indeed, in that very house had she not heard women, prominent before the country and besieging Congress, utter sentiments that fully justified the course she was marking out for herself?

They were seated now, side by side, talking with more calmness. Laura was happy, or thought she was. But it was that feverish sort of happiness which is snatched out of the black shadow of falsehood, and is at the moment recognized as fleeting and perilous, and indulged tremblingly. She loved.

She was loved. That is happiness certainly. And the black past and the troubled present and the uncertain future could not snatch that from her.

What did they say as they sat there? What nothings do people usually say in such circumstances, even if they are threescore and ten? It was enough for Laura to hear his voice and be near him. It was enough for him to be near her, and avoid committing himself as much as he could. Enough for him was the present also. Had there not always been some way out of such scrapes?

And yet Laura could not be quite content without prying into to-morrow. *How* could the Colonel manage to free himself from his wife? Would it be long? Could he not go into some state where it would not take much time? He could not say exactly. That they must think of. That they must talk over. And so on. Did this seem like a damnable plot to Laura against the life, maybe, of a sister, a woman like herself? Probably not. It was right that this man should be hers, and there were some obstacles in the way. That was all. There are as good reasons for bad actions as for good ones, to those who commit them. When one has broken the tenth commandment, the others are not of much account.

Was it unnatural, therefore, that when George Selby departed, Laura should watch him from the window, with an almost joyful heart as he went down the sunny square? "I shall see him to-morrow," she said, "and the next day, and the next. He is mine now."

"Damn the woman," said the Colonel, as he picked his way down the steps. "Or," he added, as his thoughts took a new turn. "I wish my wife was in New Orleans."

CHAPTER IX.

HOW WASHINGTON NEWS LEAKS OUT

Open your ears; for which of you will stop
The vent of hearing, when loud Rumor speaks?
I, from the Orient to the drooping West,
Making the wind my post-horse, still unfold
The acts commencèd on this ball of earth:
Upon my tongues continual slanders ride;
The which in every language I pronounce,
Stuffing the ears of men with false reports.
King Henry IV.

AS may be readily believed, Colonel Beriah Sellers was by this time one of the best-known men in Washington. For the first time in his life his talents had a fair field.

He was now at the center of the manufacture of gigantic schemes, of speculations of all sorts, of political and social gossip. The atmosphere was full of little and big rumors and of vast, undefined expectations. Everybody was in haste, too, to push on his private plan, and feverish in his haste, as if in constant apprehension that to-morrow would be Judgment Day. Work while Congress is in session, said the uneasy spirit, for in the recess there is no work and no device.

(88)

The Colonel enjoyed this bustle and confusion amazingly; he thrived in the air of indefinite expectation. All his own schemes took larger shape and more misty and majestic proportions; and in this congenial air the Colonel seemed even to himself to expand into something large and mysterious. If he respected himself before, he almost worshiped Beriah Sellers now, as a superior being. If he could have chosen an official position out of the highest, he would have been embarrassed in the selection. The Presidency of the republic seemed too limited and cramped in the constitutional restrictions. If he could have been Grand Llama of the United States, that might have come the nearest to his idea of a position. And next to that he would have luxuriated in the irresponsible omniscience of the special correspondent.

Colonel Sellers knew the President very well, and had access to his presence when officials were kept cooling their heels in the waiting-room. The President liked to hear the Colonel talk, his voluble ease was a refreshment after the decorous dullness of men who only talked business and government, and everlastingly expounded their notions of justice and the distribution of patronage. The Colonel was as much a lover of farming and of horses as Thomas Jefferson was. He talked to the President by the hour about his magnificent stud, and his plantation at Hawkeye, a kind of principality he represented it. He urged the President to pay him a visit during the recess, and see his stock farm.

"The President's table is well enough," he used to say, to the loafers who gathered about him at Willard's, "well enough for a man on a salary, but, God bless my soul, I should like him to see a little old-fashioned hospitality — open house, you know. A person seeing me at home might think I paid no attention to what was in the house, just let things flow in and out. He'd be mistaken. What I look to is quality, sir. The President has variety enough, but the quality! Vegetables, of course, you can't expect here. I'm very particular about mine. Take celery, now — there's only one spot in this country where celery will grow. But I *am* surprised about the wines. I should think they were manufactured in the New York Custom House. I must send the President some from my cellar. I was really mortified the other day at dinner to see Blacque Bey leave his standing in the glasses."

When the Colonel first came to Washington he had thoughts of taking the mission to Constantinople, in order to be on the spot to look after the dissemination of his Eye Water, but as that invention was not yet quite ready, the project shrank a little in the presence of vaster schemes. Besides he felt that he could do the country more good by remaining at home. He was one of the Southerners who were constantly quoted as heartily "accepting the situation."

" I'm whipped," he used to say with a jolly laugh, " the government was too many for me; I'm cleaned out, done for, except my plantation and private mansion. We played for a big thing, and lost it, and I don't whine, for one. I go for putting the old flag on all the vacant lots. I said to the President, says I, ' Grant, why don't you take Santo Domingo, annex the whole thing, and settle the bill afterwards.' That's my way. I'd take the job to manage Congress. The South would come into it. You've got to conciliate the South, consolidate the two debts, pay 'em off in greenbacks, and go ahead. That's my notion. Boutwell's got the right notion about the value of paper, but he lacks courage. I *should* like to run the treasury department about six months. I'd make things plenty, and business look up."

The Colonel had access to the departments. He knew all the Senators and Representatives, and especially the lobby. He was consequently a great favorite in Newspaper Row, and was often lounging in the offices there, dropping bits of private, official information, which were immediately caught up and telegraphed all over the country. But it used to surprise even the Colonel when he read it; it was embellished to that degree that he hardly recognized it, and the hint was not lost on him. He began to exaggerate his heretofore simple conversation to suit the newspaper demand.

People used to wonder in the winters of 187- and

187–, where the "Specials" got that remarkable information with which they every morning surprised the country, revealing the most secret intentions of the President and his cabinet, the private thoughts of political leaders, the hidden meaning of every movement. This information was furnished by Colonel Sellers.

When he was asked, afterward, about the stolen copy of the Alabama Treaty which got into the "New York Tribune," he only looked mysterious, and said that neither he nor Senator Dilworthy knew anything about it. But those whom he was in the habit of meeting occasionally felt almost certain that he did know.

It must not be supposed that the Colonel in his general patriotic labors neglected his own affairs. The Columbus River navigation scheme absorbed only a part of his time, so he was enabled to throw quite a strong reserve force of energy into the Tennessee Land plan, a vast enterprise commensurate with his abilities, and in the prosecution of which he was greatly aided by Mr. Henry Brierly, who was buzzing about the Capitol and the hotels day and night, and making capital for it in some mysterious way.

"We must create a public opinion," said Senator Dilworthy. "My only interest in it is a public one, and if the country wants the institution, Congress will have to yield."

It may have been after a conversation between

the Colonel and Senator Dilworthy that the following
special dispatch was sent to a New York newspaper:

"We understand that a philanthropic plan is on foot in relation to
the colored race that will, if successful, revolutionize the whole character of Southern industry. An experimental institution is in contempla-
tion in Tennessee which will do for that state what the Industrial School
at Zurich did for Switzerland. We learn that approaches have been
made to the heirs of the late Hon. Silas Hawkins, of Missouri, in refer-
erence to a lease of a portion of their valuable property in East Tennessee. Senator Dilworthy, it is understood, is inflexibly opposed to
any arrangement that will not give the government absolute control.
Private interests must give way to the public good. It is to be hoped
that Col. Sellers, who represents the heirs, will be led to see the matter
in this light."

When Washington Hawkins read this dispatch,
he went to the Colonel in some anxiety. He was
for a lease, he didn't want to surrender anything.
What did he think the government would offer?
Two millions?

"Maybe three, maybe four," said the Colonel,
"it's worth more than the Bank of England."

"If they will not lease," said Washington, "let
'em make it two millions for an undivided half. I'm
not going to throw it away, not the whole of it."

Harry told the Colonel that they must drive the
thing through, he couldn't be dallying round Washington when spring opened. Phil wanted him, Phil
had a great thing on hand up in Pennsylvania.

"What is that?" inquired the Colonel, always
ready to interest himself in anything large.

"A mountain of coal; that's all. He's going to
run a tunnel into it in the spring."

7**

"Does he want any capital?" asked the Colonel, in the tone of a man who is given to calculating carefully before he makes an investment.

"No. Old man Bolton's behind him. He has capital, but I judged that he wanted my experience in starting."

"If he wants me, tell him I'll come, after Congress adjourns. I should like to give him a little lift. He lacks enterprise — now, about that Columbus River. He doesn't see his chances. But he's a good fellow, and you can tell him that Sellers won't go back on him."

"By the way," asked Harry, "who is that rather handsome party that's hanging 'round Laura? I see him with her everywhere, at the Capitol, in the horse cars, and he comes to Dilworthy's. If he weren't lame, I should think he was going to run off with her."

"Oh, that's nothing. Laura knows her business. He has a cotton claim. Used to be at Hawkeye during the war — Selby's his name, was a Colonel. Got a wife and family. Very respectable people, the Selbys."

"Well, that's all right," said Harry, "if it's business. But if a woman looked at me as I've seen her at Selby, I should understand it. And it's talked about, I can tell you."

Jealousy had, no doubt, sharpened this young gentleman's observation. Laura could not have treated him with more lofty condescension if she had been the Queen of Sheba, on a royal visit to the great republic. And he resented it, and was "huffy" when he was with her, and ran her errands, and brought her gossip, and bragged of his intimacy with the lovely creature among the fellows at Newspaper Row.

Laura's life was rushing on now in the full stream of intrigue and fashionable dissipation. She was conspicuous at the balls of the fastest set, and was suspected of being present at those doubtful suppers that began late and ended early. If Senator Dilworthy remonstrated about appearances, she had a way of silencing him. Perhaps she had some hold on him, perhaps she was necessary to his plan for ameliorating the condition of the colored race.

She saw Colonel Selby, when the public knew and when it did not know. She would see him, whatever excuses he made, and however he avoided her. She was urged on by a fever of love and hatred and jealousy, which alternately possessed her. Sometimes she petted him, and coaxed him, and tried all her fascinations. And again she threatened him and reproached him. What was he doing? Why had he taken no steps to free himself? Why didn't he send his wife home? She should have *money* soon. They could go to Europe,— anywhere. What did she care for talk?

And he promised, and lied, and invented fresh excuses for delay, like a cowardly gambler and roué as he was, fearing to break with her, and half the time unwilling to give her up.

"That woman doesn't know what fear is," he said to himself, "and she watches me like a hawk."

He told his wife that this woman was a lobbyist, whom he had to tolerate and use in getting through his claims, and that he should pay her and have done with her, when he succeeded.

CHAPTER X.

HARRY HOPELESSLY IN LOVE

وَزَادَهُ كَلَفًا فِى الحُبِّ أَنْ مَنَعَتْ
وَحَبَّ شَيْئًا اَلَى الانْسَانِ مَا مُنِعَا

Táj el-'Aroos.

Egundano yçan daya ni baydienetacoric?
Ny amoriac enu mayte, nic hura ecin gayecxi.

Bern. d'Echeparre.

HENRY BRIERLY was at the Dilworthys' constantly and on such terms of intimacy that he
came and went without question. The Senator was
not an inhospitable man, he liked to have guests in
his house, and Harry's gay humor and rattling way
entertained him; for even the most devout men and
busy statesmen must have hours of relaxation.

Harry himself believed that he was of great service
in the university business, and that the success of
the scheme depended upon him to a great degree.
He spent many hours in talking it over with the
Senator after dinner. He went so far as to consider
whether it would be worth his while to take the pro-
fessorship of civil engineering in the new institution.

7   (97)

But it was not the Senator's society nor his dinners — at which this scapegrace remarked that there was too much grace and too little wine — which attracted him to the house. The fact was, the poor fellow hung around there day after day for the chance of seeing Laura for five minutes at a time. For her presence at dinner he would endure the long bore of the Senator's talk afterward, while Laura was off at some assembly, or excused herself on the plea of fatigue. Now and then he accompanied her to some reception, and rarely, on off nights, he was blessed with her company in the parlor, when he sang, and was chatty and vivacious and performed a hundred little tricks of imitation and ventriloquism, and made himself as entertaining as a man could be.

It puzzled him not a little that all his fascinations seemed to go for so little with Laura; it was beyond his experience with women. Sometimes Laura was exceedingly kind, and petted him a little, and took the trouble to exert her powers of pleasing, and to entangle him deeper and deeper. But this, it angered him afterward to think, was in private; in public she was beyond his reach, and never gave occasion to the suspicion that she had any affair with him. He was never permitted to achieve the dignity of a serious flirtation with her in public.

"Why do you treat me so?" he once said, reproachfully.

"Treat you how?" asked Laura in a sweet voice, lifting her eyebrows.

' You know well enough. You let other fellows monopolize you in society, and you are as indifferent to me as if we were strangers."

"Can I help it if they are attentive, can I be rude? But we are such old friends, Mr. Brierly, that I didn't suppose you would be jealous."

"I think I must be a very old friend, then, by your conduct toward me. By the same rule, I should judge that Colonel Selby must be very new."

Laura looked up quickly, as if about to return an indignant answer to such impertinence, but she only said, "Well, what of Colonel Selby, sauce-box?"

"Nothing, probably, you'll care for. Your being with him so much is the town talk, that's all."

"What do people say?" asked Laura calmly.

"Oh, they say a good many things. You are offended, though, to have me speak of it?"

"Not in the least. You are my true friend. I feel that I can trust you. You wouldn't deceive me, Harry?" throwing into her eyes a look of trust and tenderness that melted away all his petulance and distrust. "What do they say?"

"Some say that you've lost your head about him; others that you don't care any more for him than you do for a dozen others, but that he is completely fascinated with you and about to desert his wife; and others say it is nonsense to suppose you would entangle yourself with a married man, and that your intimacy only arises from the matter of the cotton claims, for which he wants your influence with Dil-

G

worthy. But you know everybody is talked about more or less in Washington. I shouldn't care; but I wish you wouldn't have so much to do with Selby, Laura," continued Harry, fancying that he was now upon such terms that his advice would be heeded.

"And you believed these slanders?"

"I don't believe anything against you, Laura, but Col. Selby does not mean you any good. I know you wouldn't be seen with him if you knew his reputation."

"Do you know him?" Laura asked, as indifferently as she could.

"Only a little. I was at his lodgings in Georgetown a day or two ago, with Colonel Sellers. Sellers wanted to talk with him about some patent remedy he has, Eye Water, or something of that sort, which he wants to introduce into Europe. Selby is going abroad very soon."

Laura started, in spite of her self-control.

"And his wife? Does he take his family? Did you see his wife?"

"Yes. A dark little woman, rather worn — must have been pretty once, though. Has three or four children, one of them a baby. They'll all go, of course. She said she should be glad enough to get away from Washington. You know Selby has got his claim allowed, and they say he has had a run of luck lately at Morrissey's."

Laura heard all this in a kind of stupor, looking straight at Harry, without seeing him. Is it possible, she was thinking, that this base wretch, after all his promises, will take his wife and children and leave me? Is it possible the town is saying all these things about me? And — a look of bitterness coming into her face — does the fool think he can escape so?

"You are angry with me, Laura," said Harry, not comprehending in the least what was going on in her mind.

"Angry?" she said, forcing herself to come back to his presence. "With you? Oh, no. I'm angry with the cruel world, which pursues an independent woman as it never does a man. I'm grateful to you, Harry; I'm grateful to you for telling me of that odious man."

And she rose from her chair and gave him her pretty hand, which the silly fellow took, and kissed and clung to. And he said many silly things, before she disengaged herself gently, and left him, saying it was time to dress for dinner.

And Harry went away, excited, and a little hopeful, but only a little. The happiness was only a gleam, which departed and left him thoroughly miserable. She never would love him, and she was going to the devil, besides. He couldn't shut his eyes to what he saw, nor his ears to what he heard of her.

What had come over this trifling young ladykiller? It was a pity to see such a gay butterfly broken on a wheel. Was there something good in him, after all, that had been touched? He was, in fact, madly in love with this woman. It is not for us to analyze the passion and say whether it was a worthy one. It absorbed his whole nature and made him wretched enough. If he deserved punishment, what more would you have? Perhaps this love was kindling a new heroism in him.

He saw the road on which Laura was going clearly enough, though he did not believe the worst he heard of her. He loved her too passionately to credit that for a moment. And it seemed to him that if he could compel her to recognize her position and his own devotion, she might love him, and that he could save her. His love was so far ennobled, and become a very different thing from its beginning in Hawkeye. Whether he ever thought that if he could save her from ruin, he could give her up himself, is doubtful. Such a pitch of virtue does not occur often in real life, especially in such natures as Harry's, whose generosity and unselfishness were matters of temperament rather than habits or principles.

He wrote a long letter to Laura, an incoherent, passionate letter, pouring out his love as he could not do in her presence, and warning her as plainly as he dared of the dangers that surrounded her, and the risks she ran of compromising herself in many ways.

Laura read the letter, with a little sigh, maybe, as she thought of other days, but with contempt also, and she put it into the fire with the thought, "They are all alike."

Harry was in the habit of writing to Philip freely, and boasting also about his doings, as he could not help doing and remain himself. Mixed up with his own exploits, and his daily triumphs as a lobbyist, especially in the matter of the new university, in which Harry was to have something handsome, were amusing sketches of Washington society, hints about Dilworthy, stories about Colonel Sellers, who had become a well-known character, and wise remarks upon the machinery of private legislation for the public good, which greatly entertained Philip in his convalescence.

Laura's name occurred very often in these letters, at first in casual mention as the belle of the season, carrying everything before her with her wit and beauty, and then more seriously, as if Harry did not exactly like so much general admiration of her, and was a little nettled by her treatment of him. This was so different from Harry's usual tone about women, that Philip wondered a good deal over it. Could it be possible that he was seriously affected? Then came stories about Laura, town talk, gossip which Harry denied the truth of indignantly; but he was evidently uneasy, and at length wrote in such miserable spirits that Philip asked him squarely what the trouble was; was he in love?

Upon this, Harry made a clean breast of it, and told Philip all he knew about the Selby affair, and Laura's treatment of him, sometimes encouraging him and then throwing him off, and finally his belief

that she would go to the bad if something was not
done to arouse her from her infatuation. He wished
Philip was in Washington. He knew Laura, and
she had a great respect for his character, his opinions, his judgment. Perhaps he, as an uninterested
person in whom she would have some confidence,
and as one of the public, could say something to
her that would show her where she stood.

Philip saw the situation clearly enough. Of Laura
he knew not much, except that she was a woman of
uncommon fascination, and he thought from what
he had seen of her in Hawkeye, her conduct toward
him and toward Harry, of not too much principle.
Of course he knew nothing of her history; he knew
nothing seriously against her, and if Harry was
desperately enamored of her, why should he not win
her if he could. If, however, she had already become what Harry uneasily felt she might become,
was it not his duty to go to the rescue of his friend
and try to save him from any rash act on account of
a woman that might prove to be entirely unworthy
of him; for, trifler and visionary as he was, Harry
deserved a better fate than this.

Philip determined to go to Washington and see
for himself. He had other reasons also. He began
to know enough of Mr. Bolton's affairs to be uneasy.
Pennybacker had been there several times during the
winter, and he suspected that he was involving Mr.
Bolton in some doubtful scheme. Pennybacker was
in Washington, and Philip thought he might perhaps,

find out something about him, and his plans, that would be of service to Mr. Bolton.

Philip had enjoyed his winter very well, for a man with his arm broken and his head smashed. With two such nurses as Ruth and Alice, illness seemed to him rather a nice holiday, and every moment of his convalescence had been precious and all too fleeting. With a young fellow of the habits of Philip, such injuries cannot be counted on to tarry long, even for the purpose of love-making, and Philip found himself getting strong with even disagreeable rapidity.

During his first weeks of pain and weakness, Ruth was unceasing in her ministrations; she quietly took charge of him, and with a gentle firmness resisted all attempts of Alice or any one else to share to any great extent the burden with her. She was clear, decisive and peremptory in whatever she did; but often when Philip opened his eyes in those first days of suffering and found her standing by his bedside, he saw a look of tenderness in her anxious face that quickened his already feverish pulse, a look that remained in his heart long after he closed his eyes. Sometimes he felt her hand on his forehead, and did not open his eyes for fear she would take it away. He watched for her coming to his chamber; he could distinguish her light footstep from all others. If this is what is meant by women practicing medicine, thought Philip to himself, I like it.

" Ruth," said he one day when he was getting to be quite himself, " I believe in it."

" Believe in what?"

" Why, in women physicians."

" Then I'd better call in Mrs. Dr. Longstreet."

" Oh, no. One will do, one at a time. I think
I should be well to-morrow, if I thought I should
never have any other."

" Thy physician thinks thee mustn't talk, Philip,"
said Ruth, putting her finger on his lips.

" But Ruth, I want to tell you that I should wish
I never had got well if ——"

" There, there, thee must *not* talk. Thee is
wandering again," and Ruth closed his lips, with a
smile on her own that broadened into a merry laugh
as she ran away.

Philip was not weary, however, of making these
attempts; he rather enjoyed it. But whenever he
inclined to be sentimental, Ruth would cut him off,
with some such gravely conceived speech as, " Does
thee think that thy physician will take advantage of
the condition of a man who is as weak as thee is? I
will call Alice, if thee has any dying confessions to
make."

As Philip convalesced, Alice more and more took
Ruth's place as his entertainer, and read to him by
the hour, when he did not want to talk — to talk
about Ruth, as he did a good deal of the time. Nor
was this altogether unsatisfactory to Philip. He
was always happy and contented with Alice. She
was the most restful person he knew. Better informed than Ruth and with a much more varied

culture, and bright and sympathetic, he was never weary of her company, if he was not greatly excited by it. She had upon his mind that peaceful influence that Mrs. Bolton had when, occasionally, she sat by his bedside with her work. Some people have this influence, which is like an emanation. They bring peace to a house, they diffuse serene content in a room full of mixed company, though they may say very little, and are apparently unconscious of their own power.

Not that Philip did not long for Ruth's presence all the same. Since he was well enough to be about the house, she was busy again with her studies. Now and then her teasing humor came again. She always had a playful shield against his sentiment. Philip used sometimes to declare that she had no sentiment; and then he doubted if he should be pleased with her after all if she were at all sentimental; and he rejoiced that she had, in such matters, what he called the airy grace of sanity. She was the most gay serious person he ever saw.

Perhaps he was not so much at rest or so contented with her as with Alice. But then he loved her. And what have rest and contentment to do with love?

CHAPTER XI.

MR. TROLLOP IS TRAPPED AND BECOMES AN ALLY

Subtle. Would I were hang'd then! I'll conform myself.
Dol. Will you, sir? Do so then, and quickly: swear.
Sub. What should I swear?
Dol. To leave your faction, sir,
    And labour kindly in the common work.

Ben. Jonson. The Alchemist.

Eku edue mfine, ata eku: miduehe mfine, mfine itaha.

MR. BUCKSTONE'S campaign was brief — much briefer than he supposed it would be. He began it purposing to win Laura without being won himself; but his experience was that of all who had fought on that field before him; he diligently continued his effort to win her, but he presently found that while as yet he could not feel entirely certain of having won her, it was very manifest that she had won him. He had made an able fight, brief as it was, and that at least was to his credit. He was in good company, now; he walked in a leash of conspicuous captives. These unfortunates followed Laura helplessly, for whenever she took a prisoner he remained her slave henceforth. Sometimes they

(108)

chafed in their bondage; sometimes they tore themselves free and said their serfdom was ended; but sooner or later they always came back penitent and worshiping. Laura pursued her usual course; she encouraged Mr. Buckstone by turns, and by turns she harassed him; she exalted him to the clouds at one time, and at another she dragged him down again. She constituted him chief champion of the Knobs University bill, and he accepted the position, at first reluctantly, but later as a valued means of serving her — he even came to look upon it as a piece of great good fortune, since it brought him into such frequent contact with her.

Through him she learned that the Hon. Mr. Trollop was a bitter enemy of her bill. He urged her not to attempt to influence Mr. Trollop in any way, and explained that whatever she might attempt in that direction would surely be used against her and with damaging effect.

She at first said she knew Mr. Trollop, "and was aware that he had a Blank-Blank;"* but Mr. Buckstone said that while he was not able to conceive what so curious a phrase as Blank-Blank might mean, and had no wish to pry into the matter, since it was probably private, he "would, nevertheless, venture the blind assertion that *nothing* would answer in this particular case and during this particular session but to be exceedingly wary and keep clear away from Mr. Trollop; any other course would be fatal."

---

* Her private figure of speech for Brother — or Son-in-law.

8**

It seemed that nothing could be done. Laura was seriously troubled. Everything was looking well, and yet it was plain that one vigorous and determined enemy might eventually succeed in overthrowing all her plans. A suggestion came into her mind presently and she said:

"Can't you fight against his great Pension bill and bring him to terms?"

"Oh, never; he and I are sworn brothers on that measure; we work in harness and are very loving — I do everything I possibly can for him there. But I work with might and main against his Immigration bill, — as pertinaciously and as vindictively, indeed, as he works against our university. We hate each other through half a conversation and are all affection through the other half. We understand each other. He is an admirable worker outside the Capitol; he will do more for the Pension bill than any other man could do; I wish he would make the great speech on it which he wants to make — and then I would make another and we would be safe."

"Well, if he wants to make a great speech why doesn't he do it?"

Visitors interrupted the conversation and Mr. Buckstone took his leave. It was not of the least moment to Laura that her question had not been answered, inasmuch as it concerned a thing which did not interest her; and yet, human being like, she thought she would have liked to know. An opportunity occurring presently, she put the same question to another person and got an answer that satisfied her. She pondered a good while, that night, after she had gone to bed, and when she finally turned over to go to sleep, she had thought out a new scheme. The next evening at Mrs. Gloverson's party, she said to Mr. Buckstone:

"I want Mr. Trollop to make his great speech on the Pension bill."

"*Do* you! But you remember I was interrupted, and did not explain to you ——"

"Never mind, I know. You must make him make that speech. I very particularly desire it."

"Oh, it is easy to say make him do it, but *how* am I to make him?"

"It is perfectly easy; I have thought it all out."

She then went into the details. At length Mr. Buckstone said:

"I see now. I can manage it, I am sure. Indeed, I wonder he never thought of it himself — there are no end of precedents. But how is this going to benefit you, after I *have* managed it? There is where the mystery lies."

"But I will take care of that. It will benefit me a great deal."

"I only wish I could see how; it is the oddest freak. You seem to go the furthest around to get at a thing — but you are in earnest, aren't you?"

"Yes, I am, indeed."

"Very well, I will do it — but why not tell me how you imagine it is going to help you?"

" I will, by and by. Now there is nobody talking to him. Go straight and do it, there's a good fellow."

A moment or two later the two sworn friends of the Pension bill were talking together, earnestly, and seemingly unconscious of the moving throng about them. They talked an hour, and then Mr. Buckstone came back and said:

" He hardly fancied it at first, but he fell in love with it after a bit. And we have made a compact, too. I am to keep his secret and he is to spare me, in future, when he gets ready to denounce the supporters of the University bill — and I can easily believe he will keep his word on this occasion."

A fortnight elapsed, and the University bill had gathered to itself many friends, meantime. Senator Dilworthy began to think the harvest was ripe. He conferred with Laura privately. She was able to tell him exactly how the House would vote. There was a majority — the bill would pass, unless weak members got frightened at the last, and deserted — a thing pretty likely to occur. The Senator said:

" I wish we had one more good strong man. Now Trollop ought to be on our side, for he is a friend of the negro. But he is against us, and is our bitterest opponent. If he would simply vote No, but keep quiet and not molest us, I would feel perfectly cheerful and content. But perhaps there is no use in thinking of that."

" Why, I laid a little plan for his benefit two weeks

ago. I think he will be tractable, maybe. He is to
come here to-night.''

"Look out for him, my child! He means mis-
chief, sure. It is said that he claims to know of
improper practices having been used in the interest
of this bill, and he thinks he sees a chance to make a
great sensation when the bill comes up. Be wary.
Be very, very careful, my dear. Do your very
ablest talking, now. You can convince a man of
anything, when you try. You must convince him
that if anything improper has been done, you at
least are ignorant of it and sorry for it. And if you
could only persuade him out of his hostility to the
bill, too — but don't overdo the thing; don't seem
too anxious, dear.''

"I won't; I'll be ever so careful. I'll talk as
sweetly to him as if he were my own child! You
may trust me — indeed, you may.''

The door bell rang.

"That is the gentleman now," said Laura.
Senator Dilworthy retired to his study.

Laura welcomed Mr. Trollop, a grave, carefully
dressed and very respectable looking man, with a
bald head, standing collar, and old-fashioned watch
seals.

"Promptness is a virtue, Mr. Trollop, and I perceive that you have it. You are always prompt
with me.''

"I always meet my engagements, of every kind,
Miss Hawkins.''

8

" It is a quality which is rarer in the world than it has been, I believe. I wished to see you on business, Mr. Trollop."

" I judged so. What can I do for you?"

" You know my bill — the Knobs University bill?"

" Ah, I believe it *is* your bill. I had forgotten. Yes, I know the bill."

" Well, would you mind telling me your opinion of it?"

" Indeed, since you seem to ask it without reserve, I am obliged to say that I do not regard it favorably. I have not seen the bill itself, but from what I can hear, it — it — well, it has a bad look about it. It——"

" Speak it out — never fear."

" Well, it — they say it contemplates a fraud upon the government."

" Well?" said Laura tranquilly.

" Well! *I* say ' Well?' too."

" Well, suppose it *were* a fraud — which I feel able to deny — would it be the first one?"

" You take a body's breath away! Would you — did you wish me to vote for it? Was that what you wanted to see me about?"

" Your instinct is correct. I *did* want you — I *do* want you to vote for it."

" Vote for a fr — for a measure which is generally believed to be at least questionable? I am afraid we cannot come to an understanding, Miss Hawkins."

"No, I am afraid not — if you have resumed your principles, Mr. Trollop."

"Did you send for me merely to insult me? It is time for me to take my leave, Miss Hawkins."

"No — wait a moment. Don't be offended at a trifle. Do not be offish and unsociable. The Steamship Subsidy bill was a fraud on the government. You voted for it, Mr. Trollop, though you always opposed the measure until after you had an interview one evening with a certain Mrs. McCarter at her house. She was my agent. She was acting for me. Ah, that is right — sit down again. You can be sociable, easily enough, if you have a mind to. Well? I am waiting. Have you nothing to say?"

"Miss Hawkins, I voted for that bill because when I came to examine into it——"

"Ah, yes. When you came to examine into it. Well, I only want you to examine into *my* bill. Mr. Trollop, you would not sell your vote on that subsidy bill — which was perfectly right — but you accepted of some of the stock, with the understanding that it was to stand in your brother-in-law's name."

"There is no pr — I mean, this is utterly groundless, Miss Hawkins." But the gentleman seemed somewhat uneasy, nevertheless.

"Well, not entirely so, perhaps. I and a person whom we will call Miss Blank (never mind the real name) were in a closet at your elbow all the while."

Mr. Trollop winced — then he said with dignity:

H

" Miss Hawkins, is it possible that you were capable of such a thing as that?"

" It was bad; I confess that. It *was* bad. Almost as bad as selling one's vote for — but I forget; you did not sell your vote — you only accepted a little trifle, a small token of esteem, for your brother-in-law. Oh, let us come out and be frank with each other. I know you, Mr. Trollop. I have met you on business three or four times; true, I never offered to corrupt your principles — never hinted such a thing; but always when I had finished sounding you, I manipulated you through an agent. Let us be frank. Wear this comely disguise of virtue before the public — it will count there; but here it is out of place. My dear sir, by and by there is going to be an investigation into that National Internal Improvement Directors' Relief Measure of a few years ago, and you know very well that you will be a crippled man, as likely as not, when it is completed."

" It cannot be shown that a man is a knave merely for owning that stock. I am not distressed about the National Improvement Relief Measure."

" Oh, indeed, I am not trying to distress you. I only wished to make good my assertion that I knew you. Several of you gentlemen bought of that stock (without paying a penny down) received dividends from it (think of the happy idea of receiving dividends, and very large ones, too, from stock one hasn't paid for!), and all the while your

names never appeared in the transaction; if ever
you took the stock at all, you took it in other
people's names.   Now, you see, you had to know
one of two things; namely, you either knew that
the idea of all this preposterous generosity was to
bribe you into future legislative friendship, or you
didn't know it.   That is to say, you had to be
either a knave or a — well, a fool — there was no
middle ground.   *You* are not a fool, Mr. Trollop."

   " Miss Hawkins, you flatter me.   But, seriously,
you do not forget that some of the best and purest
men in Congress took that stock in that way?"

   " Did Senator Blank?"

   " Well, no — I believe not."

   " Of course you believe not.   Do you suppose
he was ever approached on the subject?"

   " Perhaps not."

   " If *you* had approached him, for instance, fortified with the fact that some of the best men in Congress, and the purest, etc., etc., what would have
been the result?"

   " Well, what *would* have been the result?"

   " He would have shown you the door!   For Mr.
Blank is neither a knave *nor* a fool.   There are
other men in the Senate and the House whom no
one would have been hardy enough to approach with
that Relief stock in that peculiarly generous way,
but they are not of the class that *you* regard as the
best and purest.   No, I say I know you, Mr. Trollop.
That is to say, one may suggest a thing to Mr.

Trollop which it would not do to suggest to Mr. Blank. Mr. Trollop, you are pledged to support the Indigent Congressmen's Retroactive Appropriation which is to come up, either in this or the next session. You do not deny that, even in public. The man that will vote for that bill will break the eighth commandment in any *other* way, sir!''

'' But he will not vote for *your* corrupt measure, nevertheless, madam!'' exclaimed Mr. Trollop, rising from his seat in a passion.

'' Ah, but he will. Sit down again, and let me explain why. Oh, come, don't behave so. It is very unpleasant. Now be good, and you shall have the missing page of your great speech. Here it is!''— and she displayed a sheet of manuscript.

Mr. Trollop turned immediately back from the threshold. It might have been gladness that flashed into his face; it might have been something else; but, at any rate, there was much astonishment mixed with it.

'' Good! Where did you get it? Give it me!''

'' Now there is no hurry. Sit down; sit down and let us talk and be friendly.''

The gentleman wavered. Then he said:

'' No, this is only a subterfuge. I will go. It is not the missing page.''

Laura tore off a couple of lines from the bottom of the sheet.

'' Now,'' she said, '' you will know whether this is the handwriting or not. You know it *is* the handwriting. Now, if you will listen, you will know that this must be the list of statistics which was to be the ' nub ' of your great effort, and the accompanying blast the beginning of the burst of eloquence which was continued on the next page — and you will recognize that there was where you broke down.''

She read the page. Mr. Trollop said:

'' This is perfectly astounding. Still, what is all this to me? It is nothing. It does not concern me. The speech is made, and there an end. I *did* break down for a moment, and in a rather uncomfortable place, since I had led up to those statistics with some grandeur; the hiatus was pleasanter to the House and the galleries than it was to me. But it is no matter now. A week has passed; the jests about it ceased three or four days ago. The whole thing is a matter of indifference to me, Miss Hawkins.''

'' But you apologized, and promised the statistics for next day. Why didn't you keep your promise?''

'' The matter was not of sufficient consequence. The time was gone by to produce an effect with them.''

'' But I hear that other friends of the Soldiers' Pension bill desire them very much. I think you ought to let them have them.''

'' Miss Hawkins, this silly blunder of my copyist evidently has more interest for you than it has for me. I will send my private secretary to you and let him discuss the subject with you at length.''

"Did he copy your speech for you?"

"Of course he did. Why all these questions? Tell me — how did you get hold of that page of manuscript? *That* is the only thing that stirs a passing interest in my mind."

"I'm coming to that." Then she said, much as if she were talking to herself: "It does seem like taking a deal of unnecessary pains, for a body to hire another body to construct a great speech for him and then go and get still another body to copy it before it can be read in the House."

"Miss Hawkins, what do you mean by such talk as that?"

"Why, I am sure I mean no harm — no harm to anybody in the world. I am certain that I overheard the Hon. Mr. Buckstone either promise to write your great speech for you or else get some other competent person to do it."

"This is perfectly absurd, madam, perfectly absurd!" and Mr. Trollop affected a laugh of derision.

"Why, the thing has occurred before now. I mean that I have heard that Congressmen have sometimes hired literary grubs to build speeches for them. Now, didn't I overhear a conversation like that I spoke of?"

"Pshaw! Why, of course, you may have overheard some such jesting nonsense. But would one be in earnest about so farcical a thing?"

"Well, if it was only a joke, why did you make a serious matter of it? Why did you get the speech

written for you, and then read it in the House without ever having it copied?"

Mr. Trollop did not laugh this time; he seemed
seriously perplexed. He said:

"Come, play out your jest, Miss Hawkins. I
can't understand what you are contriving — but it
seems to entertain you — so please go on."

"I will, I assure you; but I hope to make the
matter entertaining to you, too. Your private
secretary never copied your speech."

"Indeed? Really you seem to know my affairs
better than I do myself."

"I believe I do. You can't name your own
amanuensis, Mr. Trollop."

"That is sad, indeed. Perhaps Miss Hawkins
can?"

"Yes, I *can*. *I* wrote your speech myself, and
you read it from my manuscript. There, now!"

Mr. Trollop did not spring to his feet and smite
his brow with his hands while a cold sweat broke
out all over him and the color forsook his face —
no, he only said, "Good God!" and looked greatly
astonished.

Laura handed him her commonplace book and
called his attention to the fact that the handwriting
there and the handwriting of this speech were the
same. He was shortly convinced. He laid the
book aside and said, composedly:

"Well, the wonderful tragedy is done, and it
transpires that I am indebted to you for my late

eloquence. What of it? What was all this for, and what does it amount to, after all? What do you propose to do about it?"

"Oh, nothing. It is only a bit of pleasantry. When I overheard that conversation I took an early opportunity to ask Mr. Buckstone if he knew of anybody who might want a speech written — I had a friend, and so forth and so on. *I* was the friend, myself; I thought I might do you a good turn then and depend on you to do me one by and by. I never let Mr. Buckstone have the speech till the last moment, and when you hurried off to the House with it, you did not know there was a missing page, of course, but I did."

"And now perhaps you think that if I refuse to support your bill, you will make a grand exposure?"

"Well, I had not thought of that. I only kept back the page for the mere fun of the thing; but since you mention it, I don't know but I might do something if I were angry."

"My dear Miss Hawkins, if you were to give out that you composed my speech, you know very well that people would say it was only your raillery, your fondness for putting a victim in the pillory and amusing the public at his expense. It is too flimsy, Miss Hawkins, for a person of your fine inventive talent — contrive an abler device than that. Come!"

"It is easily done, Mr. Trollop. I will hire a man, and pin this page on his breast, and label it,

'The Missing Fragment of the Hon. Mr. Trollop's Great Speech — which speech was written and composed by Miss Laura Hawkins under a secret understanding for one hundred dollars — and the money has not been paid.'   And I will pin round about it notes in my handwriting, which I will procure from prominent friends of mine for the occasion; also your printed speech in the *Globe*, showing the connection between its bracketed hiatus and my Fragment; and I give you my word of honor that I will stand that human bulletin board in the rotunda of the Capitol and make him stay there a week! You see you are premature, Mr. Trollop, the wonderful tragedy is not done yet, by any means. Come, now, doesn't it improve?"

Mr. Trollop opened his eyes rather widely at this novel aspect of the case. He got up and walked the floor and gave himself a moment for reflection. Then he stopped and studied Laura's face a while, and ended by saying:

"Well, I am obliged to believe you *would* be reckless enough to do that."

"Then don't put me to the test, Mr. Trollop. But let's drop the matter. I have had my joke and you've borne the infliction becomingly enough. It spoils a jest to harp on it after one has had one's laugh. I would much rather talk about my bill."

"So would I, now, my clandestine amanuensis. Compared with some other subjects, even your bill is a pleasant topic to discuss."

"Very good, indeed! I thought I could persuade you. Now I am sure you will be generous to the poor negro and vote for that bill."

"Yes, I feel more tenderly toward the oppressed colored man than I did. Shall we bury the hatchet and be good friends and respect each other's little secrets, on condition that I vote Aye on the measure?"

"With all my heart, Mr. Trollop. I give you my word of that."

"It is a bargain. But isn't there something else you could give me, too?"

Laura looked at him inquiringly a moment, and then she comprehended.

"Oh, yes! You may have it now. I haven't any more use for it." She picked up the page of manuscript, but she reconsidered her intention of handing it to him, and said, "But never mind; I will keep it close; no one shall see it; you shall have it as soon as your vote is recorded."

Mr. Trollop looked disappointed, but presently made his adieux, and had got as far as the hall, when something occurred to Laura. She said to herself, "I don't simply want his vote; under compulsion — he might vote Aye, but work against the bill in secret, for revenge; that man is unscrupulous enough to do anything. I must have his hearty cooperation as well as his vote. There is only one way to get that."

She called him back, and said:

"I value your vote, Mr. Trollop, but I value your influence more. You are able to help a measure along in many ways, if you choose. I want to ask you to work for the bill as well as vote for it."

"It takes so much of one's time, Miss Hawkins — and time is money, you know."

'Yes, I know it is — especially in Congress. Now there is no use in you and I dealing in pretenses and going at matters in roundabout ways. We know each other — disguises are nonsense. Let us be plain. I will make it an object to you to work for the bill."

"Don't make it unnecessarily plain, please. There are little proprieties that are best preserved. What do you propose?"

"Well, this." She mentioned the names of several prominent Congressmen. "Now," said she, "these gentlemen are to vote and work for the bill, simply out of love for the negro — and out of pure generosity I have put in a relative of each as a member of the university incorporation. They will handle a million or so of money, officially, but will receive no salaries. A larger number of statesmen are to vote and work for the bill — also out of love for the negro — gentlemen of but moderate influence, these — and out of pure generosity I am to see that relatives of theirs have positions in the university, *with* salaries, and good ones, too. You will vote and work for the bill, from mere affection

9**

for the negro, and I desire to testify my gratitude becomingly. Make free choice. Have you any friend whom you would like to present with a salaried or unsalaried position in our institution?"

" Well, I have a brother-in-law ——"

" That same old brother-in-law, you good unselfish provider! I have heard of him often, through my agents. How regularly he does ' turn up,' to be sure. He could deal with those millions virtuously, and withal with ability, too — but, of course, you would rather he had a salaried position?"

" Oh, no," said the gentleman, facetiously, " we are very humble, very humble in our desires; we want no money; we labor solely for our country and require no reward but the luxury of an applauding conscience. Make him one of those poor hardworking unsalaried corporators, and let him do everybody good with those millions — and go hungry himself! I will try to exert a little influence in favor of the bill."

Arrived at home, Mr. Trollop sat down and thought it all over — something after this fashion: it is about the shape it might have taken if he had spoken it aloud.

" My reputation is getting a little damaged, and I meant to clear it up brilliantly with an exposure of this bill at the supreme moment, and ride back into Congress on the éclat of it; and if I had that bit of manuscript, I would do it yet. It would be more money in my pocket, in the end, than my brother-in-law will get out of that incorporatorship, fat as it is. But that sheet of paper is out of my reach — she will never let that get out of her hands. And what a mountain it is! It blocks up *my* road, completely. She was going to hand it to me, once. Why *didn't* she! Must be a deep woman. Deep devil! That is what she is; a beautiful devil — and perfectly fearless, too. The idea of her pinning that paper on a man and standing him up in the rotunda looks absurd at a first glance. But she would do it! She is capable of doing anything. I went there hoping she would try to bribe me — good solid capital that would be in the exposure. Well, my prayer was answered; she did try to bribe me; and I made the best of a bad bargain and let her. I am checkmated. I must contrive something fresh to get back to Congress on. Very well; a bird in the hand is worth two in the bush; I will work for the bill — the incorporatorship will be a very good thing.''

As soon as Mr. Trollop had taken his leave, Laura ran to Senator Dilworthy and began to speak, but he interrupted her and said distressfully, without even turning from his writing to look at her:

"Only half an hour! You gave it up early, child. However, it was best, it was best — I'm sure it was best — and safest.''

"Give it up! *I!*''

The Senator sprang up, all aglow:

"My child, you can't mean that you ———''

"I've made him promise on honor to think about a compromise to-night and come and tell me his decision in the morning."

"Good! There's hope yet that——"

"Nonsense, uncle. I've made him engage to let the Tennessee Land bill utterly alone!"

"*Impossible!* You——"

"I've made him promise to vote with us!"

"INCREDIBLE! Abso——"

"I've made him swear that he'll *work* for us!"

"PRE — POSTEROUS! — Utterly pre — break a window, child, before I suffocate!"

"No matter, it's true anyway. Now we can march into Congress with drums beating and colors flying!"

"Well — well — well. I'm sadly bewildered, sadly bewildered. I can't understand it at all — the most extraordinary woman that ever — it's a great day, it's a great day. There — there — let me put my hand in benediction on this precious head. Ah, my child, the poor negro will bless——"

"Oh, bother the poor negro, uncle! Put it in your speech. Good-night, good-bye — we'll marshal our forces and march with the dawn!"

Laura reflected a while, when she was alone, and then fell to laughing, peacefully.

"Everybody works for me," — so ran her thought. "It was a good idea to make Buckstone lead Mr. Trollop on to get a great speech written for him; and it was a happy part of the same idea for me to copy the speech after Mr. Buckstone had written it, and then keep back a page. Mr. B. was very complimentary to me when Trollop's breakdown in the House showed him the *object* of my mysterious scheme; I think he will say still finer things when I tell him the triumph the sequel to it has gained for us.

" But what a coward the man was, to believe I would have exposed that page in the rotunda, and so exposed myself. However, I don't know — I don't know. I will think a moment. Suppose he voted No; suppose the bill failed; that is to suppose this stupendous game lost forever, that I have played so desperately for; suppose people came around pitying me — odious! And he could have saved me by his single voice. Yes, I *would* have exposed him! What would I care for the talk that that would have made about me when I was gone to Europe with Selby and all the world was busy with my history and my dishonor? It would be almost happiness to spite somebody at such a time."

CHAPTER XII.

NEWSPAPERS ATTACK THE UNIVERSITY BILL

"Ikkaké gidiamuttu Wamallitakoanti likissitu anissia ukunnaria ni rubu kurru naussa abbanu aboahüddunnua namonnua."

THE very next day, sure enough, the campaign opened. In due course, the Speaker of the House reached that order of business which is termed "Notices of Bills," and then the Hon. Mr. Buckstone rose in his place and gave notice of a bill "To Found and Incorporate the Knobs Industrial University," and then sat down without saying anything further. The busy gentlemen in the reporters' gallery jotted a line in their notebooks, ran to the telegraphic desk in a room which communicated with their own writing-parlor, and then hurried back to their places in the gallery; and by the time they had resumed their seats, the line which they had delivered to the operator had been read in telegraphic offices in towns and cities hundreds of miles away. It was distinguished by frankness of language as well as by brevity:

"The child is born. Buckstone gives notice of the thieving Knobs University job. It is said the noses have been counted, and enough votes have been bought to pass it."

For some time the correspondents had been posting their several journals upon the alleged disreputable nature of the bill, and furnishing daily reports of the Washington gossip concerning it. So the next morning, nearly every newspaper of character in the land assailed the measure and hurled broadsides of invective at Mr. Buckstone. The Washington papers were more respectful, as usual — and conciliatory, also, as usual. They generally supported measures, when it was possible; but when they could not they " deprecated " violent expressions of opinion in other journalistic quarters. They always deprecated, when there was trouble ahead.

However, *The Washington Daily Love-Feast* hailed the bill with warm approbation. This was Senator Balaam's paper — or, rather, " Brother " Balaam, as he was popularly called, for he had been a clergyman, in his day; and he himself and all that he did still emitted an odor of sanctity now that he had diverged into journalism and politics. He was a power in the Congressional prayer meeting, and in all movements that looked to the spread of religion and temperance. His paper supported the new bill with gushing affection; it was a noble measure; it was a just measure; it was a generous measure; it was a pure measure, and that surely should recommend it in these corrupt times; and, finally, if the nature of the bill were not known at all, the *Love-Feast* would support it anyway, and unhesitatingly, for the fact that Senator Dilworthy was the originator

I

of the measure was a guaranty that it contemplated a worthy and righteous work.

Senator Dilworthy was so anxious to know what the New York papers would say about the bill, that he had arranged to have synopses of their editorials telegraphed to him; he could not wait for the papers themselves to crawl along down to Washington by a mail train which has never run over a cow since the road was built, for the reason that it has never been able to overtake one. It carries the usual " cow-catcher " in front of the locomotive, but this is mere ostentation. It ought to be attached to the rear car, where it could do some good; but instead, no provision is made there for the protection of the traveling public, and hence it is not a matter of sur-prise that cows so frequently climb aboard that train and among the passengers.

The Senator read his dispatches aloud at the breakfast table. Laura was troubled beyond meas-ure at their tone, and said that that sort of comment would defeat the bill; but the Senator said:

' Oh, not at all, not at all, my child. It is just what we want. Persecution is the one thing need-ful, now — all the other forces are secured. Give us newspaper persecution enough, and we are safe. Vigorous persecution will alone carry a bill some-times, dear; and when you start with a strong vote in the first place, persecution comes in with double effect. It scares off some of the weak supporters, true, but it soon turns strong ones into stubborn

ones. And then, presently, it changes the tide of
public opinion. The great public is weak-minded;
the great public is sentimental; the great public
always turns around and weeps for an odious murderer, and prays for him, and carries flowers to his
prison, and besieges the governor with appeals to his
clemency, as soon as the papers begin to howl for
that man's blood. In a word, the great putty-hearted
public loves to 'gush,' and there is no such darling
opportunity to gush as a case of persecution affords.''

"Well, uncle, dear, if your theory is right, let us
go into raptures, for nobody can ask a heartier
persecution than these editorials are furnishing."

"I am not so sure of that, my daughter. I don't
entirely like the tone of some of these remarks.
They lack vim, they lack venom. Here is one calls
it a 'questionable measure.' Bah, there is no
strength in that. This one is better; it calls it
'highway robbery.' That sounds something like.
But now this one seems satisfied to call it an 'iniquitous scheme!'—'Iniquitous' does not exasperate
anybody; it is weak — puerile. The ignorant will
imagine it to be intended for a compliment. But
this other one — the one I read last — has the true
ring: 'This vile, dirty effort to rob the public
treasury, by the kites and vultures that now infest
the filthy den called Congress'— that is admirable,
admirable! We must have more of that sort. But
it will come — no fear of that; they're not warmed
up, yet. A week from now you'll see."

"Uncle, you and Brother Balaam are bosom friends — why don't you get his paper to persecute us, too?"

"It isn't worth while, my daughter. His support doesn't hurt a bill. Nobody reads his editorials but himself. But I wish the New York papers would talk a little plainer. It is annoying to have to wait a week for them to warm up. I expected better things at their hands — and time is precious, now."

At the proper hour, according to his previous notice, Mr. Buckstone duly introduced his bill, entitled "An Act to Found and Incorporate the Knobs Industrial University," moved its proper reference, and sat down.

The Speaker of the House rattled off this observation:

"'Fnobjectionbilltakuzhlcourssoreferred!'"

Habitués of the House comprehended that this long, lightning-heeled word signified that if there was no objection, the bill would take the customary course of a measure of its nature, and be referred to the Committee on Benevolent Appropriations, and that it was accordingly so referred. Strangers merely supposed that the Speaker was taking a gargle for some affection of the throat.

The reporters immediately telegraphed the introduction of the bill. And they added:

"The assertion that the bill will pass was premature. It is said that many favorers of it will desert when the storm breaks upon them from the public press."

The storm came, and during ten days it waxed more and more violent day by day. The great "Negro University Swindle" became the one absorbing topic of conversation throughout the Union. Individuals denounced it, journals denounced it, public meetings denounced it, the pictorial papers caricatured its friends, the whole nation seemed to be growing frantic over it. Meantime, the Washington correspondents were sending such telegrams as these abroad in the land: Under date of —

SATURDAY. — "Congressmen Jex and Fluke are wavering; it is believed they will desert the execrable bill."

MONDAY. — "Jex and Fluke *have* deserted!"

THURSDAY. — "Tubbs and Huffy left the sinking ship last night."

Later on:

"Three desertions. The University thieves are getting scared, though they will not own it."

Later:

"The leaders are growing stubborn — they swear they can carry it, but it is now almost certain that they no longer have a majority!"

After a day or two of reluctant and ambiguous telegrams:

"Public sentiment seems changing, a trifle, in favor of the bill — but only a trifle."

And still later:

"It is whispered that the Hon. Mr. Trollop has gone over to the pirates. It is probably a canard. Mr. Trollop has all along been the bravest and most efficient champion of virtue and the people against the bill, and the report is without doubt a shameless invention."

Next day:

"With characteristic treachery, the truckling and pusillanimous reptile, Crippled-Speech Trollop, has gone over to the enemy. It is contended, now, that *he has been a friend to the bill, in secret, since the day it was introduced,* and has had bankable reasons for being so; but he himself declares that he has gone over because the malignant persecution of the bill by the newspapers caused him to study its provisions with more care than he had previously done, and this close examination revealed the fact that the measure is one in every way worthy of support. (Pretty thin!) It cannot be denied that this desertion has had a damaging effect. Jex and Fluke have returned to their iniquitous allegiance, with six or eight others of lesser calibre, and it is reported and believed that Tubbs and Huffy are ready to go back. It is feared that the University swindle is stronger to-day than it has ever been before."

Later — midnight:

"It is said that the committee will report the bill back to-morrow. Both sides are marshaling their forces, and the fight on this bill is evidently going to be the hottest of the session. All Washington is boiling."

CHAPTER XIII.

PHILIP SHOWS HIS FRIENDSHIP FOR BRIERLY

Capienda rebus in malis præceps via est.

Seneca.

Et enim ipsi se impellunt, ubi semel a ratione discessum est: ipsaque sibi imbecillitas indulget, in altumque provehitur imprudenter: nec reperit locum consistendi.

Cicero.

"IT'S easy enough for another fellow to talk," said Harry, despondingly, after he had put Philip in possession of his view of the case. "It's easy enough to say 'give her up,' if you don't care for her. What am I going to do to give her up?"

It seemed to Harry that it was a situation requiring some active measures. He couldn't realize that he had fallen hopelessly in love without some rights accruing to him for the possession of the object of his passion. Quiet resignation under relinquishment of anything he wanted was not in his line. And when it appeared to him that his surrender of Laura would be the withdrawal of the one barrier that kept her from ruin, it was unreasonable to expect that he could see how to give her up.

Harry had the most buoyant confidence in his

own projects always; he saw everything connected with himself in a large way and in rosy hues. This predominance of the imagination over the judgment gave that appearance of exaggeration to his conversation and to his communications with regard to himself, which sometimes conveyed the impression that he was not speaking the truth. His acquaintances had been known to say that they invariably allowed a half for shrinkage in his statements, and held the other half under advisement for confirmation.

Philip in this case could not tell from Harry's story exactly how much encouragement Laura had given him, nor what hopes he might justly have of winning her. He had never seen him desponding before. The " brag" appeared to be all taken out of him, and his airy manner only asserted itself now and then in a comical imitation of its old self.

Philip wanted time to look about him before he decided what to do. He was not familiar with Washington, and it was difficult to adjust his feelings and perceptions to its peculiarities. Coming out of the sweet sanity of the Bolton household, this was by contrast the maddest Vanity Fair one could conceive. It seemed to him a feverish, unhealthy atmosphere in which lunacy would be easily developed. He fancied that everybody attached to himself an exaggerated importance, from the fact of being at the national capital, the center of political influence, the fountain of patronage, preferment, jobs, and opportunities.

People were introduced to each other as from this or that state, not from cities or towns, and this gave a largeness to their representative feeling. All the women talked politics as naturally and glibly as they talk fashion or literature elsewhere. There was always some exciting topic at the Capitol, or some huge slander was rising up like a miasmatic exhalation from the Potomac, threatening to settle no one knew exactly where. Every other person was an aspirant for a place, or, if he had one, for a better place, or more pay; almost every other one had some claim or interest or remedy to urge; even the women were all advocates for the advancement of some person, and they violently espoused or denounced this or that measure as it would affect some relative, acquaintance, or friend.

Love, travel, even death itself, waited on the chances of the dies daily thrown in the two Houses, and the committee-rooms there. If the measure went through, love could afford to ripen into marriage, and longing for foreign travel would have fruition; and it must have been only eternal hope springing in the breast that kept alive numerous old claimants who for years and years had besieged the doors of Congress, and who looked as if they needed not so much an appropriation of money as six feet of ground. And those who stood so long waiting for success to bring them death were usually those who had a just claim.

Representing states and talking of national and

even international affairs, as familiarly as neighbors
at home talk of poor crops and the extravagance of
their ministers, was likely at first to impose upon
Philip as to the importance of the people gathered
here.

There was a little newspaper editor from Phil's
native town, the assistant on a Peddletonian weekly,
who made his little annual joke about the " first egg
laid on our table," and who was the menial of every
tradesman in the village and under bonds to him for
frequent "puffs," except the undertaker, about
whose employment he was recklessly facetious. In
Washington he was an important man, correspondent, and clerk of two house committees, a " worker "
in politics, and a confident critic of every woman
and every man in Washington. He would be a consul, no doubt, by and by, at some foreign port, of
the language of which he was ignorant; though if
ignorance of language were a qualification he might
have been a consul at home. His easy familiarity
with great men was beautiful to see, and when Philip
learned what a tremendous underground influence
this little ignoramus had, he no longer wondered at
the queer appointments and the queerer legislation.

Philip was not long in discovering that people in
Washington did not differ much from other people;
they had the same meannesses, generosities, and
tastes. A Washington boarding-house had the odor
of a boarding-house the world over.

Colonel Sellers was as unchanged as any one

Philip saw whom he had known elsewhere. Washington appeared to be the native element of this man. His pretensions were equal to any he encountered there. He saw nothing in its society that equaled that of Hawkeye; he sat down to no table that could not be unfavorably contrasted with his own at home; the most airy scheme inflated in the hot air of the capital only reached in magnitude some of his lesser fancies, the by-play of his constructive imagination.

"The country is getting along very well," he said to Philip, "but our public men are too timid. What we want is more money. I've told Boutwell so. Talk about basing the currency on gold; you might as well base it on pork. Gold is only one product. Base it on everything! You've got to do something for the West. How am I to move my crops? We must have improvements. Grant's got the idea. We want a canal from the James River to the Mississippi. Government ought to build it."

It was difficult to get the Colonel off from these large themes when he was once started, but Philip brought the conversation round to Laura and her reputation in the city.

"No," he said, "I haven't noticed much. We've been so busy about this university. It will make Laura rich with the rest of us, and she has done nearly as much as if she were a man. She has great talent, and will make a big match. I see the foreign

10**

ministers and that sort after her.   Yes, there is talk,
always will be about a pretty woman so much in
public as she is.   Tough stories come to me, but I
put 'em away.   'Taint likely one of Si. Hawkins'
children would do that — for she is the same as a child
of his.   I told her, though, to go slow," added the
Colonel, as if that mysterious admonition from him
would set everything right.

"Do you know anything about a Colonel Selby?"

"Know all about him.   Fine fellow.   But he's
got a wife; and I told him, as a friend, he'd better
sheer off from Laura.   I reckon he thought better
of it and did."

But Philip was not long in learning the truth.
Courted as Laura was by a certain class and still admitted into society, that, nevertheless, buzzed with
disreputable stories about her, she had lost character
with the best people.   Her intimacy with Selby was
open gossip, and there were winks and thrustings of
the tongue in any group of men when she passed
by.   It was clear enough that Harry's delusion must
be broken up, and that no such feeble obstacle as
his passion could interpose would turn Laura from
her fate.   Philip determined to see her, and put
himself in possession of the truth, as he suspected
it, in order to show Harry his folly.

Laura, after her last conversation with Harry, had
a new sense of her position.   She had noticed before
the signs of a change in manner toward her, a little
less respect perhaps from men, and an avoidance by

women. She had attributed this latter partly to jealousy of her, for no one is willing to acknowledge a fault in himself when a more agreeable motive can be found for the estrangement of his acquaintances. But, now, if society had turned on her, she would defy it. It was not in her nature to shrink. She knew she had been wronged, and she knew that she had no remedy.

What she heard of Colonel Selby's proposed departure alarmed her more than anything else, and she calmly determined that if he was deceiving her the second time it should be the last. Let society finish the tragedy if it liked; she was indifferent what came after. At the first opportunity, she charged Selby with his intention to abandon her. He unblushingly denied it. He had not thought of going to Europe. He had only been amusing himself with Sellers' schemes. He swore that as soon as she succeeded with her bill, he would fly with her to any part of the world.

She did not quite believe him, for she saw that he feared her, and she began to suspect that his were the protestations of a coward to gain time. But she showed him no doubts. She only watched his movements day by day, and always held herself ready to act promptly.

When Philip came into the presence of this attractive woman, he could not realize that she was the subject of all the scandal he had heard. She received him with quite the old Hawkeye openness and cordiality, and fell to talking at once of their little acquaintance there; and it seemed impossible that he could ever say to her what he had come determined to say. Such a man as Philip has only one standard by which to judge women.

Laura recognized that fact, no doubt. The better part of her woman's nature saw it. Such a man might, years ago, not now, have changed her nature, and made the issue of her life so different, even after her cruel abandonment. She had a dim feeling of this, and she would like now to stand well with him. The spark of truth and honor that was left in her was elicited by his presence. It was this influence that governed her conduct in this interview.

"I have come," said Philip in his direct manner, "from my friend Mr. Brierly. You are not ignorant of his feeling toward you?"

"Perhaps not."

"But perhaps you do not know, you who have so much admiration, how sincere and overmastering his love is for you?" Philip would not have spoken so plainly, if he had in mind anything except to draw from Laura something that would end Harry's passion.

"And is sincere love so rare, Mr. Sterling?" asked Laura, moving her foot a little, and speaking with a shade of sarcasm.

"Perhaps not in Washington," replied Philip, tempted into a similar tone. "Excuse my bluntness," he continued, "but would the knowledge of his love, would his devotion, make any difference to you in your Washington life?"

"In respect to what?" asked Laura quickly.

"Well, to others. I won't equivocate — to Colonel Selby?"

Laura's face flushed with anger, or shame; she looked steadily at Philip and began:

"By what right, sir ——"

"By the right of friendship," interrupted Philip stoutly. "It may matter little to you. It is everything to him. He has a Quixotic notion that you would turn back from what is before you for his sake. You cannot be ignorant of what all the city is talking of." Philip said this determinedly and with some bitterness.

It was a full minute before Laura spoke. Both had risen, Philip as if to go, and Laura in suppressed excitement. When she spoke her voice was very unsteady, and she looked down.

"Yes, I know. I perfectly understand what you mean. Mr. Brierly is nothing — simply nothing. He is a moth singed, that is all — the trifler with women thought he was a wasp. I have no pity for him, not the least. You may tell him not to make a fool of himself, and to keep away. I say this on your account, not his. You are not like him. It is enough for me that you want it so. Mr. Sterling," she continued, looking up, and there were tears in her eyes that contradicted the hardness of her language, "you might not pity him if you knew my

10

history; perhaps you would not wonder at some things you hear. No; it is useless to ask me why it must be so. You can't make a life over — society wouldn't let you if you would — and mine must be lived as it is. There, sir, I'm not offended; but it is useless for you to say anything more."

Philip went away with his heart lightened about Harry, but profoundly saddened by the glimpse of what this woman might have been. He told Harry all that was necessary of the conversation — she was bent on going her own way, he had not the ghost of a chance — he was a fool, she had said, for thinking he had.

And Harry accepted it meekly, and made up his own mind that Philip didn't know much about women.

CHAPTER XIV.

WHY MR. BUCKSTONE SUPPORTED THE UNIVERSITY BILL

—Nakila cu ch'y cu yao chike, chi ka togobah cu y vach, x-e u chax-cut?—Utz, chi ka ya puvak chyve, x-e cha-cu ri amag.

Popol Vuh.

THE galleries of the House were packed, on the momentous day, not because the reporting of an important bill back by a committee was a thing to be excited about, if the bill were going to take the ordinary course afterward; it would be like getting excited over the empaneling of a coroner's jury in a murder case, instead of saving up one's emotions for the grander occasion of the hanging of the accused, two years later, after all the tedious forms of law had been gone through with.

But suppose you understand that this coroner's jury is going to turn out to be a vigilance committee in disguise, who will hear testimony for an hour and then hang the murderer on the spot? That puts a different aspect upon the matter. Now it was whispered that the legitimate forms of procedure usual in the House, and which keep a bill hanging along for days, and even weeks, before it is finally passed upon, were going to be overruled in this case, and

J

(147)

short work made of the measure; and so, what was
beginning as a mere inquest might turn out to be
something very different.

In the course of the day's business the order of
"Reports of Committees" was finally reached, and
when the weary crowds heard that glad announcement issue from the Speaker's lips they ceased to
fret at the dragging delay, and plucked up spirit.
The chairman of the Committee on Benevolent Appropriations rose and made his report, and just then
a blue-uniformed brass-mounted little page put a
note into his hand. It was from Senator Dilworthy,
who had appeared upon the floor of the House for
a moment and flitted away again:

> "Everybody expects a grand assault in force; no doubt you believe
> as I certainly do, that it is the thing to do; we are strong, and every-
> thing is hot for the contest. Trollop's espousal of our cause has im-
> mensely helped us and we grow in power constantly. Ten of the
> opposition were called away from town about noon (*but*— so it is said —
> *only for one day*). Six others are sick, but expect to be about again
> *to-morrow or next day* a friend tells me. A bold onslaught is worth try-
> ing. Go for a suspension of the rules! You will find we can swing a
> two-thirds vote — I am perfectly satisfied of it. The Lord's truth will
> prevail.
>
> "*Dilworthy.*"

Mr. Buckstone had reported the bills from his
committee, one by one, leaving *the* bill to the last.
When the House had voted upon the acceptance or
rejection of the report upon all but it, and the question now being upon *its* disposal—

Mr. Buckstone begged that the House would give
its attention to a few remarks which he desired to

make. His committee had instructed him to report the bill favorably; he wished to explain the nature of the measure, and thus justify the committee's action; the hostility roused by the press would then disappear, and the bill would shine forth in its true and noble character. He said that its provisions were simple. It incorporated the Knobs Industrial University, locating it in East Tennessee, declaring it open to all persons without distinction of sex, color, or religion, and committing its management to a board of perpetual trustees, with power to fill vacancies in their own number. It provided for the erection of certain buildings for the university, dormitories, lecture halls, museums, libraries, laboratories, workshops, furnaces, and mills. It provided also for the purchase of sixty-five thousand acres of land (fully described) for the purposes of the university, in the Knobs of East Tennessee. And it appropriated [blank] dollars for the purchase of the land, which should be the property of the national trustees in trust for the uses named.

Every effort had been made to secure the refusal of the whole amount of the property of the Hawkins heirs in the Knobs, some seventy-five thousand acres, Mr. Buckstone said. But Mr. Washington Hawkins (one of the heirs) objected. He was, indeed, very reluctant to sell any part of the land at any price; and, indeed, this reluctance was justifiable when one considers how constantly and how greatly the property is rising in value.

What the South needed, continued Mr. Buckstone, was skilled labor. Without that it would be
unable to develop its mines, build its roads, work to
advantage and without great waste its fruitful land,
establish manufactures or enter upon a prosperous
industrial career. Its laborers were almost altogether
unskilled. Change them into intelligent, trained
workmen, and you increased at once the capital, the
resources of the entire South, which would enter
upon a prosperity hitherto unknown. In five years
the increase in local wealth would not only reimburse
the government for the outlay in this appropriation,
but pour untold wealth into the treasury.

This was the material view, and the least important
in the honorable gentleman's opinion. [Here he
referred to some notes furnished him by Senator
Dilworthy, and then continued.] God had given us
the care of these colored millions. What account
should we render to Him of our stewardship? We
had made them free. Should we leave them ignorant?
We had cast them upon their own resources.
Should we leave them without tools? We could not
tell what the intentions of Providence are in regard
to these peculiar people, but our duty was plain.
The Knobs Industrial University would be a vast
school of modern science and practice, worthy of a
great nation. It would combine the advantages of
Zurich, Freiburg, Creuzot, and the Sheffield Scien-
tific. Providence had apparently reserved and set
apart the Knobs of East Tennessee for this purpose.

What else were they for? Was it not wonderful that for more than thirty years, over a generation, the choicest portion of them had remained in one family, untouched, as if consecrated for some great use!

It might be asked why the government should buy this land, when it had millions of acres, more than the railroad companies desired, which it might devote to this purpose? He answered, that the government had no such tract of land as this. It had nothing comparable to it for the purposes of the university. This was to be a school of mining, of engineering, of the working of metals, of chemistry, zoology, botany, manufactures, agriculture: in short, of all the complicated industries that make a state great. There was no place for the location of such a school like the Knobs of East Tennessee. The hills abounded in metals of all sorts, iron in all its combinations, copper, bismuth, gold and silver in small quantities, platinum he believed, tin, aluminium; it was covered with forests and strange plants; in the woods were found the coon, the opossum, the fox, the deer, and many other animals who roamed in the domain of natural history; coal existed in enormous quantity and no doubt oil; it was such a place for the practice of agricultural experiments that any student who had been successful there would have an easy task in any other portion of the country.

No place offered equal facilities for experiments

in mining, metallurgy, engineering. He expected to live to see the day when the youth of the South would resort to its mines, its workshops, its laboratories, its furnaces and factories for practical instruction in all the great industrial pursuits.

A noisy and rather ill-natured debate followed now, and lasted hour after hour. The friends of the bill were instructed by the leaders to *make no effort to check this;* it was deemed better strategy to tire out the opposition; it was decided to vote down every proposition to adjourn, and so continue the sitting in to the night; opponents might desert, then, one by one and weaken their party, for they had no personal stake in the bill.

Sunset came, and still the fight went on; the gas was lit, the crowd in the galleries began to thin, but the contest continued; the crowd returned, by and by, with hunger and thirst appeased, and aggravated the hungry and thirsty House by looking contented and comfortable; but still the wrangle lost nothing of its bitterness. Recesses were moved plaintively by the opposition, and invariably voted down by the university army.

At midnight the House presented a spectacle calculated to interest a stranger. The great galleries were still thronged — though only with men now; the bright colors that had made them look like hanging gardens were gone, with the ladies. The reporters' gallery was merely occupied by one or two watchful sentinels of the quill-driving guild;

the main body cared nothing for a debate that had
dwindled to a mere vaporing of dull speakers and
now and then a brief quarrel over a point of order;
but there was an unusually large attendance of
journalists in the reporters' waiting-room, chatting,
smoking, and keeping on the *qui vive* for the general
irruption of the Congressional volcano that must
come when the time was ripe for it. Senator Dilworthy and Philip were in the diplomatic gallery;
Washington sat in the public gallery, and Colonel
Sellers was not far away. The Colonel had been
flying about the corridors and buttonholing Congressmen all the evening, and believed that he had
accomplished a world of valuable service; but fatigue
was telling upon him now, and he was quiet and
speechless — for once. Below, a few Senators
lounged upon the sofas set apart for visitors, and
talked with idle Congressmen. A dreary member
was speaking; the presiding officer was nodding;
here and there little knots of members stood in the
aisles, whispering together; all about the House
others sat in all the various attitudes that express
weariness; some, tilted back, had one or more legs
disposed upon their desks; some sharpened pencils
indolently; some scribbled aimlessly; some yawned
and stretched; a great many lay upon their breasts
upon the desks, sound asleep and gently snoring.
The flooding gaslight from the fancifully wrought
roof poured down upon the tranquil scene. Hardly
a sound disturbed the stillness, save the monotonous

eloquence of the gentleman who occupied the floor.
Now and then a warrior of the opposition broke
down under the pressure, gave it up and went home.

Mr. Buckstone began to think it might be safe,
now, to "proceed to business." He consulted with
Trollop and one or two others. Senator Dilworthy
descended to the floor of the House and they went
to meet him. After a brief comparison of notes,
the Congressmen sought their seats and sent pages
about the House with messages to friends. These
latter instantly roused up, yawned, and began to
look alert. The moment the floor was unoccupied,
Mr. Buckstone rose, with an injured look, and said
it was evident that the opponents of the bill were
merely talking against time, hoping in this unbe-
coming way to tire out the friends of the measure
and so defeat it. Such conduct might be respectable enough in a village debating society, but it was
trivial among statesmen, it was out of place in so
august an assemblage as the House of Representatives of the United States. The friends of the bill
had been not only willing that its opponents should
express their opinions, but had strongly desired it.
They courted the fullest and freest discussion; but
it seemed to him that this fairness was but illy ap-
preciated, since gentlemen were capable of taking
advantage of it for selfish and unworthy ends. This
trifling had gone far enough. He called for the
question.

The instant Mr. Buckstone sat down, the storm

burst forth. A dozen gentlemen sprang to their feet.

" Mr. Speaker!"

' Mr. Speaker!"

" Mr. Speaker!"

" Order! Order! Order! Question! Question!"

The sharp blows of the Speaker's gavel rose above the din.

The " previous question," that hated gag, was moved and carried. All debate came to a sudden end, of course. Triumph No. 1.

Then the vote was taken on the adoption of the report, and it carried by a surprising majority.

Mr. Buckstone got the floor again and moved that the rules be suspended and the bill read a first time.

Mr. Trollop —" Second the motion!"

The Speaker —" It is moved and ——"

Clamor of Voices. " Move we adjourn! Second the motion! Adjourn! Adjourn! Order! Order!"

The Speaker (after using his gavel vigorously) — " It is moved and seconded that the House do now adjourn. All those in favor ——"

Voices —" Division! Division! Ayes and nays! Ayes and nays!"

It was decided to vote upon the adjournment by ayes and nays. This was war in earnest. The excitement was furious. The galleries were in commotion in an instant, the reporters swarmed to their places, idling members of the House flocked to their

seats, nervous gentlemen sprang to their feet, pages
flew hither and thither, life and animation were
visible everywhere, all the long ranks of faces in the
building were kindled.

" This thing decides it !" thought Mr. Buckstone;
" but let the fight proceed."

The voting began, and every sound ceased but the
calling of the names and the " Aye !"   " No !"
'No !"   " Aye !" of the responses.   There was
not a movement in the House; the people seemed
to hold their breath.

The voting ceased, and then there was an interval
of dead silence while the clerk made up his count.
There was a two-thirds vote on the university side —
and two over !

The Speaker—" The rules are suspended, the
motion is carried — first reading of the *bill !*"

By one impulse the galleries broke forth into
stormy applause, and even some of the members of
the House were not wholly able to restrain their
feelings.   The Speaker's gavel came to the rescue
and his clear voice followed:

" Order, gentlemen !   The House will come to
order !   If spectators offend again, the Sergeant-at-
arms will clear the galleries !"

Then he cast his eyes aloft and gazed at some
object attentively for a moment.   All eyes followed
the direction of the Speaker's, and then there was a
general titter.   The Speaker said:

" Let the Sergeant-at-arms inform the gentleman

that his conduct is an infringement of the dignity of the House — and one which is not warranted by the state of the weather.''

Poor Sellers was the culprit. He sat in the front seat of the gallery, with his arms and his tired body overflowing the balustrade — sound asleep, dead to all excitements, all disturbances. The fluctuations of the Washington weather had influenced his dreams, perhaps, for during the recent tempest of applause he had hoisted his gingham umbrella and calmly gone on with his slumbers. Washington Hawkins had seen the act, but was not near enough at hand to save his friend, and no one who was near enough desired to spoil the effect. But a neighbor stirred up the Colonel, now that the House had its eye upon him, and the great speculator furled his tent like the Arab. He said:

'' Bless my soul, I'm so absent-minded when I get to thinking! I never wear an umbrella in the house — did anybody notice it? What — asleep? Indeed? And did you wake me, sir? Thank you — thank you very much, indeed. It might have fallen out of my hands and been injured. Admirable article, sir — present from a friend in Hong Kong; one doesn't come across silk like that in this country — it's the real Young Hyson, I'm told.''

By this time the incident was forgotten, for the House was at war again. Victory was almost in sight, now, and the friends of the bill threw themselves into their work with enthusiasm. They soon

11**

moved and carried its second reading, and after a
strong, sharp fight, carried a motion to go into committee of the whole.   The Speaker left his place, of
course, and a chairman was appointed.

Now the contest raged hotter than ever — for the
authority that compels order when the House sits *as*
a House, is greatly diminished when it sits as a
committee.   The main fight came upon the filling
of the blanks with the sum to be appropriated for
the purchase of the land, of course.

Mr. Buckstone —" Mr. Chairman, I move you,
sir, that the words *three millions of* be inserted."

Mr. Hadley —" Mr. Chairman, I move that the
words *two and a half dollars* be inserted."

Mr. Clawson —" Mr. Chairman, I move the in-
sertion of the words *five and twenty cents*, as representing the true value of this barren and isolated
tract of desolation."

The question, according to rule, was taken upon
the smallest sum first.   It was lost.

Then upon the next smallest sum.   Lost also.

And then upon the three millions.   After a vigorous battle that lasted a considerable time, this motion
was carried.

Then, clause by clause, the bill was read, discussed, and amended in trifling particulars, and now
the committee rose and reported.

The moment the House had resumed its functions
and received the report, Mr. Buckstone moved and
carried the third reading of the bill.

The same bitter war over the sum to be paid was fought over again, and now that the ayes and nays could be called and placed on record, every man was compelled to vote by name on the three millions, and, indeed, on every paragraph of the bill from the enacting clause straight through. But, as before, the friends of the measure stood firm and voted in a solid body every time, and so did its enemies.

The supreme moment was come now, but so sure was the result that not even a voice was raised to interpose an adjournment. The enemy were totally demoralized. The bill was put upon its final passage almost without dissent, and the calling of the ayes and nays began. When it was ended the triumph was complete — the two-thirds vote held good, and a veto was impossible, as far as the House was concerned!

Mr. Buckstone resolved that now that the nail was driven home, he would clinch it on the other side and make it stay forever. He moved a reconsideration of the vote by which the bill had passed. The motion was lost, of course, and the great Industrial University act was an accomplished fact as far as it was in the power of the House of Representatives to make it so.

There was no need to move an adjournment. The instant the last motion was decided, the enemies of the university rose and flocked out of the hall, talking angrily, and its friends flocked after them jubilant and congratulatory. The galleries disgorged their burden, and presently the House was silent and deserted.

When Colonel Sellers and Washington stepped out of the building they were surprised to find that the daylight was old and the sun well up. Said the Colonel:

"Give me your hand, my boy! You're all right at last! You're a millionaire! At least you're going to be. The thing is dead sure. Don't you bother about the Senate. Leave me and Dilworthy to take care of that. Run along home, now, and tell Laura. Lord, it's magnificent news — perfectly magnificent! Run, now. I'll telegraph my wife. She must come here and help me build a house. Everything's all right now!"

Washington was so dazed by his good fortune and so bewildered by the gaudy pageant of dreams that was already trailing its long ranks through his brain, that he wandered he knew not where, and so loitered by the way that when at last he reached home he woke to a sudden annoyance in the fact that his news must be old to Laura, now, for of course Senator Dilworthy must have already been home and told her an hour before. He knocked at her door, but there was no answer.

"That is like the Duchess," said he. "Always cool. A body can't excite her — can't keep her excited, anyway. Now she has gone off to sleep again, as comfortably as if she were used to picking up a million dollars every day or two."

Then he went to bed. But he could not sleep;
so he got up and wrote a long, rapturous letter to
Louise, and another to his mother. And he closed
both to much the same effect:

"Laura will be queen of America, now, and she will be applauded,
and honored and petted by the whole nation. Her name will be in
every one's mouth more than ever, and how they will court her and
quote her bright speeches. And mine, too, I suppose; though they do
that more already, than they really seem to deserve. Oh, the world is
so bright, now, and so cheery; the clouds are all gone, our long struggle
is ended, our troubles are all over. Nothing can ever make us unhappy
any more. Your dear faithful ones will have the reward of your patient
waiting now. How father's wisdom is proven at last! And how I re-
pent me that there have been times when I lost faith and said the blessing he stored up for us a tedious generation ago was but a long-drawn
curse, a blight upon us all. But everything is well now — we are done
with poverty, and toil, weariness and heart-breakings; all the world is
filled with sunshine."

CHAPTER XV.

LAURA KILLS COLONEL SELBY

Forte è l'aceto di vin dolce.

Ne bið swylc cwénlíc þeaw
idese to efnanne,
þeáh ðe hió ænlícu sy,
þætte freoðu-webbe
feores onsæce,
æfter lig-torne,
leófne mannan.

Beowulf.

PHILIP left the Capitol and walked up Pennsylvania Avenue in company with Senator Dilworthy. It was a bright spring morning; the air was soft and inspiring; in the deepening wayside green, the pink flush of the blossoming peach trees, the soft suffusion on the heights of Arlington, and the breath of the warm south wind, was apparent the annual miracle of the resurrection of the earth.

The Senator took off his hat and seemed to open his soul to the sweet influences of the morning. After the heat and noise of the chamber, under its dull gas-illuminated glass canopy, and the all-night

(162)

struggle of passion and feverish excitement there, the open, tranquil world seemed like Heaven. The Senator was not in an exultant mood, but rather in a condition of holy joy, befitting a Christian states- man, whose benevolent plans Providence has made its own and stamped with approval. The great battle had been fought, but the measure had still to encounter the scrutiny of the Senate, and Providence sometimes acts differently in the two Houses. Still, the Senator was tranquil, for he knew that there is an *esprit de corps* in the Senate which does not exist in the House, the effect of which is to make the members complaisant toward the projects of each other, and to extend a mutual aid which in a more vulgar body would be called " log-rolling."

" It is, under Providence, a good night's work, Mr. Sterling. The government has founded an in- stitution which will remove half the difficulty from the Southern problem. And it is a good thing for the Hawkins heirs, a very good thing. Laura will be almost a millionaire."

" Do you think, Mr. Dilworthy, that the Haw- kinses will get much of the money?" asked Philip innocently, remembering the fate of the Columbus River appropriation.

The Senator looked at his companion scrutiniz- ingly for a moment to see if he meant anything personal, and then replied:

" Undoubtedly, undoubtedly. I have had their interests greatly at heart. There will, of course, be

K

a few expenses, but the widow and orphans will realize all that Mr. Hawkins dreamed of for them.''

The birds were singing as they crossed the Presidential square, now bright with its green turf and tender foliage. After the two had gained the steps of the Senator's house they stood a moment, looking upon the lovely prospect.

"It is like the peace of God," said the Senator devoutly.

Entering the house, the Senator called a servant and said: "Tell Miss Laura that we are waiting to see her. I ought to have sent a messenger on horseback half an hour ago," he added to Philip. "She will be transported with our victory. You must stop to breakfast, and see the excitement." The servant soon came back, with a wondering look and reported:

"Miss Laura ain't dah, sah. I reckon she hain't been dah all night."

The Senator and Philip both started up. In Laura's room there were the marks of a confused and hasty departure, drawers half open, little articles strewn on the floor. The bed had not been disturbed. Upon inquiry it appeared that Laura had not been at dinner, excusing herself to Mrs. Dilworthy on the plea of a violent headache; that she made a request to the servants that she might not be disturbed.

The Senator was astounded. Philip thought at once of Colonel Selby. Could Laura have run away

" MISS LAURA AIN'T DAH, SAH "

with him? The Senator thought not. In fact, it could not be. General Leffenwell, the member from New Orleans, had casually told him at the house last night that Selby and his family went to New York yesterday morning and were to sail for Europe to-day.

Philip had another idea which he did not mention. He seized his hat, and saying that he would go and see what he could learn, ran to the lodgings of Harry, whom he had not seen since yesterday afternoon, when he left him to go to the House.

Harry was not in. He had gone out with a hand bag before six o'clock yesterday, saying that he had to go to New York, but should return next day. In Harry's room on the table Philip found this note:

"Dear Mr. Brierly:—Can you meet me at the six o'clock train, and be my escort to New York? I have to go about this University bill, the vote of an absent member we must have here. Senator Dilworthy cannot go. Yours &c., L. H."

"Confound it," said Philip, "the noodle has fallen into her trap. And she promised me she would let him alone."

He only stopped to send a note to Senator Dilworthy, telling him what he had found, and that he should go at once to New York, and then hastened to the railway station. He had to wait an hour for a train, and when it did start it seemed to go at a snail's pace.

Philip was devoured with anxiety. Where could they have gone? What was Laura's object in taking Harry? Had the flight anything to do with Selby?

Would Harry be such a fool as to be dragged into some public scandal?

It seemed as if the train would never reach Baltimore. Then there was a long delay at Havre de Grace. A hot box had to be cooled at Wilmington. Would it never get on? Only in passing around the city of Philadelphia did the train not seem to go slow. Philip stood upon the platform and watched for the Boltons' house, fancied he could distinguish its roof among the trees, and wondered how Ruth would feel if she knew he was so near her.

Then came Jersey, everlasting Jersey, stupid, irritating Jersey, where the passengers are always asking which line they are on, and where they are to come out, and whether they have yet reached Elizabeth. Launched into Jersey, one has a vague notion that he is on many lines and no one in particular, and that he is liable at any moment to come to Elizabeth. He has no notion what Elizabeth is, and always resolves that the next time he goes that way he will look out of the window and see what it is like; but he never does. Or, if he does, he probably finds that it is Princeton or something of that sort. He gets annoyed, and never can see the use of having different names for stations in Jersey. By and by there is Newark, three or four Newarks, apparently; then marshes, then long rock cuttings devoted to the advertisements of patent medicines and ready-made clothing and New York tonics for Jersey agues, and — Jersey City is reached.

On the ferry-boat Philip bought an evening paper from a boy crying " 'Ere's the *Evening Gram*, all about the murder," and with breathless haste ran his eyes over the following:

SHOCKING MURDER! ! !

TRAGEDY IN HIGH LIFE! !   A BEAUTIFUL WOMAN SHOOTS A DISTIN-
   GUISHED CONFEDERATE SOLDIER AT THE SOUTHERN HOTEL! ! !
   JEALOUSY THE CAUSE! ! ! !

This morning occurred another of those shocking murders which have become the almost daily food of the newspapers, the direct result of the socialistic doctrines and woman's rights agitations, which have made every woman the avenger of her own wrongs, and all society the hunting ground for her victims.

About nine o'clock a lady deliberately shot a man dead in the public parlor of the Southern Hotel, coolly remarking, as she threw down her revolver and permitted herself to be taken into custody, " He brought it on himself." Our reporters were immediately dispatched to the scene of the tragedy, and gathered the following particulars.

Yesterday afternoon arrived at the hotel from Washington, Col. George Selby and family, who had taken passage and were to sail at noon to-day in the steamer *Scotia* for England. The Colonel was a handsome man about forty, a gentleman of wealth and high social posi-tion, a resident of New Orleans. He served with distinction in the confederate army, and received a wound in the leg from which he has never entirely recovered, being obliged to use a cane in locomotion.

This morning at about nine o'clock, a lady, accompanied by a gentle-man, called at the office of the hotel and asked for Col. Selby. The Colonel was at breakfast. Would the clerk tell him that a lady and gentleman wished to see him for a moment in the parlor? The clerk says that the gentleman asked her, " What do you want to see *him* for?" and that she replied, " He is going to Europe, and I ought to just say good by."

Col. Selby was informed, and the lady and gentleman were shown to the parlor, in which were at the time three or four other persons. Five minutes after two shots were fired in quick succession, and there was a rush to the parlor from which the reports came.

Col. Selby was found lying on the floor, bleeding, but not dead. Two gentlemen, who had just come in, had seized the lady, who made no resistance, and she was at once given in charge of a police officer who arrived. The persons who were in the parlor agree substantially as to what occurred. They had happened to be looking towards the door when the man—Col. Selby—entered with his cane, and they looked at him, because he stopped as if surprised and frightened, and made a backward movement. At the same moment the lady in the bonnet advanced towards him and said something like "George, will you come with me?" He replied, throwing up his hand and retreating, "My God! I can't, don't fire," and the next instant two shots were heard and he fell. The lady appeared to be beside herself with rage or excitement, and trembled very much when the gentlemen took hold of her; it was to them she said, "He brought it on himself."

Col. Selby was carried at once to his room and Dr. Puffer, the eminent surgeon, was sent for. It was found that he was shot through the breast and through the abdomen. Other aid was summoned, but the wounds were mortal, and Col. Selby expired in an hour, in pain, but his mind was clear to the last, and he made a full deposition. The substance of it was that his murderess is a Miss Laura Hawkins, whom he had known at Washington as a lobbyist, and had had some business with her. She had followed him with her attentions and solicitations, and had endeavored to make him desert his wife and go to Europe with her. When he resisted and avoided her, she had threatened him. Only the day before he left Washington she had declared that he should never go out of the city alive without her.

It seems to have been a deliberate and premeditated murder, the woman following him from Washington on purpose to commit it.

We learn that the murderess, who is a woman of dazzling and transcendent beauty and about twenty-six or seven, is a niece of Senator Dilworthy, at whose house she has been spending the winter. She belongs to a high Southern family, and has the reputation of being an heiress. Like some other great beauties and belles in Washington however there have been whispers that she had something to do with the lobby. If we mistake not we have heard her name mentioned in connection with the sale of the Tennessee Lands to the Knobs University, the bill for which passed the House last night.

Her companion is Mr. Harry Brierly, a New York dandy, who has been in Washington. His connection with her and with this tragedy is not known, but he was also taken into custody, and will be detained at least as a witness.

P. S.   One of the persons present in the parlor says that after Laura Hawkins had fired twice, she turned the pistol towards herself, but that Brierly sprang and caught it from her hand, and that it was he who threw it on the floor.

Further particulars with full biographies of all the parties in our next edition.

Philip hastened at once to the Southern Hotel, where he found still a great state of excitement, and a thousand different and exaggerated stories passing from mouth to mouth. The witnesses of the event had told it over so many times that they had worked it up into a most dramatic scene, and embellished it with whatever could heighten its awfulness. Outsiders had taken up invention also. The Colonel's wife had gone insane, they said. The children had rushed into the parlor and rolled themselves in their father's blood. The hotel clerk said that he noticed there was murder in the woman's eye when he saw her. A person who had met the woman on the stairs felt a creeping sensation. Some thought Brierly was an accomplice, and that he had set the woman on to kill his rival. Some said the woman showed the calmness and indifference of insanity.

Philip learned that Harry and Laura had both been taken to the city prison, and he went there; but he was not admitted. Not being a newspaper reporter, he could not see either of them that night; but the officer questioned him suspiciously and asked him who he was. He might perhaps see Brierly in the morning.

The latest editions of the evening papers had the result of the inquest. It was a plain enough case for the jury, but they sat over it a long time, listening to the wrangling of the physicians. Dr. Puffer insisted that the man died from the effects of the wound in the chest. Dr. Dobb as strongly insisted that the wound in the abdomen caused death. Dr. Golightly suggested that, in his opinion, death ensued from a complication of the two wounds and perhaps other causes. He examined the table waiter, as to whether Colonel Selby ate any breakfast, and what he ate, and if he had any appetite.

The jury finally threw themselves back upon the indisputable fact that Selby was dead, that either wound would have killed him (admitted by the doctors), and rendered a verdict that he died from pistol-shot wounds inflicted by a pistol in the hands of Laura Hawkins.

The morning papers blazed with big type, and overflowed with details of the murder. The accounts in the evening papers were only the premonitory drops to this mighty shower. The scene was dramatically worked up in column after column. There were sketches, biographical and historical. There were long "specials" from Washington, giving a full history of Laura's career there, with the names of men with whom she was said to be intimate, a description of Senator Dilworthy's residence and of his family, and of Laura's room in his house, and a sketch of the Senator's appearance and what he said. There was a great deal about her beauty, her accomplishments, and her brilliant position in society, and her doubtful position in society. There was also an interview with Colonel Sellers and another with Washington Hawkins, the brother of the murderess. One journal had a long dispatch from Hawkeye, reporting the excitement in that quiet village and the reception of the awful intelligence.

All the parties had been " interviewed." There were reports of conversations with the clerk at the hotel, with the call-boy, with the waiter at table, with all the witnesses, with the policeman, with the landlord (who wanted it understood that nothing of that sort had ever happened in his house before, although it had always been frequented by the best Southern society), and with Mrs. Colonel Selby. There were diagrams illustrating the scene of the shooting, and views of the hotel and street, and portraits of the parties.

There were three minute and different statements from the doctors about the wounds, so technically worded that nobody could understand them. Harry and Laura had also been " interviewed," and there was a statement from Philip himself, which a reporter had knocked him up out of bed at midnight to give, though how he found him, Philip never could conjecture.

What some of the journals lacked in suitable length for the occasion, they made up in encyclopædic information about other similar murders and shootings.

The statement from Laura was not full, in fact it was fragmentary, and consisted of nine parts of the reporter's valuable observations to one of Laura's, and it was, as the reporter significantly remarked, "incoherent." But it appeared that Laura claimed to be Selby's wife, or to have been his wife, that he had deserted her and betrayed her, and that she was going to follow him to Europe. When the reporter asked:

"What made you shoot him, Miss Hawkins?" Laura's only reply was, very simply,

"Did I shoot him? Do they say I shot him?" And she would say no more.

The news of the murder was made the excitement of the day. Talk of it filled the town. The facts reported were scrutinized, the standing of the parties was discussed, the dozen different theories of the motive, broached in the newspapers, were disputed over.

During the night subtle electricity had carried the tale over all the wires of the continent and under the sea; and in all villages and towns of the Union, from the Atlantic to the Territories, and away up and down the Pacific slope, and as far as London and Paris and Berlin, that morning the name of Laura Hawkins was spoken by millions and millions of people, while the owner of it — the sweet child of years ago, the beautiful queen of Washington drawing rooms — sat shivering on her cot-bed in the darkness of a damp cell in the Tombs.

CHAPTER XVI.

LAURA IN THE TOMBS

— Mana qo c'u x-opon-vi ri v'oyeualal, ri v'achihilal! ahcarroc cah, ahcarroc uleu! la quitzih varal in camel, in zachel varal chuxmut cah, chuxmut uleu!

Rabinal-Achi.

PHILIP'S first effort was to get Harry out of the Tombs. He gained permission to see him, in the presence of an officer, during the day, and he found that hero very much cast down.

"I never intended to come to such a place as this, old fellow," he said to Philip; "it's no place for a gentleman, they've no idea how to treat a gentleman. Look at that provender," pointing to his uneaten prison ration. "They tell me I am detained as a witness, and I passed the night among a lot of cut-throats and dirty rascals — a pretty witness I'd be in a month spent in such company."

"But what under heavens," asked Philip, "induced you to come to New York with Laura! What was it for?"

"What for? Why, she wanted me to come. I didn't know anything about that cursed Selby. She said it was lobby business for the University. I'd

no idea what she was dragging me into that con-
founded hotel for. I suppose she knew that the
Southerners all go there, and thought she'd find her
man. Oh! Lord, I wish I'd taken your advice.
You might as well murder somebody and have the
credit of it, as get into the newspapers the way I
have. She's pure devil, that girl. You ought to
have seen how sweet she was on me. What an ass I
am!''

"Well, I'm not going to dispute a poor prisoner.
But the first thing is to get you out of this. I've
brought the note Laura wrote you, for one thing,
and I've seen your uncle, and explained the truth
of the case to him. He will be here soon.''

Harry's uncle came, with other friends, and in the
course of the day made such a showing to the
authorities that Harry was released, on giving bonds
to appear as a witness when wanted. His spirits
rose with their usual elasticity as soon as he was out
of Centre Street, and he insisted on giving Philip
and his friends a royal supper at Delmonico's, an excess which was perhaps excusable in the rebound of
his feelings, and which was committed with his usual
reckless generosity. Harry ordered the supper, and
it is perhaps needless to say that Philip paid the bill.

Neither of the young men felt like attempting to
see Laura that day, and she saw no company except
the newspaper reporters, until the arrival of Colonel
Sellers and Washington Hawkins, who had hastened
to New York with all speed.

They found Laura in a cell in the upper tier of the woman's department. The cell was somewhat larger than those in the men's department, and might be eight feet by ten square, perhaps a little longer. It was of stone, floor and all, and the roof was oven shaped. A narrow slit in the roof admitted sufficient light, and was the only means of ventilation; when the window was opened there was nothing to prevent the rain coming in. The only means of heating being from the corridor, when the door was ajar, the cell was chilly and at this time damp. It was whitewashed and clean, but it had a slight jail odor; its only furniture was a narrow iron bedstead, with a tick of straw and some blankets, not too clean.

When Colonel Sellers was conducted to the cell by the matron and looked in, his emotions quite overcame him, the tears rolled down his cheeks and his voice trembled so that he could hardly speak. Washington was unable to say anything; he looked from Laura to the miserable creatures who were walking in the corridor with unutterable disgust. Laura was alone calm and self-contained, though she was not unmoved by the sight of the grief of her friends.

"Are you comfortable, Laura?" was the first word the Colonel could get out.

"You see," she replied. "I can't say it's exactly comfortable."

"Are you cold?"

" It is pretty chilly. The stone floor is like ice. It chills me through to step on it. I have to sit on the bed."

" Poor thing! poor thing! And can you eat anything?"

" No, I am not hungry. I don't know that I could eat anything. I can't eat *that*."

" Oh dear," continued the Colonel, " it's dreadful. But cheer up, dear, cheer up; " and the Colonel broke down entirely.

" But," he went on, " we'll stand by you. We'll do everything for you. I know you couldn't have meant to do it. It must have been insanity, you know, or something of that sort. You never did anything of the sort before."

Laura smiled very faintly and said:

" Yes, it was something of that sort. It's all a whirl. He was a villain; you don't know."

" I'd rather have killed him myself, in a duel you know, all fair. I wish I had. But don't you be down. We'll get you off — the best counsel, the lawyers in New York can do anything; I've read of cases. But you must be comfortable now. We've brought some of your clothes, at the hotel. What else can we get for you? "

Laura suggested that she would like some sheets for her bed, a piece of carpet to step on, and her meals sent in; and some books and writing materials if it was allowed. The Colonel and Washington promised to procure all these things, and then took their sorrowful leave, a great deal more affected than the criminal was, apparently, by her situation.

The Colonel told the matron as he went away that if she would look to Laura's comfort a little it shouldn't be the worse for her; and to the turnkey who let them out he patronizingly said,

"You've got a big establishment here, a credit to the city. I've got a friend in there — I shall see you again, sir."

By the next day something more of Laura's own story began to appear in the newspapers, colored and heightened by reporter's rhetoric. Some of them cast a lurid light upon the Colonel's career, and represented his victim as a beautiful avenger of her murdered innocence; and others pictured her as his willing paramour and pitiless slayer. Her communications to the reporters were stopped by her lawyers as soon as they were retained and visited her, but this fact did not prevent — it may have facilitated — the appearance of casual paragraphs here and there which were likely to beget popular sympathy for the poor girl.

The occasion did not pass without "improvement" by the leading journals; and Philip preserved the editorial comments of three or four of them which pleased him most. These he used to read aloud to his friends afterwards and ask them to guess from which journal each of them had been cut. One began in this simple manner:—

12

History never repeats itself, but the kaleidoscopic combinations of the pictured present often seem to be constructed out of the broken fragments of antique legends. Washington is not Corinth, and Lais, the beautiful daughter of Timandra, might not have been the prototype of the ravishing Laura, daughter of the plebeian house of Hawkins; but the orators and statesmen who were the purchasers of the favors of the one, may have been as incorruptible as the Republican statesmen who learned how to love and how to vote from the sweet lips of the Washington lobbyist; and perhaps the modern Lais would never have departed from the national Capital if there had been there even one republican Xenocrates who resisted her blandishments. But here the parallel fails. Lais, wandering away with the youth Hippostratus, is slain by the women who are jealous of her charms. Laura, straying into her Thessaly with the youth Brierly, slays her other lover and becomes the champion of the wrongs of her sex.

Another journal began its editorial with less lyrical beauty, but with equal force. It closed as follows:—

With Laura Hawkins, fair, fascinating, and fatal, and with the dissolute Colonel of a lost cause, who has reaped the harvest he sowed, we have nothing to do. But as the curtain rises on this awful tragedy, we catch a glimpse of the society at the capital under this Administration, which we cannot contemplate without alarm for the fate of the Republic.

A third newspaper took up the subject in a different tone. It said: —

Our repeated predictions are verified. The pernicious doctrines which we have announced as prevailing in American society have been again illustrated. The name of the city is becoming a reproach. We may have done something in averting its ruin in our resolute exposure of the Great Frauds; we shall not be deterred from insisting that the outraged laws for the protection of human life shall be vindicated now, so that a person can walk the streets or enter the public houses, at least in the day-time, without the risk of a bullet through his brain.

A fourth journal began its remarks as follows: —

The fullness with which we present our readers this morning the details of the Selby-Hawkins homicide is a miracle of modern journalism. Subsequent investigation can do little to fill out the picture. It is the old story. A beautiful woman shoots her absconding lover in cold blood; and we shall doubtless learn in due time that if she was not as mad as a hare in this month of March, she was at least laboring under what is termed "momentary insanity."

It would not be too much to say that upon the first publication of the facts of the tragedy, there was an almost universal feeling of rage against the murderess in the Tombs, and that reports of her beauty only heightened the indignation. It was as if she presumed upon that and upon her sex, to defy the law; and there was a fervent hope that the law would take its plain course.

Yet Laura was not without friends, and some of them very influential, too. She had in her keeping a great many secrets and a great many reputations, perhaps. Who shall set himself up to judge human motives? Why, indeed, might we not feel pity for a woman whose brilliant career had been so suddenly extinguished in misfortune and crime? Those who had known her so well in Washington might find it impossible to believe that the fascinating woman could have had murder in her heart, and would readily give ear to the current sentimentality about the temporary aberration of mind under the stress of personal calamity.

Senator Dilworthy was greatly shocked, of course, but he was full of charity for the erring.

"We shall all need mercy," he said. "Laura as an inmate of my family was a most exemplary

L

female, amiable, affectionate, and truthful, perhaps too fond of gayety, and neglectful of the externals of religion, but a woman of principle. She may have had experiences of which I am ignorant, but she could not have gone to this extremity if she had been in her own right mind."

To the Senator's credit be it said, he was willing to help Laura and her family in this dreadful trial. She, herself, was not without money, for the Washington lobbyist is not seldom more fortunate than the Washington claimant, and she was able to procure a good many luxuries to mitigate the severity of her prison life. It enabled her also to have her own family near her, and to see some of them daily. The tender solicitude of her mother, her childlike grief, and her firm belief in the real guilt-lessness of her daughter, touched even the custodians of the Tombs, who are enured to scenes of pathos.

Mrs. Hawkins had hastened to her daughter as soon as she received money for the journey. She had no reproaches, she had only tenderness and pity. She could not shut out the dreadful facts of the case, but it had been enough for her that Laura had said, in their first interview, "Mother, I did not know what I was doing." She obtained lodgings near the prison and devoted her life to her daughter, as if she had been really her own child. She would have remained in the prison day and night if it had been permitted. She was aged and feeble, but this great necessity seemed to give her new life.

The pathetic story of the old lady's ministrations, and her simplicity and faith, also got into the newspapers in time, and probably added to the pathos of this wrecked woman's fate, which was beginning to be felt by the public. It was certain that she had champions who thought that her wrongs ought to be placed against her crime, and expressions of this feeling came to her in various ways. Visitors came to see her, and gifts of fruit and flowers were sent, which brought some cheer into her hard and gloomy cell.

Laura had declined to see either Philip or Harry, somewhat to the former's relief, who had a notion that she would necessarily feel humiliated by seeing him after breaking faith with him, but to the discomfiture of Harry, who still felt her fascination, and thought her refusal heartless. He told Philip that of course he had got through with such a woman, but he wanted to see her.

Philip, to keep him from some new foolishness, persuaded him to go with him to Philadelphia, and give his valuable services in the mining operations at Ilium.

The law took its course with Laura. She was indicted for murder in the first degree, and held for trial at the summer term. The two most distinguished criminal lawyers in the city had been retained for her defense, and to that the resolute woman devoted her days, with a courage that rose as she consulted with her counsel and understood the methods of criminal procedure in New York.

She was greatly depressed, however, by the news from Washington. Congress had adjourned and her bill had failed to pass the Senate. It must wait for the next session.

CHAPTER XVII.

MR. BIGLER HELPED OUT WHILE MR. BOLTON RUNS IN DEBT

> — In our werking, nothing us availle;
> For lost is all our labour and travaille,
> And all the cost a twenty devil way
> Is lost also, which we upon it lay.
>
> *Chaucer.*
>
> He moonihoawa ka aie.
>
> *Hawaiian Proverb.*

IT had been a bad winter, somehow, for the firm of Pennybacker, Bigler, and Small. These celebrated contractors usually made more money during the session of the legislature at Harrisburg than upon all their summer work, and this winter had been unfruitful. It was unaccountable to Bigler.

"You see, Mr. Bolton," he said, and Philip was present at the conversion, "it puts us all out. It looks as if politics was played out. We'd counted on the year of Simon's re-election. And now he's re-elected, and I've yet to see the first man who's the better for it."

"You don't mean to say," asked Philip, "that he went in without paying anything?"

"Not a cent, not a dash cent, as I can hear," repeated Mr. Bigler, indignantly. "I call it a swindle

on the state. How it was done gets me. I never
saw such a tight time for money in Harrisburg.''

''Were there no combinations, no railroad jobs,
no mining schemes put through in connection with
the election?''

'' Not that I know,'' said Bigler, shaking his head
in disgust. '' In fact, it was openly said that there
was no money in the election. It's perfectly un-
heard of.''

'' Perhaps,'' suggested Philip, '' it was effected on
what the insurance companies call the ' endowment,'
or the ' paid-up,' plan, by which a policy is secured
after a certain time without further payment.''

''You think, then,'' said Mr. Bolton smiling,
'' that a liberal and sagacious politician might own a
legislature after a time, and not be bothered with
keeping up his payments?''

''Whatever it is,'' interrupted Mr. Bigler, '' it's
devilish ingenious, and goes ahead of my calculations; it's cleaned me out, when I thought we had a
dead sure thing. I tell you what it is, gentlemen,
I shall go in for reform. Things have got pretty
mixed when a legislature will give away a United
States Senatorship.''

It was melancholy, but Mr. Bigler was not a man
to be crushed by one misfortune, or to lose his confidence in human nature on one exhibition of apparent honesty. He was already on his feet again, or
would be if Mr. Bolton could tide him over the shoal
water for ninety days.

"We've got something with money in it," he explained to Mr. Bolton, "got hold of it by good luck. We've got the entire contract for Dobson's Patent Pavement for the city of Mobile. See here."

Mr. Bigler made some figures: contract so much, cost of work and materials so much, profits so much. At the end of three months the city would owe the company three hundred and seventy-five thousand dollars — two hundred thousand of that would be profits. The whole job was worth at least a million to the company — it might be more. There could be no mistake in these figures; here was the contract. Mr. Bolton knew what materials were worth and what the labor would cost.

Mr. Bolton knew perfectly well from sore experience that there was always a mistake in figures when Bigler or Small made them, and he knew that he ought to send the fellow about his business. Instead of that, he let him talk.

They only wanted to raise fifty thousand dollars to carry on the contract — that expended, they would have city bonds. Mr. Bolton said he hadn't the money. But Bigler could raise it on his name. Mr. Bolton said he had no right to put his family to that risk. But the entire contract could be assigned to him — the security was ample — it was a fortune to him if it was forfeited. Besides, Mr. Bigler had been unfortunate, he didn't know where to look for the necessaries of life for his family. If he could only have one more chance, he was sure he could right himself. He begged for it.

And Mr. Bolton yielded. He could never refuse such appeals. If he had befriended a man once and been cheated by him, that man appeared to have a claim upon him forever. He shrank, however, from telling his wife what he had done on this occasion, for he knew that if any person was more odious than Small to his family it was Bigler.

" Philip tells me," Mrs. Bolton said that evening, " that the man Bigler has been with thee again to-day. I hope thee will have nothing more to do with him."

" He has been very unfortunate," replied Mr. Bolton, uneasily.

" He is always unfortunate, and he is always getting thee into trouble. But thee didn't listen to him again?"

" Well, mother, his family is in want, and I lent him my name — but I took ample security. The worst that can happen will be a little inconvenience."

Mrs. Bolton looked grave and anxious, but she did not complain or remonstrate; she knew what a " little inconvenience " meant, but she knew there was no help for it. If Mr. Bolton had been on his way to market to buy a dinner for his family with the only dollar he had in the world in his pocket, he would have given it to a chance beggar who asked him for it. Mrs. Bolton only asked (and the question showed that she was no more provident than her husband where her heart was interested):

"But has thee provided money for Philip to use in opening the coal mine?"

"Yes, I have set apart as much as it ought to cost to open the mine, as much as we can afford to lose if no coal is found. Philip has the control of it, as equal partner in the venture, deducting the capital invested. He has great confidence in his success, and I hope for his sake he won't be disappointed."

Philip could not but feel that he was treated very much like one of the Bolton family — by all except Ruth. His mother, when he went home after his recovery from his accident, had affected to be very jealous of Mrs. Bolton, about whom and Ruth she asked a thousand questions — an affectation of jealousy which, no doubt, concealed a real heartache, which comes to every mother when her son goes out into the world and forms new ties. And to Mrs. Sterling, a widow, living on a small income in a remote Massachusetts village, Philadelphia was a city of many splendors. All its inhabitants seemed highly favored, dwelling in ease and surrounded by superior advantages. Some of her neighbors had relations living in Philadelphia, and it seemed to them somehow a guarantee of respectability to have relations in Philadelphia. Mrs. Sterling was not sorry to have Philip make his way among such well-to-do people, and she was sure that no good fortune could be too good for his deserts.

"So, sir," said Ruth, when Philip came from New York, "you have been assisting in a pretty tragedy. I saw your name in the papers. Is this woman a specimen of your Western friends?"

"My only assistance," replied Philip, a little annoyed, "was in trying to keep Harry out of a bad scrape, and I failed after all. He walked into her trap, and he has been punished for it. I'm going to take him up to Ilium to see if he won't work steadily at one thing, and quit his nonsense."

"Is she as beautiful as the newspapers say she is?"

"I don't know, she has a kind of beauty — she is not like ——"

"Not like Alice?"

"Well, she is brilliant; she was called the handsomest woman in Washington — dashing, you know, and sarcastic and witty. Ruth, do you believe a woman ever becomes a devil?"

"Men do, and I don't know why women shouldn't. But I never saw one."

"Well, Laura Hawkins comes very near it. But it is dreadful to think of her fate."

"Why, do you suppose they will hang a woman? Do you suppose they will be so barbarous as that?"

"I wasn't thinking of that — it's doubtful if a New York jury would find a woman guilty of any such crime. But to think of her life if she is acquitted."

"It is dreadful," said Ruth, thoughtfully, "but the worst of it is that you men do not want women educated to do anything, to be able to earn an honest living by their own exertions. They are educated as if they were always to be petted and supported, and there was never to be any such thing as misfortune. I suppose, now, that you would all choose to have me stay idly at home, and give up my profession.''

"Oh, no," said Philip, earnestly, "I respect your resolution. But, Ruth, do you think you would be happier or do more good in following your profession than in having a home of your own?"

"What is to hinder having a home of my own?"

"Nothing, perhaps, only you never would be in it — you would be away day and night, if you had any practice; and what sort of a home would that make for your husband?"

"What sort of a home is it for the wife whose husband is always away riding about in his doctor's gig?"

"Ah, you know that is not fair. The woman makes the home."

Philip and Ruth often had this sort of discussion, to which Philip was always trying to give a personal turn. He was now about to go to Ilium for the season, and he did not like to go without some assurance from Ruth that she might perhaps love him some day, when he was worthy of it, and when he could offer her something better than a partnership in his poverty.

"I should work with a great deal better heart, Ruth," he said the morning he was taking leave, "if I knew you cared for me a little."

13**

Ruth was looking down; the color came faintly to her cheeks, and she hesitated. She needn't be looking down, he thought, for she was ever so much shorter than tall Philip.

" It's not much of a place, Ilium," Philip went on, as if a little geographical remark would fit in here as well as anything else, " and I shall have plenty of time to think over the responsibility I have taken, and —" his observation did not seem to be coming out anywhere.

But Ruth looked up, and there was a light in her eyes that quickened Phil's pulse. She took his hand, and said with serious sweetness:

" Thee mustn't lose heart, Philip." And then she added, in another mood: " Thee knows I graduate in the summer and shall have my diploma. And if anything happens — mines explode sometimes — theé can send for me. Farewell."

The opening of the Ilium coal mine was begun with energy, but without many omens of success. Philip was running a tunnel into the breast of the mountain, in faith that the coal stratum ran there as it ought to. How far he must go in he believed he knew, but no one could tell exactly. Some of the miners said that they should probably go through the mountain, and that the hole could be used for a railway tunnel. The mining camp was a busy place at any rate. Quite a settlement of board and log shanties had gone up, with a blacksmith shop, a small machine shop, and a temporary store for supplying the wants of the workmen. Philip and Harry pitched a commodious tent, and lived in the full enjoyment of the free life.

There is no difficulty in digging a hole in the ground, if you have money enough to pay for the digging, but those who try this sort of work are always surprised at the large amount of money necessary to make a small hole. The earth is never willing to yield one product, hidden in her bosom, without an equivalent for it; and when a person asks of her coal, she is quite apt to require gold in exchange.

It was exciting work for all concerned in it. As the tunnel advanced into the rock every day promised to be the golden day. This very blast might disclose the treasure.

The work went on week after week, and at length during the night as well as the daytime. Gangs relieved each other, and the tunnel was every hour, inch by inch and foot by foot, crawling into the mountain. Philip was on the stretch of hope and excitement. Every pay day he saw his funds melting away, and still there was only the faintest show of what the miners call " signs."

The life suited Harry, whose buoyant hopefulness was never disturbed. He made endless calculations, which nobody could understand, of the probable position of the vein. He stood about among the workmen with the busiest air. When he was down at Ilium he called himself the engineer of the works,

and he used to spend hours smoking his pipe with
the Dutch landlord on the hotel porch, and astonishing the idlers there with the stories of his railroad
operations in Missouri. He talked with the landlord, too, about enlarging his hotel, and about buying some village lots, in the prospect of a rise, when
the mine was opened. He taught the Dutchman
how to mix a great many cooling drinks for the
summer time, and had a bill at the hotel, the
growing length of which Mr. Dusenheimer contemplated with pleasant anticipations. Mr. Brierly
was a very useful and cheering person wherever he
went.

Midsummer arrived. Philip could report to Mr.
Bolton only progress, and this was not a cheerful
message for him to send to Philadelphia in reply to
inquiries that he thought became more and more
anxious. Philip himself was a prey to the constant
fear that the money would give out before the coal
was struck.

At this time Harry was summoned to New York,
to attend the trial of Laura Hawkins. It was possible that Philip would have to go also, her lawyer
wrote, but they hoped for a postponement. There
was important evidence that they could not yet obtain, and he hoped the judge would not force them
to a trial unprepared. There were many reasons
for a delay, reasons which of course are never
mentioned, but which it would seem that a New
York judge sometimes must understand, when he

grants a postponement upon a motion that seems to the public altogether inadequate.

Harry went, but he soon came back. The trial was put off. Every week we can gain, said the learned counsel, Braham, improves our chances. The popular rage never lasts long.

CHAPTER XVIII.

PHILIP JUST MISSES STRIKING COAL

Солнце заблистало, но не надолго: блеснуло и скрылось.

" Mofère ipa eiye nā." " Aki ije *ofere* li obbè."

"WE'VE struck it!"

This was the electric announcement at the tent door that woke Philip out of a sound sleep at dead of night, and shook all the sleepiness out of him in a trice.

"What! Where is it? When? Coal? Let me see it. What quality is it?" were some of the rapid questions that Philip poured out as he hurriedly dressed. "Harry, wake up, my boy. The coal train is coming. Struck it, eh? Let's see!"

The foreman put down his lantern, and handed Philip a black lump. There was no mistake about it, it was the hard, shining anthracite, and its freshly fractured surface glistened in the light like polished steel. Diamond never shone with such luster in the eyes of Philip.

Harry was exuberant, but Philip's natural caution found expression in his next remark.

" Now, Roberts, you are sure about this?"

" What — sure that it's coal?"

" Oh, no, sure that it's the main vein."

" Well, yes.   We took it to be that."

" Did you from the first?"

" I can't say we did at first.   No, we didn't. Most of the indications were there, but not all of them, not all of them.   So we thought we'd prospect a bit."

" Well?"

" It was tolerable thick, and looked as if it might be the vein — looked as if it *ought* to be the vein. Then we went down on it a little.   Looked better all the time."

" When did you strike it?"

" About ten o'clock."

" Then you've been prospecting about four hours."

" Yes, been sinking on it something over four hours."

" I'm afraid you couldn't go down very far in four hours — could you?"

" Oh, yes — it's a good deal broke up, nothing but picking and gadding stuff."

" Well, it *does* look encouraging, sure enough — but then the lacking indications ——"

" I'd rather we had them, Mr. Sterling, but I've seen more than one good permanent mine struck without 'em in my time."

" Well, *that* is encouraging too."

M

"Yes, there was the Union, the Alabama, and the Black Mohawk — all good, sound mines, you know — all just exactly like this one when we first struck them."

"Well, I begin to feel a good deal more easy. I guess we've really got it. I remember hearing them tell about the Black Mohawk."

"I'm free to say that *I* believe it, and the men all think so, too. They are all old hands at this business."

"Come, Harry, let's go up and look at it, just for the comfort of it," said Philip. They came back in the course of an hour, satisfied and happy.

There was no more sleep for them that night. They lit their pipes, put a specimen of the coal on the table, and made it a kind of loadstone of thought and conversation.

"Of course," said Harry, "there will have to be a branch track built, and a 'switch-back' up the hill."

"Yes, there will be no trouble about getting the money for that now. We could sell out to-morrow for a handsome sum. That sort of çoal doesn't go begging within a mile of a railroad. I wonder if Mr. Bolton would rather sell out or work it?"

"Oh, work it," says Harry, "probably the whole mountain is coal, now you've got to it."

"Possibly it might not be much of a vein, after all," suggested Philip.

"Possibly it *is ;* I'll bet it's forty feet thick. I

told you.   I knew the sort of thing as soon as I put my eyes on it.''

Philip's next thought was to write to his friends and announce their good fortune.   To Mr. Bolton he wrote a short, business letter, as calm as he could make it.   They had found coal of excellent quality, but they could not yet tell with absolute certainty what the vein was.   The prospecting was still going on.   Philip also wrote to Ruth; but though this letter may have glowed, it was not with the heat of burning anthracite.   He needed no artificial heat to warm his pen and kindle his ardor when he sat down to write to Ruth.   But it must be confessed that the words never flowed so easily before, and he ran on for an hour disporting in all the extravagance of his imagination.   When Ruth read it, she doubted if the fellow had not gone out of his senses.   And it was not until she reached the postscript that she discovered the cause of the exhilaration.   '' P. S.— We have found coal.''

The news couldn't have come to Mr. Bolton in better time.   He had never been so sorely pressed.   A dozen schemes which he had in hand, any one of which might turn up a fortune, all languished, and each needed just a little more money to save that which had been invested.   He hadn't a piece of real estate that was not covered with mortgages, even to the wild tract which Philip was experimenting on, and which had no marketable value above the incumbrance on it.

He had come home that day early, unusually
dejected.

" I am afraid," he said to his wife, " that we shall
have to give up our house. I don't care for myself,
but for thee and the children."

" That will be the least of misfortunes," said
Mrs. Bolton, cheerfully. " If thee can clear thyself
from debt and anxiety, which is wearing thee out,
we can live anywhere. Thee knows we were never
happier than when we were in a much humbler
home."

" The truth is, Margaret, that affair of Bigler and
Small's has come on me just when I couldn't stand
another ounce. They have made another failure of
it. I might have known they would; and the
sharpers, or fools, I don't know which, have contrived to involve me for three times as much as the
first obligation. The security is in my hands, but it
is good for nothing to me. I have not the money
to do anything with the contract."

Ruth heard this dismal news without great surprise. She had long felt that they were living on a
volcano, that might go into active operation at any
hour. Inheriting from her father an active brain
and the courage to undertake new things, she had
little of his sanguine temperament, which blinds one
to difficulties and possible failures. She had little
confidence in the many schemes which had been
about to lift her father out of all his embarrassments
and into great wealth, ever since she was a child; as

she grew older, she rather wondered that they were as prosperous as they seemed to be, and that they did not all go to smash amid so many brilliant projects. She was nothing but a woman, and did not know how much of the business prosperity of the world is only a bubble of credit and speculation, one scheme helping to float another which is no better than it, and the whole liable to come to naught and confusion as soon as the busy brain that conceived them ceases its power to devise, or when some accident produces a sudden panic.

"Perhaps, I shall be the stay of the family yet," said Ruth, with an approach to gayety. "When we move into a little house in town, will thee let me put a little sign on the door — DR. RUTH BOLTON? Mrs. Dr. Longstreet, thee knows, has a great income."

"Who will pay for the sign, Ruth?" asked Mr. Bolton.

A servant entered with the afternoon mail from the office. Mr. Bolton took his letters listlessly, dreading to open them. He knew well what they contained, new difficulties, more urgent demands for money.

"Oh, here is one from Philip. Poor fellow! I shall feel his disappoinment as much as my own bad luck. It is hard to bear when one is young."

He opened the letter and read. As he read his face lightened, and he fetched such a sigh of relief, that Mrs. Bolton and Ruth both exclaimed.

"Read that," he cried. "Philip has found coal!"

The world was changed in a moment. One little sentence had done it. There was no more trouble. Philip had found coal. That meant relief. That meant fortune. A great weight was taken off, and the spirits of the whole household rose magically. Good Money! beautiful demon of Money, what an enchanter thou art! Ruth felt that she was of less consequence in the household, now that Philip had found coal, and perhaps she was not sorry to feel so.

Mr. Bolton was ten years younger the next morning. He went into the city, and showed his letter on 'change. It was the sort of news his friends were quite willing to listen to. They took a new interest in him. If it was confirmed, Bolton would come right up again. There would be no difficulty about his getting all the money he wanted. The money market did not seem to be half so tight as it was the day before. Mr. Bolton spent a very pleasant day in his office, and went home revolving some new plans, and the execution of some projects he had long been prevented from entering upon by the lack of money.

The day had been spent by Philip in no less excitement. By daylight, with Philip's letters to the mail, word had gone down to Ilium that coal had been found, and very early a crowd of eager spectators had come up to see for themselves.

The " prospecting" continued day and night for upwards of a week, and during the first four or five days the indications grew more and more promising, and the telegrams and letters kept Mr. Bolton duly posted. But at last a change came, and the promises began to fail with alarming rapidity. In the end, it was demonstrated without the possibility of a doubt that the great " find " was nothing but a worthless seam.

Philip was cast down, all the more so because he had been so foolish as to send the news to Philadelphia before he knew what he was writing about. And now he must contradict it. " It turns out to be only a mere seam," he wrote, " but we look upon it as an indication of better further in."

Alas! Mr. Bolton's affairs could not wait for "indications." The future might have a great deal in store, but the present was black and hopeless. It was doubtful if any sacrifice could save him from ruin. Yet sacrifice he must make, and that instantly, in the hope of saving something from the wreck of his fortune.

His lovely country home must go. That would bring the most ready money. The house that he had built with loving thought for each one of his family, as he planned its luxurious apartments and adorned it; the grounds that he had laid out, with so much delight in following the tastes of his wife, with whom the country, the cultivation of rare trees and flowers, the care of garden and lawn and conservatories were a passion almost; this home, which he had hoped his children would enjoy long after he had done with it, must go.

The family bore the sacrifice better than he did.

They declared, in fact — women are such hypocrites — that they quite enjoyed the city (it was in August) after living so long in the country, that it was a thousand times more convenient in every respect; Mrs. Bolton said it was a relief from the worry of a large establishment, and Ruth reminded her father that she should have had to come to town anyway before long.

Mr. Bolton was relieved, exactly as a water-logged ship is lightened by throwing overboard the most valuable portion of the cargo — but the leak was not stopped. Indeed, his credit was injured instead of helped by the prudent step he had taken. It was regarded as a sure evidence of his embarrassment, and it was much more difficult for him to obtain help than if he had, instead of retrenching, launched into some new speculation.

Philip was greatly troubled, and exaggerated his own share in the bringing about of the calamity.

"You must not look at it so!" Mr. Bolton wrote him. "You have neither helped or hindered — but you know you may help by and by. It would have all happened just so, if we had never begun to dig that hole. That is only a drop. Work away. I still have hope that something will occur to relieve me. At any rate, we must not give up the mine so long as we have any show."

Alas! the relief did not come. New misfortunes came instead. When the extent of the Bigler swindle was disclosed there was no more hope that Mr. Bolton could extricate himself, and he had, as an honest man, no resource except to surrender all his property for the benefit of his creditors.

The autumn came and found Philip working with diminished force but still with hope. He had again and again been encouraged by good "indications," but he had again and again been disappointed. He could not go on much longer, and almost everybody except himself had thought it was useless to go on as long as he had been doing.

When the news came of Mr. Bolton's failure, of course the work stopped. The men were discharged, the tools were housed, the hopeful noise of pickman and driver ceased, and the mining camp had that desolate and mournful aspect which always hovers over a frustrated enterprise.

Philip sat down amid the ruins, and almost wished he were buried in them. How distant Ruth was now from him, now, when she might need him most. How changed was all the Philadelphia world, which had hitherto stood for the exemplification of happiness and prosperity.

He still had faith that there was coal in that mountain. He had made a picture of himself living there a hermit in a shanty by the tunnel, digging away with solitary pick and wheelbarrow, day after day and year after year, until he grew gray and aged, and was known in all that region as the old man of the mountain. Perhaps some day — he felt it must be so some day— he should strike coal. But what if he did? Who would be alive to care for it then?

What would he care for it then? No, a man wants riches in his youth, when the world is fresh to him. He wondered why Providence could not have reversed the usual process, and let the majority of men begin with wealth and gradually spend it, and die poor when they no longer needed it.

Harry went back to the city. It was evident that his services were no longer needed. Indeed, he had letters from his uncle, which he did not read to Philip, desiring him to go to San Francisco to look after some government contracts in the harbor there.

Philip had to look about him for something to do. He was like Adam: the world was all before him where to choose. He made, before he went elsewhere, a somewhat painful visit to Philadelphia, painful but yet not without its sweetnesses. The family had never shown him so much affection before; they all seemed to think his disappointment of more importance than their own misfortune. And there was that in Ruth's manner — in what she gave him and what she withheld — that would have made a hero of a very much less promising character than Philip Sterling.

Among the assets of the Bolton property, the Ilium tract was sold, and Philip bought it in at the vendue, for a song, for no one cared to even undertake the mortgage on it except himself. He went away the owner of it, and had ample time before he reached home in November to calculate how much poorer he was by possessing it.

CHAPTER XIX.

A BAD FIX. PHILIP SEES A WAY OUT OF IT

> þá eymdir stríða á sorgfullt sinn,
> og svipur mótgángs um vánga ríða,
> og bakivendir þér veröldin,
> og vellyst brosir að þínum qvíða;
> þeink allt er knöttótt, og hverfast lætr,
> sá hló í dag er á morgun grætr;
> Alt jafnar sig!
>
> *Sigurd Peterson.*

IT is impossible for the historian, with even the best intentions, to control events or compel the persons of his narrative to act wisely or to be successful. It is easy to see how things might have been better managed; a very little change here and there would have made a very different history of this one now in hand.

If Philip had adopted some regular profession, even some trade, he might now be a prosperous editor or a conscientious plumber, or an honest lawyer, and have borrowed money at the savings bank and built a cottage, and be now furnishing it for the occupancy of Ruth and himself. Instead of this, with only a smattering of civil engineering, he is at his mother's house, fretting and fuming over his ill-luck, and the hardness and dishonesty of men, and thinking of nothing but how to get the coal out of the Ilium hills.

If Senator Dilworthy had not made that visit to Hawkeye, the Hawkins family and Colonel Sellers would not now be dancing attendance upon Congress, and endeavoring to tempt that immaculate body into one of those appropriations, for the benefit of its members, which the members find it so difficult to explain to their constituents; and Laura would not be lying in the Tombs, awaiting her trial for murder, and doing her best, by the help of able counsel, to corrupt the pure fountain of criminal procedure in New York.

If Henry Brierly had been blown up on the first Mississippi steamboat he set foot on, as the chances were that he would be, he and Colonel Sellers never would have gone into the Columbus Navigation scheme, and probably never into the East Tennessee Land scheme, and he would not now be detained in New York from very important business operations on the Pacific coast, for the sole purpose of giving evidence to convict of murder the only woman he ever loved half as much as he loves himself.

If Mr. Bolton had said the little word " No " to Mr. Bigler, Alice Montague might now be spending the winter in Philadelphia, and Philip also (waiting to resume his mining operations in the spring) ; and Ruth would not be an assistant in a Philadelphia hospital, taxing her strength with arduous routine duties, day by day, in order to lighten a little the burdens that weigh upon her unfortunate family.

It is altogether a bad business. An honest historian who had progressed thus far, and traced everything to such a condition of disaster and suspension, might well be justified in ending his narrative and writing — "after this the deluge." His only consolation would be in the reflection that he was not responsible for either characters or events.

And the most annoying thought is that a little money, judiciously applied, would relieve the burdens and anxieties of most of these people; but affairs seem to be so arranged that money is most difficult to get when people need it most.

A little of what Mr. Bolton has weakly given to unworthy people would now establish his family in a sort of comfort, and relieve Ruth of the excessive toil for which she inherited no adequate physical vigor. A little money would make a prince of Colonel Sellers; and a little more would calm the anxiety of Washington Hawkins about Laura, for, however the trial ended, he could feel sure of extricating her in the end. And if Philip had a little money he could unlock the stone door in the mountain whence would issue a stream of shining riches. It needs a golden wand to strike that rock. If the Knobs University bill could only go through, what a change would be wrought in the condition of most of the persons in this history. Even Philip himself would feel the good effects of it; for Harry would have something and Colonel Sellers would have something; and have not both these cautious people expressed a determination to take an interest in the Ilium mine when they catch their larks?

Philip could not resist the inclination to pay a visit to Fallkill. He had not been at the Montagues' since the time he saw Ruth there, and he wanted to consult the Squire about an occupation. He was determined now to waste no more time in waiting on Providence, but to go to work at something, if it were nothing better than teaching in the Fallkill Seminary, or digging clams on Hingham beach. Perhaps he could read law in Squire Montague's office while earning his bread as a teacher in the Seminary.

It was not altogether Philip's fault, let us own, that he was in this position. There are many young men like him in American society, of his age, opportunities, education, and abilities, who have really been educated for nothing and have let themselves drift, in the hope that they will find somehow, and by some sudden turn of good luck, the golden road to fortune. He was not idle or lazy; he had energy and a disposition to carve his own way. But he was born into a time when all young men of his age caught the fever of speculation, and expected to get on in the world by the omission of some of the regular processes which have been appointed from of old. And examples were not wanting to encourage him. He saw people, all around him, poor

yesterday, rich to-day, who had come into sudden
opulence by some means which they could not have
classified among any of the regular occupations of
life. A war would give such a fellow a career and
very likely fame. He might have been a " railroad
man," or a politician, or a land speculator, or one
of those mysterious people who travel free on all rail-
roads and steamboats, and are continually crossing
and recrossing the Atlantic, driven day and night
about nobody knows what, and make a great deal of
money by so doing. Probably, at last, he sometimes thought with a whimsical smile, he should end
by being an insurance agent, and asking people to
insure their lives for his benefit.

Possibly Philip did not think how much the
attractions of Fallkill were increased by the presence
of Alice there. He had known her so long, she
had somehow grown into his life by habit, that he
would expect the pleasure of her society without
thinking much about it. Latterly, he never thought
of her without thinking of Ruth, and if he gave the
subject any attention, it was probably in an undefined consciousness that he had her sympathy in his
love, and that she was always willing to hear him
talk about it. If he ever wondered that Alice herself was not in love and never spoke of the possibility of her own marriage, it was a transient thought
— for love did not seem necessary, exactly, to one
so calm and evenly balanced and with so many
resources in herself.

14

Whatever her thoughts may have been they were unknown to Philip, as they are to these historians; if she was seeming to be what she was not, and carrying a burden heavier than any one else carried, because she had to bear it alone, she was only doing what thousands of women do, with a self-renunciation and heroism of which men, impatient and complaining, have no conception. Have not these big babies with beards filled all literature with their outcries, their griefs, and their lamentations? It is always the gentle sex which is hard and cruel and fickle and implacable.

"Do you think you would be contented to live in Fallkill, and attend the county court?" asked Alice, when Philip had opened the budget of his new programme.

"Perhaps not always," said Philip, "I might go and practice in Boston, maybe, or go to Chicago."

"Or you might get elected to Congress."

Philip looked at Alice to see if she was in earnest and not chaffing him. Her face was quite sober. Alice was one of those patriotic women in the rural districts, who think men are still selected for Congress on account of qualifications for the office.

"No," said Philip, "the chances are that a man cannot get into Congress now without resorting to arts and means that should render him unfit to go there; of course, there are exceptions; but do you know that I could not go into politics if I were a lawyer without losing standing somewhat in my profession, and without raising at least a suspicion of my intentions and unselfishness? Why, it is telegraphed all over the country and commented on as something wonderful if a Congressman votes honestly and unselfishly and refuses to take advantage of his position to steal from the government."

"But," insisted Alice, "I should think it a noble ambition to go to Congress, if it is so bad, and help reform it. I don't believe it is as corrupt as the English Parliament used to be, if there is any truth in the novels, and I suppose that is reformed."

"I'm sure I don't know where the reform is to begin. I've seen a perfectly capable, honest man, time and again, run against an illiterate trickster, and get beaten. I suppose if the people wanted decent members of Congress they would elect them. Perhaps," continued Philip, with a smile, "the women will have to vote."

"Well, I should be willing to, if it were a necessity, just as I would go to war and do what I could, if the country couldn't be saved otherwise," said Alice, with a spirit that surprised Philip, well as he thought he knew her. "If I were a young gentleman in these times ——"

Philip laughed outright. "It's just what Ruth used to say, 'if she were a man.' I wonder if all the young ladies are contemplating a change of sex."

"No, only a changed sex," retorted Alice; "we contemplate for the most part young men who don't care for anything they ought to care for."

N

"Well," said Philip, looking humble, "I care for some things, you and Ruth, for instance: perhaps I ought not to. Perhaps I ought to care for Congress and that sort of thing."

"Don't be a goose, Philip. I heard from Ruth yesterday."

"Can I see her letter?"

"No, indeed. But I am afraid her hard work is telling on her, together with her anxiety about her father."

"Do you think, Alice," asked Philip with one of those selfish thoughts that are not seldom mixed with real love, "that Ruth prefers her profession to — to marriage?"

"Philip," exclaimed Alice, rising to quit the room, and speaking hurriedly as if the words were forced from her, "you are as blind as a bat: Ruth would cut off her right hand for you this minute."

Philip never noticed that Alice's face was flushed and that her voice was unsteady; he only thought of the delicious words he had heard. And the poor girl, loyal to Ruth, loyal to Philip, went straight to her room, locked the door, threw herself on the bed, and sobbed as if her heart would break. And then she prayed that her Father in Heaven would give her strength. And after a time she was calm again, and went to her bureau drawer and took from a hiding place a little piece of paper, yellow with age. Upon it was pinned a four-leaved clover, dry and yellow also. She looked long at this foolish memento. Under the clover leaf was written in a schoolgirl's hand — *Philip, June, 186 —.*"

Squire Montague thought very well of Philip's proposal. It would have been better if he had begun the study of the law as soon as he left college, but it was not too late now, and besides he had gathered some knowledge of the world.

" But," asked the Squire, " do you mean to abandon your land in Pennsylvania?" This tract of land seemed an immense possible fortune to this New England lawyer-farmer. " Hasn't it good timber, and doesn't the railroad almost touch it?"

" I can't do anything with it now. Perhaps I can some time."

" What is your reason for supposing that there is coal there?"

" The opinion of the best geologist I could consult, my own observation of the country, and the little veins of it we found. I feel certain it is there. I shall find it some day. I know it. If I can only keep the land till I make money enough to try again."

Philip took from his pocket a map of the anthracite coal region, and pointed out the position of the Ilium mountain which he had begun to tunnel.

" Doesn't it look like it?"

" It certainly does," said the Squire, very much interested. It is not unusual for a quiet country gentleman to be more taken with such a venture than a speculator who has had more experience in its uncertainty. It was astonishing how many New England clergymen, in the time of the petroleum excitement, took chances in oil. The Wall street brokers are said to do a good deal of small business for country clergymen, who are moved, no doubt, with the laudable desire of purifying the New York stock board.

"I don't see that there is much risk," said the Squire, at length. "The timber is worth more than the mortgage; and if that coal seam does run there, it's a magnificent fortune. Would you like to try it again in the spring, Phil?"

Like to try it! If he could have a little help, he would work himself, with pick and barrow, and live on a crust. Only give him one more chance.

And this is how it came about that the cautious old Squire Montague was drawn into this young fellow's speculation, and began to have his serene old age disturbed by anxieties and by the hope of a great stroke of luck.

"To be sure, I only care about it for the boy," he said. The Squire was like everybody else; sooner or later he must "take a chance."

It is probably on account of the lack of enterprise in women that they are not so fond of stock speculations and mine ventures as men. It is only when woman becomes demoralized that she takes to any sort of gambling. Neither Alice nor Ruth were much elated with the prospect of Philip's renewal of his mining enterprise.

But Philip was exultant. He wrote to Ruth as if his fortune were already made, and as if the clouds that lowered over the house of Bolton were already in the deep bosom of a coal mine buried. Toward spring he went to Philadelphia with his plans all matured for a new campaign. His enthusiasm was irresistible.

"Philip has come, Philip has come," cried the children, as if some great good had again come into the household; and the refrain even sang itself over in Ruth's heart as she went the weary hospital rounds. Mr. Bolton felt more courage than he had had in months, at the sight of his manly face and the sound of his cheery voice.

Ruth's course was vindicated now, and it certainly did not become Philip, who had nothing to offer but a future chance against the visible result of her determination and industry, to open an argument with her. Ruth was never more certain that she was right and that she was sufficient unto herself. She, maybe, did not much heed the still small voice that sang in her maiden heart as she went about her work, and which lightened it and made it easy, "Philip has come."

"I am glad for father's sake," she said to Philip, "that thee has come. I can see that he depends greatly upon what thee can do. He thinks women won't hold out long," added Ruth, with the smile that Philip never exactly understood.

"And aren't you tired sometimes of the struggle?"

"Tired? Yes, everybody is tired, I suppose. But it is a glorious profession. And would you want me to be dependent, Philip?"

"Well, yes, a little," said Philip, feeling his way toward what he wanted to say.

"On what, for instance, just now?" asked Ruth, a little maliciously, Philip thought.

"Why, on —" he couldn't quite say it, for it occurred to him that he was a poor stick for anybody to lean on in the present state of his fortune, and that the woman before him was at least as independent as he was.

"I don't mean depend," he began again. "But I love you, that's all. Am I nothing to you?" And Philip looked a little defiant, and as if he had said something that ought to brush away all the sophistries of obligation on either side, between man and woman.

Perhaps Ruth saw this. Perhaps she saw that her own theories of a certain equality of power, which ought to precede a union of two hearts, might be pushed too far. Perhaps she had felt sometimes her own weakness and the need after all of so dear a sympathy and so tender an interest confessed, as that which Philip could give. Whatever moved her — the riddle is as old as creation — she simply looked up to Philip and said in a low voice:

"Everything."

And Philip clasping both her hands in his, and looking down into her eyes, which drank in all his tenderness with the thirst of a true woman's nature—

" Oh! Philip, come out here," shouted young Eli, throwing the door wide open.

And Ruth escaped away to her room, her heart singing again, and now as if it would burst for joy, " Philip has come."

That night Philip received a dispatch from Harry — "The trial begins to-morrow."

CHAPTER XX.

Mpethie ou sagar lou nga thia ɲawantou kone yoboul goube.
Wolof Proverb.

"Mitsoda eb volna a' te szolgád, hogy illyen nagy dolgot tselekednek?"
Királyok II. K. 8. 13.

DECEMBER, 18—, found Washington Hawkins and Colonel Sellers once more at the Capitol of the nation, standing guard over the University bill. The former gentleman was despondent, the latter hopeful. Washington's distress of mind was chiefly on Laura's account. The court would soon sit to try her case, he said, and consequently a great deal of ready money would be needed in the engineering of it. The University bill was sure to pass, this time, and that would make money plenty, but might not the help come too late? Congress had only just assembled, and delays were to be feared.

"Well," said the Colonel, "I don't know but you are more or less right, there. Now let's figure up a little on the preliminaries. I think Congress always tries to do as near right as it can, according to its lights. A man can't ask any fairer than that.

(218)

The first preliminary it always starts out on, is to clean itself, so to speak. It will arraign two or three dozen of its members, or maybe four or five dozen, for taking bribes to vote for this and that and the other bill last winter.''

"It goes up into the dozens, does it?''

"Well, yes; in a free country like ours, where any man can run for Congress and anybody can vote for him, you can't expect immortal purity all the time — it ain't in nature. Sixty or eighty or a hundred and fifty people are bound to get in who are not angels in disguise, as young Hicks the correspondent, says; but still it is a very good average; very good, indeed. As long as it averages as well as that, I think we can feel very well satisfied. Even in these days, when people growl so much and the newspapers are so out of patience, there is still a very respectable minority of honest men in Congress.''

"Why a respectable *minority* of honest men can't do any good, Colonel.''

"Oh, yes it can, too.''

"Why, how?''

"Oh, in many ways, many ways.''

"But what *are* the ways?''

"Well — I don't know — it is a question that requires time; a body can't answer every question right off-hand. But it *does* do good. I am satisfied of that.''

"All right, then; grant that it does good; go on with the preliminaries.''

" That is what I am coming to. First, as I said, they will try a lot of members for taking money for votes. That will take four weeks."

" Yes, that's like last year; and it is a sheer waste of the time for which the nation pays those men to *work* — that is what that is. And it pinches when a body's got a bill waiting."

" A waste of time, to purify the fountain of public law? Well, I never heard anybody express an idea like that before. But if it were, it would still be the fault of the minority, for the majority don't institute these proceedings. *There* is where that minority becomes an obstruction — but still one can't say it is on the wrong side. Well, after they have finished the bribery cases, they will take up cases of members who have bought their seats with money. That will take another four weeks."

" Very good; go on. You have accounted for two-thirds of the session."

" Next they will try each other for various smaller irregularities, like the sale of appointments to West Point cadetships, and that sort of thing — mere trifling pocket-money enterprises that might better be passed over in silence, perhaps; but then one of our Congresses can never rest easy till it has thoroughly purified itself of all blemishes — and that is a thing to be applauded."

" How long does it take to disinfect itself of these minor impurities?"

" Well, about two weeks, generally."

" So Congress always lies helpless in quarantine ten weeks of a session. That's encouraging. Colonel, poor Laura will never get any benefit from our bill. Her trial will be over before Congress has half purified itself. And doesn't it occur to you that by the time it has expelled all its impure members there may not be enough members left to do business legally?"

" Why, I did not say Congress would expel anybody."

" Well, *won't* it expel anybody?"

" Not necessarily. Did it last year? It never does. That would not be regular."

" Then why waste all the session in that tomfoolery of trying members?"

" It is usual; it is customary; the country requires it."

" Then the country is a fool, *I* think."

" Oh, no. The country *thinks* somebody is going to be expelled."

" Well, when nobody *is* expelled, what does the country think then?"

" By that time, the thing has strung out so long that the country is sick and tired of it and glad to have a change on any terms. But all that inquiry is not lost. It has a good moral effect."

" Who does it have a good moral effect on?"

" Well — I don't know. On foreign countries, I think. We have always been under the gaze of foreign countries. There is no country in the world,

sir, that pursues corruption as inveterately as we do.
There is no country in the world whose representatives try each other as much as ours do, or stick to
it as long on a stretch. I think there is something
great in being a model for the whole civilized world,
Washington.''

"You don't mean a model; you mean an example.''

"Well, it's all the same; it's just the same thing.
It shows that a man can't be corrupt in this country
without sweating for it, I can tell you that.''

"Hang it, Colonel, you just said we never punish
anybody for villainous practices.''

"But, good God! we *try* them, don't we? Is it
nothing to show a disposition to sift things and bring
people to a strict account? I tell you it has its
effect.''

"Oh, bother the effect! — What is it they *do* do?
How do they proceed? You know perfectly well —
and it is all bosh, too. Come, now, how do they
proceed?''

"Why they proceed right and regular — and it
ain't bosh, Washington, it ain't bosh. They appoint a committee to investigate, and that committee
hears evidence three weeks, and all the witnesses on
one side swear that the accused took money or stock
or something for his vote. Then the accused stands
up and testifies that he *may* have done it, but he
was receiving and handling a good deal of money at
the time and he doesn't remember this particular cir-

cumstance — at least with sufficient distinctness to enable him to grasp it tangibly. So of course the thing is not proven — and that is what they say in the verdict. They don't acquit, they don't condemn. They just say, ' Charge not proven.' It leaves the accused in a kind of a shaky condition before the country, it purifies Congress, it satisfies everybody, and it doesn't seriously hurt anybody. It has taken a long time to perfect our system, but it is the most admirable in the world now."

" So one of those long stupid investigations always turns out in that lame silly way. Yes, you are correct. I thought maybe you viewed the matter differently from other people. Do you think a Congress of ours could convict the devil of anything if he were a member?"

" My dear boy, don't let these damaging delays prejudice you against Congress. Don't use such strong language; you talk like a newspaper. Congress has inflicted frightful punishments on its members — now you know that. When they tried Mr. Fairoaks, and a cloud of witnesses proved him to be — well, you know what they proved him to be — and his own testimony and his own confessions gave him the same character, what did Congress do then? — come !"

" Well, what *did* Congress do?"

" You know what Congress did, Washington. Congress intimated plainly enough, that they considered him almost a stain upon their body; and without waiting ten days, hardly, to think the thing over, they rose up and hurled at him a resolution declaring that they disapproved of his conduct! Now *you* know that, Washington.''

"It *was* a terrific thing — there is no denying that. If he had been proven guilty of theft, arson, licentiousness, infanticide, and defiling graves, I believe they would have suspended him for two days.''

"You can depend on it, Washington. Congress is vindictive, Congress is savage, sir, when it gets waked up once. It will go to any length to vindicate its honor at such a time.''

"Ah, well, we have talked the morning through, just as usual in these tiresome days of waiting, and we have reached the same old result; that is to say, we are no better off than when we began. The land bill is just as far away as ever, and the trial is closer at hand. Let's give up everything and die.''

"Die and leave the Duchess to fight it out all alone? Oh, no, that won't do. Come, now, don't talk so. It is all going to come out right. Now you'll see.''

"It never will, Colonel, never in the world. Something tells me that. I get more tired and more despondent every day. I don't see any hope; life is only just a trouble. I am so miserable these days!''

The Colonel made Washington get up and walk the floor with him, arm in arm. The good old speculator wanted to comfort him, but he hardly knew how to go about it. He made many attempts, but they were lame; they lacked spirit; the words were encouraging, but they were only words — he could not get any heart into them. He could not always warm up, now, with the old Hawkeye fervor. By and by his lips trembled and his voice got unsteady. He said:

"Don't give up the ship, my boy — don't do it. The wind's bound to fetch around and set in our favor. I *know* it."

And the prospect was so cheerful that he wept. Then he blew a trumpet-blast that started the meshes of his handkerchief, and said in almost his breezy old-time way:

"Lord bless us, this is all nonsense! Night doesn't last always; day has got to break some time or other. Every silver lining has a cloud behind it, as the poet says; and that remark has always cheered me, though I never could see any meaning to it. Everybody uses it, though, and everybody gets comfort out of it. I wish they would start something fresh. Come, now, let's cheer up; there's
as good fish in the sea as there are now. It
ever be said that Beriah Sellers— Come

he telegraph boy. The Colonel reached
age and devoured its contents.

! Never give up the ship! The trial's
February, and we'll save the child yet.
what lawyers they have in New York!

Give them money to fight with, and the ghost of an excuse, and they would manage to postpone anything in this world, unless it might be the millennium or something like that. Now for work again, my boy. The trial will last till the middle of March, sure; Congress ends the fourth of March. Within three days of the end of the session they will be done putting through the preliminaries, and then they will be ready for national business. Our bill will go through in forty-eight hours, then, and we'll telegraph a million dollars to the jury — to the lawyers, I mean — and the verdict of the jury will be 'Accidental murder resulting from justifiable insanity' — or something to that effect, something to that effect. Everything is dead sure, now. Come, what is the matter? What are you wilting down like that for? You mustn't be a girl, you know."

"Oh, Colonel, I am become so used to troubles, so used to failures, disappointments, hard luck of all kinds, that a little good news breaks me right down. Everything has been so hopeless that now I can't stand good news at all. It is too good to be true, anyway. Don't you see how our bad luck worked on me? My hair is getting gray, an nights I don't sleep at all. I wish it was al we could rest. I wish we could lie do forget everything, and let it all be just is done and can't come back to trouble I am so tired."

"Ah, poor child, don't talk like t

was that they should be on hand and ready for any emergency that might come up. There was no work to do; that was all finished; this was but the second session of the last winter's Congress, and its action on the bill could have but one result — its passage. The House must do its work over again, of course, but the same membership was there to see that it did it. The Senate was secure — Senator Dilworthy was able to put all doubts to rest on that head. Indeed, it was no secret in Washington that a two-thirds vote in the Senate was ready and waiting to be cast for the University bill as soon as it should come before that body.

Washington did not take part in the gayeties of "the season," as he had done the previous winter. He had lost his interest in such things; he was oppressed with cares, now. Senator Dilworthy said to Washington that an humble deportment, under punishment, was best, and that there was but one way in which the troubled heart might find perfect repose and peace. The suggestion found a response in Washington's breast, and the Senator saw the sign of it in his face.

From that moment one could find the youth with the Senator even oftener than with Colonel Sellers. When the statesman presided at great temperance meetings, he placed Washington in the front rank of impressive dignitaries that gave tone to the occasion and pomp to the platform. His bald-headed surroundings made the youth the more conspicuous.

When the statesman made remarks in these meetings, he not infrequently alluded with effect to the encouraging spectacle of one of the wealthiest and most brilliant young favorites of society forsaking the light vanities of that butterfly existence to nobly and self-sacrificingly devote his talents and his riches to the cause of saving his hapless fellow creatures from shame and misery here and eternal regret hereafter. At the prayer meetings the Senator always brought Washington up the aisle on his arm and seated him prominently; in his prayers he referred to him in the cant terms which the Senator employed, perhaps unconsciously, and mistook, maybe, for religion, and in other ways brought him into notice. He had him out at gatherings for the benefit of the negro, gatherings for the benefit of the Indian, gatherings for the benefit of the heathen in distant lands. He had him out time and again, before Sunday-schools, as an example for emulation. Upon all these occasions the Senator made casual references to many benevolent enterprises which his ardent young friend was planning against the day when the passage of the University bill should make his ample means available for the amelioration of the condition of the unfortunate among his fellow-men of all nations and all climes. Thus, as the weeks rolled on, Washington grew up into an imposing lion once more, but a lion that roamed the peaceful fields of religion and temperance, and revisited the glittering domain of fashion no more. A great moral influence was thus brought to bear in favor of the bill; the weightiest of friends flocked to its standard; its most energetic enemies said it was useless to fight longer; they had tacitly surrendered while as yet the day of battle was not come.

CHAPTER XXII.

DILWORTHY AT SAINT'S REST, PREPARES FOR RE-ELECTION

—He seekes, of all his drifte the aymed end :
Thereto his subtile engins he does bend,
His practick witt and his fayre fylèd tongue,
With thousand other sleightes ; for well he kend
His credit now in doubtful ballaunce hong :
For hardly could bee hurt, who was already stong.

Faerie Queene.

Selons divers besoins, il est une science
D'étendre les liens de notre conscience,
Et de rectifier le mal de l'action
Avec la pureté de notre intention.

La Tartuffe, a. 4, sc. 5.

THE session was drawing toward its close. Senator Dilworthy thought he would run out West
and shake hands with his constituents and let them
look at him. The legislature whose duty it would
be to re-elect him to the United States Senate was
already in session. Mr. Dilworthy considered his re-
election certain, but he was a careful, painstaking
man, and if, by visiting his State, he could find the
opportunity to persuade a few more legislators to
vote for him, he held the journey to be well worth
taking. The University bill was safe, now ; he
could leave it without fear ; it needed his presence

(232)

and his watching no longer.   But there was a person in his State legislature who did need watching — a person who, Senator Dilworthy said, was a narrow, grumbling, uncomfortable malcontent — a person who was stolidly opposed to reform, and progress and *him* — a person who, he feared, had been bought with money to combat him, and through him the commonwealth's welfare and its political purity.

" If this person Noble," said Mr. Dilworthy, in a little speech at a dinner party given him by some of his admirers, " merely desired to sacrifice *me*, I would willingly offer up my political life on the altar of my dear State's weal, I would be glad and grateful to do it; but when he makes of me but a cloak to hide his deeper designs, when he proposes to strike *through* me at the heart of my beloved State, all the lion in me is aroused — and I say, Here I stand, solitary and alone, but unflinching, unquailing, thrice armed with my sacred trust; and whoso passes, to do evil to this fair domain that looks to me for protection, must do so over my dead body."

He further said that if this Noble were a pure man, and merely misguided, he could bear it, but that he should succeed in his wicked designs through a base use of money would leave a blot upon his State which would work untold evil to the morals of the people, and *that* he would not suffer; the public morals must not be contaminated.   He would seek this man Noble; he would argue, he would persuade, he would appeal to his honor.

When he arrived on the ground he found his friends unterrified; they were standing firmly by him and were full of courage. Noble was working hard, too, but matters were against him; he was not making much progress. Mr. Dilworthy took an early opportunity to send for Mr. Noble; he had a midnight interview with him, and urged him to forsake his evil ways; he begged him to come again and again, which he did. He finally sent the man away at 3 o'clock one morning; and when he was gone, Mr. Dilworthy said to himself,

"I feel a good deal relieved, now, a great deal relieved."

The Senator now turned his attention to matters touching the souls of his people. He appeared in church; he took a leading part in prayer meetings; he met and encouraged the temperance societies; he graced the sewing-circles of the ladies with his presence, and even took a needle now and then and made a stitch or two upon a calico shirt for some poor Bibleless pagan of the South Seas, and this act enchanted the ladies, who regarded the garments thus honored as in a manner sanctified. The Senator wrought in Bible classes, and nothing could keep him away from the Sunday-schools — neither sickness nor storms nor weariness. He even traveled a tedious thirty miles in a poor little rickety stage coach to comply with the desire of the miserable hamlet of Cattleville that he would let its Sunday-school look upon him.

All the town was assembled at the stage office
when he arrived, two bonfires were burning, and a
battery of anvils was popping exultant broadsides;
for a United States Senator was a sort of god in the
understanding of these people, who never had seen
any creature mightier than a county judge.   To
them a United States Senator was a vast, vague
colossus, an awe-inspiring unreality.

Next day, everybody was at the village church a
full half-hour before time for Sunday-school to
open; ranchmen and farmers had come with their
families from five miles around, all eager to get a
glimpse of the great man — the man who had been
to Washington; the man who had seen the President
of the United States, and had even talked with him;
the man who had seen the actual Washington
Monument — perhaps touched it with his hands.

When the Senator arrived the church was crowded,
the windows were full, the aisles were packed, so
was the vestibule, and so, indeed, was the yard in
front of the building. As he worked his way
through to the pulpit on the arm of the minister and
followed by the envied officials of the village, every
neck was stretched and every eye twisted around
intervening obstructions to get a glimpse. Elderly
people directed each other's attention and said,
"There! that's him, with the grand, noble forehead!" Boys nudged each other and said, "Hi,
Johnny, here he is! There, that's him, with the
peeled head!"

The Senator took his seat in the pulpit, with the minister on one side of him and the superintendent of the Sunday-school on the other. The town dignitaries sat in an impressive row within the altar railings below. The Sunday-school children occupied ten of the front benches, dressed in their best and most uncomfortable clothes, and with hair combed and faces too clean to feel natural. So awed were they by the presence of a living United States Senator, that during three minutes not a " spit-ball " was thrown. After that they began to come to themselves by degrees, and presently the spell was wholly gone and they were reciting verses and pulling hair.

The usual Sunday-school exercises were hurried through, and then the minister got up and bored the house with a speech built on the customary Sunday-school plan; then the superintendent put in his oar; then the town dignitaries had their say. They all made complimentary reference to " their friend, the Senator," and told what a great and illustrious man he was and what he had done for his country and for religion and temperance, and exhorted the little boys to be good and diligent and try to become like him some day. The speakers won the deathless hatred of the house by these delays, but at last there was an end and hope revived; inspiration was about to find utterance.

Senator Dilworthy rose and beamed upon the assemblage for a full minute in silence. Then he smiled

with an access of sweetness upon the children and
began:

"My little friends — for I hope that all these
bright-faced little people are my friends and will let
me be their friend — my little friends, I have traveled much, I have been in many cities and many
states, everywhere in our great and noble country,
and by the blessing of Providence I have been permitted to see many gatherings like this — but I am
proud, I am truly proud to say that I never have
looked upon so much intelligence, so much grace,
such sweetness of disposition as I see in the charming young countenances I see before me at this
moment. I have been asking myself, as I sat here,
Where am I? Am I in some far-off monarchy,
looking upon little princes and princesses? No.
Am I in some populous center of my own country,
where the choicest children of the land have been
selected and brought together as at a fair for a
prize? No. Am I in some strange foreign clime
where the children are marvels that we know not
of? No. Then where am I? Yes — where am I?
I am in a simple, remote, unpretending settlement
of my own dear state, and these are the children of
the noble and virtuous men who have made me what
I am! My soul is lost in wonder at the thought!
And I humbly thank Him to whom we are but as
worms of the dust, that He has been pleased to
call me to serve such men! Earth has no higher,
no grander position for me. Let kings and em-

16**

perors keep their tinsel crowns, I want them not; my heart is here!

"Again I thought, Is this a theater? No. Is it a concert or a gilded opera? No. Is it some other vain, brilliant, beautiful temple of soul-staining amusement and hilarity? No. Then what is it? What did my consciousness reply? I ask you, my little friends, What did my consciousness reply? It replied, It is the temple of the Lord! Ah, think of that, now. I could hardly keep the tears back, I was so grateful. Oh, how beautiful it is to see these ranks of sunny little faces assembled here to learn the way of life; to learn to be good; to learn to be useful; to learn to be pious; to learn to be great and glorious men and women; to learn to be props and pillars of the state and shining lights in the councils and the households of the nation; to be bearers of the banner and soldiers of the cross in the rude campaigns of life, and ransomed souls in the happy fields of Paradise hereafter.

"Children, honor your parents and be grateful to them for providing for you the precious privileges of a Sunday-school.

"Now, my dear little friends, sit up straight and pretty — there, that's it — and give me your attention and let me tell you about a poor little Sunday-school scholar I once knew. He lived in the Far West, and his parents were poor. They could not give him a costly education, but they were good and wise and they sent him to the Sunday-school. He loved the Sunday-school. I hope you love your Sunday-school — ah, I see by your faces that you do! That is right.

"Well, this poor little boy was always in his place when the bell rang, and he always knew his lesson; for his teachers wanted him to learn and he loved his teachers dearly. Always love your teachers, my children, for they love you more than you can know, now. He would not let bad boys persuade him to go to play on Sunday. There was one little bad boy who was always trying to persuade him, but he never could.

"So this poor little boy grew up to be a man, and had to go out in the world, far from home and friends to earn his living. Temptations lay all about him, and sometimes he was about to yield, but he would think of some precious lesson he learned in his Sunday-school a long time ago, and that would save him. By and by he was elected to the legislature. Then he did everything he could for Sunday-schools. He got laws passed for them; he got Sunday-schools established wherever he could.

"And by and by the people made him governor — and he said it was all owing to the Sunday-school.

"After a while the people elected him a Representative to the Congress of the United States, and he grew very famous. Now temptations assailed him on every hand. People tried to get him to drink wine, to dance, to go to theaters; they even tried to buy his vote; but no, the memory of his

Sunday-school saved him from all harm; he remembered the fate of the bad little boy who used to try to get him to play on Sunday, and who grew up and became a drunkard and was hanged. He remembered that, and was glad he never yielded and played on Sunday.

"Well, at last, what do you think happened? Why the people gave him a towering, illustrious position, a grand, imposing position. And what do you think it was? What should you say it was, children? It was Senator of the United States! That poor little boy that loved his Sunday-school became that man. *That man stands before you!* All that he is, he owes to the Sunday-school.

"My precious children, love your parents, love your teachers, love your Sunday-school, be pious, be obedient, be honest, be diligent, and then you will succeed in life and be honored of all men. Above all things, my children, be honest. Above all things be pure-minded as the snow. Let us join in prayer."

When Senator Dilworthy departed from Cattleville, he left three dozen boys behind him arranging a campaign of life whose objective point was the United States Senate.

When he arrived at the State capital at midnight Mr. Noble came and held a three-hours conference with him, and then as he was about leaving said:

"I've worked hard, and I've got them at last. Six of them haven't got quite backbone enough to slew around and come right out for you on the first ballot to-morrow, but they're going to vote against you on the first for the sake of appearances, and then come out for you all in a body on the second — I've fixed all that! By supper time to-morrow you'll be re-elected. You can go to bed and sleep easy on that."

After Mr. Noble was gone, the Senator said:

" Well, to bring about a complexion of things like this was worth coming West for."

CHAPTER XXIII.

LAURA'S TRIAL. AN INTELLIGENT JURY AND MODEL JUDGE

भेदस्तमसो ऽष्टाविधो मोहस्य च दशविधो महामोहः
तामिस्रो ऽष्टादशधा तथा भवत्यन्धतामिस्रः

Sânkhya Kârikâ, xlviii.

Ny byd ynat nep yr dysc; yr adysco dyn byth ny byd ynat ony byd doethineb yny callon; yr doethet uyth uo dyn ny byd ynat ony byd dysc gyt ar doethineb.

Cyvreithian Cymru.

THE case of the State of New York against Laura Hawkins was finally set down for trial on the 15th day of February, less than a year after the shooting of George Selby.

If the public had almost forgotten the existence of Laura and her crime, they were reminded of all the details of the murder by the newspapers, which for some days had been announcing the approaching trial. But they had not forgotten. The sex, the age, the beauty of the prisoner, her high social position in Washington, the unparalleled calmness with which the crime was committed, had all conspired to fix the event in the public mind, although nearly three hundred and sixty-five subsequent murders had occurred to vary the monotony of metropolitan life.

No, the public read from time to time of the lovely prisoner, languishing in the city prison, the tortured victim of the law's delay; and as the months went by it was natural that the horror of her crime should become a little indistinct in memory, while the heroine of it should be invested with a sort of sentimental interest. Perhaps her counsel had calculated on this. Perhaps it was by their advice that Laura had interested herself in the unfortunate criminals who shared her prison confinement, and had done not a little to relieve, from her own purse, the necessities of some of the poor creatures. That she had done this, the public read in the journals of the day, and the simple announcement cast a softening light upon her character.

The court room was crowded at an early hour, before the arrival of judges, lawyers, and prisoner. There is no enjoyment so keen to certain minds as that of looking upon the slow torture of a human being on trial for life, except it be an execution; there is no display of human ingenuity, wit, and power so fascinating as that made by trained lawyers in the trial of an important case, nowhere else is exhibited such subtlety, acumen, address, eloquence. All the conditions of intense excitement meet in a _____. The awful issue at stake gives signifi-_____ word or look. How the quick _____ rove from the stolid jury to the keen lawyers, the impassive judge, the anxious prisoner. Nothing is lost of the sharp wrangle of the counsel on points of law, the measured decisions of the bench, the duels between the attorneys and the witnesses. The crowd sways with the rise and fall of the shifting testimony, in sympathetic interest, and hangs upon the dicta of the judge in breathless silence. It speedily takes sides for or against the accused, and recognizes as quickly its favorites among the lawyers. Nothing delights it more than the sharp retort of a witness and the discomfiture of an obnoxious attorney. A joke, even if it be a lame one, is nowhere so keenly relished or quickly applauded as in a murder trial.

Within the bar the young lawyers and the privileged hangers-on filled all the chairs except those reserved at the table for those engaged in the case. Without, the throng occupied all the seats, the window ledges, and the standing room. The atmosphere was already something horrible. It was the peculiar odor of a criminal court, as if it were tainted by the presence, in different persons, of all the crimes that men and women can commit.

There was a little stir when the prosecuting attorney, with two assistants, made his way in, seated himself at the table, and spread his papers before him. There was more stir when the counsel of the defense appeared. They were Mr. Br senior, and Mr. Quiggle and M juniors.

Everybody in the court room knew Mr. Braham,
the great criminal lawyer, and he was not unaware
that he was the object of all eyes as he moved to his
place, bowing to his friends in the bar. A large but
rather spare man, with broad shoulders and a mas-
sive head, covered with chestnut curls which fell
down upon his coat collar and which he had a habit
of shaking as a lion is supposed to shake his mane.
His face was clean shaven, and he had a wide mouth
and rather small dark eyes, set quite too near together. Mr. Braham wore a brown frock coat but-
toned across his breast, with a rosebud in the upper
buttonhole, and light pantaloons. A diamond stud
was seen to flash from his bosom, and as he seated
himself and drew off his gloves a heavy seal ring was
displayed upon his white left hand. Mr. Braham
having seated himself, deliberately surveyed the entire house, made a remark to one of his assistants,
and then taking an ivory-handled knife from his
pocket began to pare his finger-nails, rocking his
chair backward and forward slowly.

A moment later Judge O'Shaunnessy entered at
the rear door and took his seat in one of the chairs
behind the bench; a gentleman in black broadcloth,
with sandy hair, inclined to curl, a round, reddish
and rather jovial face, sharp rather than intellectual,
and with a self-sufficient air. His career had noth-
murder tria remarkable in it. He was descended from a
cance to the ligh Irish Kings, and he was the first one of
eyes of the spectators ver come into his kingdom — the

P

kingdom of such being the city of New York. He had, in fact, descended so far and so low that he found himself, when a boy, a sort of street Arab in that city; but he had ambition and native shrewdness, and he speedily took to boot-polishing, and newspaper hawking, became the office and errand boy of a law firm, picked up knowledge enough to get some employment in police courts, was admitted to the bar, became a rising young politician, went to the legislature, and was finally elected to the bench which he now honored. In this democratic country he was obliged to conceal his royalty under a plebeian aspect. Judge O'Shaunnessy never had a lucrative practice nor a large salary, but he had prudently laid away money — believing that a dependent judge can never be impartial — and he had lands and houses to the value of three or four hundred thousand dollars. Had he not helped to build and furnish this very court-house? Did he not know that the very " spittoon " which his judgeship used cost the city the sum of one thousand dollars?

As soon as the judge was seated, the court was opened, with the " oi yis, oi yis " of the officer in his native language, the case called, and the sheriff was directed to bring in the prisoner. In the midst of a profound hush Laura entered, leaning on the arm of the officer, and was conducted to a seat by her counsel. She was followed by her mother and by Washington Hawkins, who were given seats near her.

Laura was very pale, but this pallor heightened

the luster of her large eyes and gave a touching sadness to her expressive face. She was dressed in simple black, with exquisite taste, and without an ornament. The thin lace veil which partially covered her face did not so much conceal as heighten her beauty. She would not have entered a drawing-room with more self-poise, nor a church with more haughty humility. There was in her manner or face neither shame nor boldness, and when she took her seat in full view of half the spectators, her eyes were downcast. A murmur of admiration ran through the room. The newspaper reporters made their pencils fly. Mr. Braham again swept his eyes over the house as if in approval. When Laura at length raised her eyes a little, she saw Philip and Harry within the bar, but she gave no token of recognition.

The clerk then read the indictment, which was in the usual form. It charged Laura Hawkins, in effect, with the premeditated murder of George Selby, by shooting him with a pistol, with a revolver, shot-gun, rifle, repeater, breech-loader, cannon, six-shooter, with a gun, or some other weapon; with killing him with a slung-shot, a bludgeon, carving knife, bowie knife, penknife, rolling-pin, car hook, dagger, hairpin, with a hammer, with a screw-driver, with a nail, and with all other weapons and utensils whatsover, at the Southern hotel and in all other hotels and places wheresoever, on the thirteenth day of March and all other days of the Christian era whensoever.

Laura stood while the long indictment was read, and at the end, in response to the inquiry of the judge, she said in a clear, low voice, "Not guilty." She sat down and the court proceeded to impanel a jury.

The first man called was Michael Lanigan, saloon-keeper.

"Have you formed or expressed any opinion on this case, and do you know any of the parties?"

"Not any," said Mr. Lanigan.

"Have you any conscientious objections to capital punishment?"

"No, sir, not to my knowledge."

"Have you read anything about this case?"

"To be sure, I read the papers, y'r Honor."

Objected to by Mr. Braham, for cause, and discharged.

Patrick Coughlin.

"What is your business?"

"Well—I haven't got any particular business."

"Haven't any particular business, eh? Well, what's your general business? What do you do for a living?"

"I own some terriers, sir."

"Own some terriers, eh? Keep a rat pit?"

"Gentlemen comes there to have a little sport. *I* never fit 'em, sir."

"Oh, I see — you are probably the amusement committee of the city council. Have you ever heard of this case?"

"Not till this morning, sir."

"Can you read?"

"Not fine print, y'r Honor."

The man was about to be sworn, when Mr. Braham asked:

"Could your father read?"

"The old gentleman was mighty handy at that, sir."

Mr. Braham submitted that the man was disqualified. Judge thought not. Point argued. Challenged peremptorily, and set aside.

Ethan Dobb, cart-driver.

"Can you read?"

"Yes, but haven't a habit of it."

"Have you heard of this case?"

"I think so — but it might be another. I have no opinion about it."

Dist. A. "Tha — tha — there! Hold on a bit! Did anybody tell you to say you had no opinion about it?"

"N-n-o, sir."

"Take care now, take care. Then what suggested it to you to volunteer that remark?"

"They've always asked that, when I was on juries."

"All right, then. Have you any conscientious scruples about capital punishment?"

"Any which?"

"Would you object to finding a person guilty of murder on evidence?"

"I might, sir, if I thought he wan't guilty."

The district attorney thought he saw a point.

"Would this feeling rather incline you against a capital conviction?"

The juror said he hadn't any feeling, and didn't know any of the parties.   Accepted and sworn.

Dennis Laflin, laborer. Had neither formed nor expressed an opinion. Never had heard of the case. Believed in hangin' for them that deserved it. Could read if it was necessary.

Mr. Braham objected. The man was evidently bloody-minded.   Challenged peremptorily.

Larry O'Toole, contractor.   A showily-dressed man of the style known as "vulgar genteel," had a sharp eye and a ready tongue. Had read the newspaper reports of the case, but they made no impression on him. Should be governed by the evidence. Knew no reason why he could not be an impartial juror.

Question by district attorney.

"How is it that the reports made no impression on you?"

"Never believe anything I see in the newspapers."

(Laughter from the crowd, approving smiles from his Honor and Mr. Braham.) Juror sworn in.   Mr. Braham whispered to O'Keefe, "That's the man."

Avery Hicks, peanut peddler. Did he ever hear of this case? The man shook his head.

"Can you read?"

"No."

"Any scruples about capital punishment?"

" No."

He was about to be sworn, when the district attorney turning to him carelessly remarked:

" Understand the nature of an oath?"

" Outside," said the man, pointing to the door.

" I say, do you know what an oath is?"

" Five cents," explained the man.

" Do you mean to insult me?" roared the prosecuting officer. " Are you an idiot?"

" Fresh baked. I'm deefe. I don't hear a word
you say."

The man was discharged. " He wouldn't have
made a bad juror, though," whispered Braham. " I
saw him looking at the prisoner sympathizingly.
That's a point you want to watch for."

The result of the whole day's work was the selection of only two jurors. These, however, were
satisfactory to Mr. Braham. He had kept off all
those he did not know. No one knew better than
this great criminal lawyer that the battle was fought
on the selection of the jury. The subsequent examination of witnesses, the eloquence expended on
the jury are all for effect outside. At least that is
the theory of Mr. Braham. But human nature is a
queer thing, he admits; sometimes jurors are unac-
countably swayed, be as careful as you can in
choosing them.

It was four weary days before this jury was made
up, but when it was finally complete, it did great
credit to the counsel for the defense. So far as Mr.

Braham knew, only two could read, one of whom
was the foreman, Mr. Braham's friend, the showy
contractor.   Low foreheads and heavy faces they all
had; some had a look of animal cunning, while the
most were only stupid.   The entire panel formed
that boasted heritage commonly described as the
"bulwark of our liberties."

The district attorney, Mr. McFlinn, opened the
case for the state.   He spoke with only the slightest
accent, one that had been inherited but not cultivated.
He contented himself with a brief statement of the
case.   The state would prove that Laura Hawkins,
the prisoner at the bar, a fiend in the form of a beautiful woman, shot dead George Selby, a Southern
gentleman, at the time and place described.   That
the murder was in cold blood, deliberate and without
provocation; that it had been long premeditated and
threatened; that she had followed the deceased from
Washington to commit it.   All this would be proved
by unimpeachable witnesses.   The attorney added
that the duty of the jury, however painful it might
be, would be plain and simple.   They were citizens,
husbands, perhaps fathers.   They knew how in-
secure life had become in the metropolis.   To-
morrow their own wives might be widows, their own
children orphans, like the bereaved family in yonder
hotel, deprived of husband and father by the jealous
hand of some murderous female.   The attorney sat
down, and the clerk called:

"Henry Brierly."

CHAPTER XXIV.

THE LEARNED COUNSEL

"Dyden i Midten," sagde Fanden, han sad imellem to Procutorer.

Eur breûtaer brâz eo! Ha klevet hoc'h eûz-hu hé vreût?

HENRY BRIERLY took the stand. Requested by the district attorney to tell the jury all he knew about the killing, he narrated the circumstances substantially as the reader already knows them.

He accompanied Miss Hawkins to New York at her request, supposing she was coming in relation to a bill then pending in Congress, to secure the attendance of absent members. Her note to him was here shown. She appeared to be very much excited at the Washington station. After she had asked the conductor several questions, he heard her say, "He can't escape." Witness asked her "Who?" and she replied "Nobody." Did not see her during the night. They traveled in a sleeping car. In the morning she appeared not to have slept, said she had a headache. In crossing the ferry she asked him about the shipping in sight; he pointed out where the Cunarders lay when in port. They took a cup of coffee that morning at a restaurant. She

17**   (253)

said she was anxious to reach the Southern Hotel where Mr. Simons, one of the absent members, was staying, before he went out. She was entirely self-possessed, and beyond unusual excitement did not act unnaturally. After she had fired twice at Colonel Selby, she turned the pistol toward her own breast, and witness snatched it from her. She had been a great deal with Selby in Washington, appeared to be infatuated with him.

(Cross-examined by Mr. Braham.) "Mist-er. . . . er Brierly!" (Mr. Braham had in perfection this lawyer's trick of annoying a witness, by drawling out the "Mister," as if unable to recall the name, until the witness is sufficiently aggravated, and then suddenly, with a rising inflection, flinging his name at him with startling unexpectedness.) "Mist-er. . . . er Brierly! What is your occupation?"

"Civil engineer, sir."

"Ah, *civil* engineer (with a glance at the jury). Following that occupation with Miss Hawkins?" (Smiles by the jury.)

"No, sir," said Harry, reddening.

"How long have you known the prisoner?"

"Two years, sir. I made her acquaintance in Hawkeye, Missouri."

"'M. . . m. .m. Mist-er. . . .er Brierly! Were you not a lover of Miss Hawkins?"

Objected to. "I submit, your Honor, that I have the right to establish the relation of this unwilling witness to the prisoner." Admitted.

"Well, sir," said Harry hesitatingly, "we were friends."

"You act like a friend!" (sarcastically.) The jury were beginning to hate this neatly dressed young sprig. "Mist-er....er Brierly! Didn't Miss Hawkins refuse you?"

Harry blushed and stammered and looked at the judge. "You must answer, sir," said his Honor.

"She — she — didn't accept me."

"No. I should think not. Brierly! do you dare tell the jury that you had not an interest in the removal of your rival, Colonel Selby?" roared Mr. Braham in a voice of thunder.

"Nothing like this, sir, nothing like this," protested the witness.

"That's all, sir," said Mr. Braham severely.

"One word," said the district attorney. "Had you the least suspicion of the prisoner's intention, up to the moment of the shooting?"

"Not the least," answered Harry earnestly.

"Of course not, of course not," nodded Mr. Braham to the jury.

The prosecution then put upon the stand the other witnesses of the shooting at the hotel, and the clerk and the attending physicians. The fact of the homicide was clearly established. Nothing new was elicited, except from the clerk, in reply to a question by Mr. Braham, the fact that when the prisoner inquired for Colonel Selby she appeared excited and there was a wild look in her eyes.

The dying deposition of Colonel Selby was then produced. It set forth Laura's threats, but there was a significant addition to it, which the newspaper report did not have. It seemed that after the deposition was taken as reported, the Colonel was told for the first time by his physicians that his wounds were mortal. He appeared to be in great mental agony and fear, and said he had not finished his deposition. He added, with great difficulty and long pauses these words. "I — have — not — told — all. I must tell — put — it — down — I —wronged — her. Years — ago — I — can't — see — O — God — I — deserved —" That was all. He fainted and did not revive again.

The Washington railway conductor testified that the prisoner had asked him if a gentleman and his family went out on the evening train, describing the persons he had since learned were Colonel Selby and family.

Susan Cullum, colored servant at Senator Dilworthy's, was sworn. Knew Colonel Selby. Had seen him come to the house often, and be alone in the parlor with Miss Hawkins. He came the day but one before he was shot. She let him in. He appeared flustered like. She heard talking in the parlor, 'peared like it was quarrelin'. Was afeared sumfin' was wrong. Just put her ear to the keyhole of the back parlor door. Heard a man's voice, " I can't, I can't, Good God," quite beggin' like. Heard young Miss' voice, "Take your choice, then. If you 'bandon me, you knows what to 'spect.'' Then he rushes outen the house. I goes in and I says, '' Missis, did you ring?'' She was a standin', like a tiger, her eyes flashin'. I come right out.

This was the substance of Susan's testimony, which was not shaken in the least by a severe cross-examination. In reply to Mr. Braham's question, if the prisoner did not look insane, Susan said, '' Lord, no, sir, just mad as a hawnet.''

Washington Hawkins was sworn. The pistol, identified by the officer as the one used in the homicide, was produced. Washington admitted that it was his. She had asked him for it one morning, saying she thought she had heard burglars the night before. Admitted that he never had heard burglars in the house. Had anything unusual happened just before that? Nothing that he remembered. Did he accompany her to a reception at Mrs. Schoonmaker's a day or two before? Yes. What occurred? Little by little it was dragged out of the witness that Laura had behaved strangely there, appeared to be sick, and he had taken her home. Upon being pushed he admitted that she had afterward confessed that she saw Selby there. And Washington volunteered the statement that Selby was a black-hearted villain.

The district attorney said, with some annoyance, '' There — there ! That will do.''

The defense declined to examine Mr. Hawkins at present. The case for the prosecution was closed. Of the murder there could not be the least doubt, or

17

that the prisoner followed the deceased to New York with a murderous intent. On the evidence the jury must convict, and might do so without leaving their seats. This was the condition of the case two days after the jury had been selected. A week had passed since the trial opened, and a Sunday had intervened. The public who read the reports of the evidence saw no chance for the prisoner's escape. The crowd of spectators who had watched the trial were moved with the most profound sympathy for Laura.

Mr. Braham opened the case for the defense. His manner was subdued, and he spoke in so low a voice that it was only by reason of perfect silence in the court room that he could be heard. He spoke very distinctly, however, and if his nationality could be discovered in his speech it was only in a certain richness and breadth of tone.

He began by saying that he trembled at the responsibility he had undertaken; and he should altogether despair, if he did not see before him a jury of twelve men of rare intelligence, whose acute minds would unravel all the sophistries of the prosecution, men with a sense of honor, which would revolt at the remorseless persecution of this hunted woman by the state, men with hearts to feel for the wrongs of which she was the victim. Far be it from him to cast any suspicion upon the motives of the able, eloquent, and ingenious lawyers of the state; they act officially; their business is to convict. It is our business, gentlemen, to see that justice is done.

"It is my duty, gentlemen, to unfold to you one of the most affecting dramas in all the history of misfortune. I shall have to show you a life, the sport of fate and circumstances, hurried along through shifting storm and sun, bright with trusting innocence and anon black with heartless villainy, a career which moves on in love and desertion and anguish, always hovered over by the dark spectre of INSANITY, — an insanity hereditary and induced by mental torture,— until it ends, if end it must in your verdict, by one of those fearful accidents which are inscrutable to men and of which God alone knows the secret.

"Gentlemen, I shall ask you to go with me away from this court room and its minions of the law, away from the scene of this tragedy, to a distant, I wish I could say a happier, day. The story I have to tell is of a lovely little girl, with sunny hair and laughing eyes, traveling with her parents, evidently people of wealth and refinement, upon a Mississippi steamboat. There is an explosion, one of those terrible catastrophes which leave the imprint of an unsettled mind upon the survivors. Hundreds of mangled remains are sent into eternity. When the wreck is cleared away this sweet little girl is found among the panic-stricken survivors, in the midst of a scene of horror enough to turn the steadiest brain. Her parents have disappeared. Search even for their bodies is in vain. The bewildered, stricken child — who can say what changes the fearful event

Q

wrought in her tender brain? — clings to the first person who shows her sympathy. It is Mrs. Hawkins, this good lady who is still her loving friend. Laura is adopted into the Hawkins family. Perhaps she forgets in time that she is not their child. She is an orphan. No, gentlemen, I will not deceive you, she is *not* an orphan. Worse than that. There comes another day of agony. She knows that her father lives. But who is he, where is he? Alas, I cannot tell you. Through the scenes of this painful history he flits here and there, a lunatic! If he seeks his daughter, it is the purposeless search of a lunatic, as one who wanders bereft of reason, crying, Where is my child? Laura seeks her father. In vain! Just as she is about to find him, again and again he disappears, he is gone, he vanishes.

"But this is only the prologue to the tragedy. Bear with me while I relate it. (Mr. Braham takes out his handkerchief, unfolds it slowly, crushes it in his nervous hand, and throws it on the table.) Laura grew up in her humble Southern home, a beautiful creature, the joy of the house, the pride of the neighborhood, the loveliest flower in all the sunny South. She might yet have been happy; she was happy. But the destroyer came into this paradise. He plucked the sweetest bud that grew there, and having enjoyed its odor, trampled it in the mire beneath his feet. George Selby, the deceased, a handsome, accomplished Confederate Colonel, was this human fiend. He deceived her with a mock marriage; after some months he brutally abandoned her, and spurned her as if she were a contemptible thing; all the time he had a wife in New Orleans. Laura was crushed. For weeks, as I shall show you by the testimony of her adopted mother and brother, she hovered over death in delirium. Gentlemen, did she ever emerge from this delirium? I shall show you that when she recovered her health, her mind was changed, she was not what she had been. You can judge yourselves whether the tottering reason ever recovered its throne.

"Years pass. She is in Washington, apparently the happy favorite of a brilliant society. Her family have become enormously rich by one of those sudden turns in fortune that the inhabitants of America are familiar with — the discovery of immense mineral wealth in some wild lands owned by them. She is engaged in a vast philanthropic scheme for the benefit of the poor, by the use of this wealth. But, alas, even here and now, the same relentless fate pursued her. The villain Selby appears again upon the scene, as if on purpose to complete the ruin of her life. He appeared to taunt her with her dishonor, he threatened exposure if she did not become again the mistress of his passion. Gentlemen, do you wonder if this woman, thus pursued, lost her reason, was beside herself with fear, and that her wrongs preyed upon her mind until she was no longer responsible for her acts? I turn away my head as one who would not willingly look even upon the just vengeance of Heaven. (Mr. Braham paused as if overcome by his emotions. Mrs. Hawkins and Washington were in tears, as were many of the spectators also. The jury looked scared.)

" Gentlemen, in this condition of affairs it needed but a spark — I do not say a suggestion, I do not say a hint — from this butterfly Brierly, this rejected rival, to cause the explosion. I make no charges, but if this woman was in her right mind when she fled from Washington and reached this city in company with Brierly, then I do not know what insanity is."

When Mr. Braham sat down, he felt that he had the jury with him. A burst of applause followed, which the officer promptly suppressed. Laura, with tears in her eyes, turned a grateful look upon her counsel. All the women among the spectators saw the tears and wept also. They thought as they also looked at Mr. Braham, How handsome he is!

Mrs. Hawkins took the stand. She was somewhat confused to be the target of so many eyes, but her honest and good face at once told in Laura's favor.

" Mrs. Hawkins," said Mr. Braham, " will you be kind enough to state the circumstances of your finding Laura?"

" I object," said Mr. McFlinn, rising to his feet. " This has nothing whatever to do with the case, your Honor. I am surprised at it, even after the extraordinary speech of my learned friend."

" How do you propose to connect it, Mr Braham?" asked the judge.

"If it please the court," said Mr. Braham, rising impressively, "your Honor has permitted the prosecution, and I have submitted without a word, to go into the most extraordinary testimony to establish a motive. Are we to be shut out from showing that the motive attributed to us could not by reason of certain mental conditions exist? I purpose, may it please your Honor, to show the cause and the origin of an aberration of mind, to follow it up with other like evidence, connecting it with the very moment of the homicide, showing a condition of the intellect of the prisoner that precludes responsibility."

"The state must insist upon its objections," said the district attorney. "The purpose evidently is to open the door to a mass of irrelevant testimony, the object of which is to produce an effect upon the jury your Honor well understands."

"Perhaps," suggested the judge, "the court ought to hear the testimony, and exclude it afterward, if it is irrelevant."

"Will your Honor hear argument on that?"

"Certainly."

And argument his Honor did hear, or pretend to, for two whole days, from all the counsel in turn, in the course of which the lawyers read contradictory decisions enough to perfectly establish both sides, from volume after volume, whole libraries, in fact, until no mortal man could say what the rules were. The question of insanity in all its legal aspects was, of course, drawn into the discussion, and its application affirmed and denied. The case was felt to turn upon the admission or rejection of this evidence. It was a sort of test trial of strength between the lawyers. At the end the judge decided to admit the testimony, as the judge usually does in such cases, after a sufficient waste of time in what are called arguments.

Mrs. Hawkins was allowed to go on.

CHAPTER XXV.

PROGRESS OF THE TRIAL

—Voyre mais (demandoit Trinquamelle) mon amy, comment procedez vous en action criminelle, la partie coupable prinse *flagrante crimine ?* — Comme vous aultres Messieurs (respondit Bridoye)—

"Hag eunn drâ-bennâg hoc'h eûz-hu da lavaroud évid hé wennidigez?"

MRS. HAWKINS, slowly and conscientiously, as if every detail of her family history was important, told the story of the steamboat explosion, of the finding and adoption of Laura. Silas, that is Mr. Hawkins, and she always loved Laura as if she had been their own child.

She then narrated the circumstances of Laura's supposed marriage, her abandonment and long illness, in a manner that touched all hearts. Laura had been a different woman since then.

Cross-examined. At the time of first finding Laura on the steamboat, did she notice that Laura's mind was at all deranged? She couldn't say that she did. After the recovery of Laura from her long illness, did Mrs. Hawkins think there were any signs of insanity about her? Witness confessed that she did not think of it *then*.

(265)

Re-direct examination. " But she was different after that? "

" Oh, yes, sir."

Washington Hawkins corroborated his mother's testimony as to Laura's connection with Colonel Selby. He was at Harding during the time of her living there with him. After Colonel Selby's desertion she was almost dead, never appeared to know anything rightly for weeks. He added that he never saw such a scoundrel as Selby. (Checked by district attorney.) Had he noticed any change in Laura after her illness? Oh, yes. Whenever any allusion was made that might recall Selby to mind, she looked awful — as if she could kill him.

" You mean," said Mr. Braham, " that there was an unnatural, insane gleam in her eyes? "

" Yes, certainly," said Washington in confusion.

All this was objected to by the district attorney, but it was got before the jury, and Mr. Braham did not care how much it was ruled out after that.

Beriah Sellers was the next witness called. The Colonel made his way to the stand with majestic, yet bland deliberation. Having taken the oath and kissed the Bible with a smack intended to show his great respect for that book, he bowed to his Honor with dignity, to the jury with familiarity, and then turned to the lawyers and stood in an attitude of superior attention.

" Mr. Sellers, I believe? " began Mr. Braham.

" Beriah Sellers, Missouri," was the courteous acknowledgment that the lawyer was correct.

" Mr. Sellers, you know the parties here, you are a friend of the family?"

" Know them all, from infancy, sir. It was me, sir, that induced Silas Hawkins, Judge Hawkins, to come to Missouri, and make his fortune. It was by my advice and in company with me, sir, that he went into the operation of —"

" Yes, yes. Mr. Sellers, did you know a Major Lackland?"

" Knew him well, sir, knew him and honored him, sir. He was one of the most remarkable men of our country, sir. A member of Congress. He was often at my mansion, sir, for weeks. He used to say to me, ' Colonel Sellers, if you would go into politics, if I had you for a colleague, we should show Calhoun and Webster that the brain of the country didn't lie east of the Alleghanies .' But I said —"

" Yes, yes. I believe Major Lackland is not living, Colonel?"

There was an almost imperceptible sense of pleasure betrayed in the Colonel's face at this prompt acknowledgment of his title.

" Bless you, no. Died years ago, a miserable death, sir, a ruined man, a poor sot. He was suspected of selling his vote in Congress, and probably he did; the disgrace killed him, he was an outcast, sir, loathed by himself and by his constituents. And I think, sir —"

The Judge. " You will confine yourself, Colonel Sellers, to the questions of the counsel."

"Of course, your Honor. This," continued the Colonel in confidential explanation, "was twenty years ago. I shouldn't have thought of referring to such a trifling circumstance *now*. If I remember rightly, sir "—

A bundle of letters was here handed to the witness.

"Do you recognize that handwriting?"

"As if it was my own, sir. It's Major Lackland's. I was knowing to these letters when Judge Hawkins received them. [The Colonel's memory was a little at fault here. Mr. Hawkins had never gone into details with him on this subject.] He used to show them to me, and say, ' Colonel Sellers, you've a mind to untangle this sort of thing.' Lord, how everything comes back to me! Laura was a little thing then. The Judge and I were just laying our plans to buy the Pilot Knob, and —"

"Colonel, one moment. Your Honor, we put these letters in evidence."

The letters were a portion of the correspondence of Major Lackland with Silas Hawkins; parts of them were missing and important letters were referred to that were not here. They related, as the reader knows, to Laura's father. Lackland had come upon the track of a man who was searching for a lost child in a Mississippi steamboat explosion years before. The man was lame in one leg, and appeared to be flitting from place to place. It seemed that Major Lackland got so close track of him that he was able to describe his personal appearance and learn his name. But the letter containing these particulars was lost. Once he heard of him at a hotel in Washington; but the man departed, leaving an empty trunk, the day before the major went there. There was something very mysterious in all his movements.

Colonel Sellers, continuing his testimony, said that he saw this lost letter, but could not now recall the name. Search for the supposed father had been continued by Lackland, Hawkins, and himself for several years, but Laura was not informed of it till after the death of Hawkins, for fear of raising false hopes in her mind.

Here the district attorney arose and said:

"Your Honor, I must positively object to letting the witness wander off into all these irrelevant details."

Mr. Braham. "I submit, your Honor, that we cannot be interrupted in this manner. We have suffered the state to have full swing. Now here is a witness, who has known the prisoner from infancy, and is competent to testify upon the one point vital to her safety. Evidently, he is a gentleman of character, and his knowledge of the case cannot be shut out without increasing the aspect of persecution which the state's attitude toward the prisoner already has assumed."

The wrangle continued, waxing hotter and hotter. The Colonel, seeing the attention of the counsel and court entirely withdrawn from him, thought he per-

18**

ceived here his opportunity. Turning and beaming
upon the jury, he began simply to talk, but as the
grandeur of his position grew upon him his talk
broadened unconsciously into an oratorial vein.

"You see how she was situated, gentlemen: poor
child, it might have broken her heart to let her mind
get to running on such a thing as that. You see,
from what we could make out her father was lame in
the left leg and had a deep scar on his left forehead.
And so ever since the day she found out she *had*
another father, she never could run across a lame
stranger without being taken all over with a shiver,
and almost fainting where she stood. And the next
minute she would go right after that man. Once
she stumbled on a stranger with a game leg, and she
was the most grateful thing in this world — but it
was the wrong leg, and it was days and days before
she could leave her bed. Once she found a man
with a scar on his forehead, and she was just going
to throw herself into his arms, but he stepped out
just then, and there wasn't anything the matter with
his legs. Time and time again, gentlemen of the
jury, has this poor suffering orphan flung herself on
her knees with all her heart's gratitude in her eyes
before some scarred and crippled veteran, but
always, always to be disappointed, always to be
plunged into new despair — if his legs were right his
scar was wrong, if his scar was right his legs were
wrong. Never could find a man that would fill the
bill. Gentlemen of the jury, you have hearts, you

have feelings, you have warm human sympathies, you can feel for this poor suffering child. Gentlemen of the jury, if I had time, if I had the opportunity, if I might be permitted to go on and tell you the thousands and thousands and thousands of mutilated strangers this poor girl has started out of cover, and hunted from city to city, from state to state, from continent to continent, till she has run them down and found they wan't the ones, I know your hearts——"

By this time the Colonel had become so warmed up, that his voice had reached a pitch above that of the contending counsel; the lawyers suddenly stopped, and they and the judge turned toward the Colonel and remained for several seconds too surprised at this novel exhibition to speak. In this interval of silence, an appreciation of the situation gradually stole over the audience, and an explosion of laughter followed, in which even the court and the bar could hardly keep from joining.

Sheriff. "Order in the court."

The Judge. "The witness will confine his remarks to answers to questions."

The Colonel turned courteously to the judge and said:

"Certainly, your Honor, certainly. I am not well acquainted with the forms of procedure in the courts of New York, but in the West, sir, in the West——"

The Judge. "There, there, that will do, that will do!"

"You see, your Honor, there were no questions asked me, and I thought I would take advantage of the lull in the proceedings to explain to the jury a very significant train of ——"

The Judge. "That will *do*, sir! Proceed, Mr. Braham."

"Colonel Sellers, have you any reason to suppose that this man is still living?"

"Every reason, sir, every reason."

"State why."

"I have never heard of his death, sir. It has never come to my knowledge. In fact, sir, as I once said to Governor ——"

"Will you state to the jury what has been the effect of the knowledge of this wandering and evidently unsettled being, supposed to be her father, upon the mind of Miss Hawkins for so many years?"

Question objected to. Question ruled out.

Cross-examined. "Major Sellers, what is your occupation?"

The Colonel looked about him loftily, as if casting in his mind what would be the proper occupation of a person of such multifarious interests, and then said with dignity:

"A gentleman, sir. My father used to always say, sir ——"

"Capt. Sellers, did you ever see this man, this supposed father?"

"No, sir. But upon one occasion, old Senator

Thompson said to me, 'It's my opinion, Colonel Sellers —— ' ''

" Did you ever see anybody who *had* seen him?"

" No, sir. It was reported around at one time, that ——"

" That is all."

The defense then spent a day in the examination of medical experts in insanity, who testified, on the evidence heard, that sufficient causes had occurred to produce an insane mind in the prisoner. Numerous cases were cited to sustain this opinion. There was such a thing as momentary insanity, in which the person, otherwise rational to all appearances, was for the time actually bereft of reason, and not responsible for his acts. The causes of this momentary possession could often be found in the person's life. [It afterward came out that the chief expert for the defense was paid a thousand dollars for looking into the case.]

The prosecution consumed another day in the examination of experts refuting the notion of insanity. These causes might have produced insanity, but there was no evidence that they have produced it in this case, or that the prisoner was not at the time of the commission of the crime in full possession of her ordinary faculties.

The trial had now lasted two weeks. It required four days now for the lawyers to " sum up." These arguments of the counsel were very important to their friends, and greatly enhanced their reputa-

18

tion at the bar; but they have small interest to us. Mr. Braham, in his closing speech, surpassed himself; his effort is still remembered as the greatest in the criminal annals of New York.

Mr. Braham re-drew for the jury the picture of Laura's early life; he dwelt long upon that painful episode of the pretended marriage and the desertion. Colonel Selby, he said, belonged, gentlemen, to what is called the "upper classes." It is the privilege of the "upper classes" to prey upon the sons and daughters of the people. The Hawkins family, though allied to the best blood of the South, were at the time in humble circumstances. He commented upon her parentage. Perhaps her agonized father, in his intervals of sanity, was still searching for his lost daughter. Would he one day hear that she had died a felon's death? Society had pursued her, fate had pursued her, and in a moment of delirium she had turned and defied fate and society. He dwelt upon the admission of base wrong in Colonel Selby's dying statement. He drew a vivid picture of the villain at last overtaken by the vengeance of Heaven. Would the jury say that this retributive justice, inflicted by an outraged, a deluded woman, rendered irrational by the most cruel wrongs, was in the nature of a foul, premeditated murder? "Gentlemen, it is enough for me to look upon the life of this most beautiful and accomplished of her sex, blasted by the heartless villainy of man, without seeing, at the end of it, the horrible spectacle of a gibbet. Gentlemen, we are all human, we have all sinned, we all have need of mercy. But I do not ask mercy of you who are the guardians of society and of the poor waifs, its sometimes wronged victims; I ask only that justice which you and I shall need in that last dreadful hour, when death will be robbed of half its terrors if we can reflect that we have never wronged a human being. Gentlemen, the life of this lovely and once happy girl, this now stricken woman, is in your hands.''

The jury were visibly affected. Half the court room was in tears. If a vote of both spectators and jury could have been taken *then*, the verdict would have been, "Let her go, she has suffered enough.''

But the district attorney had the closing argument. Calmly and without malice or excitement he reviewed the testimony. As the cold facts were unrolled, fear settled upon the listeners. There was no escape from the murder or its premeditation. Laura's character as a lobbyist in Washington, which had been made to appear incidentally in the evidence, was also against her. The whole body of the testimony of the defense was shown to be irrelevant, introduced only to excite sympathy, and not giving a color of probability to the absurd supposition of insanity. The attorney then dwelt upon the insecurity of life in the city, and the growing immunity with which women committed murders. Mr. McFlinn made a very able speech, convincing the reason without touching the feelings.

R

The judge in his charge reviewed the testimony with great show of impartiality. He ended by saying that the verdict must be acquital or murder in the first degree. If you find that the prisoner committed a homicide, in possession of her reason and with premeditation, your verdict will be accordingly. If you find she was not in her right mind, that she was the victim of insanity, hereditary or momentary, as it has been explained, your verdict will take that into account.

As the judge finished his charge, the spectators anxiously watched the faces of the jury. It was not a remunerative study. In the court room the general feeling was in favor of Laura, but whether this feeling extended to the jury, their stolid faces did not reveal. The public outside hoped for a conviction, as it always does; it wanted an example; the newspapers trusted the jury would have the courage to do its duty. When Laura was convicted, then the public would turn around and abuse the governor if he did not pardon her.

The jury went out. Mr. Braham preserved his serene confidence, but Laura's friends were dispirited. Washington and Colonel Sellers had been obliged to go to Washington, and they had departed under the unspoken fear that the verdict would be unfavorable,— a disagreement was the best they could hope for, and money was needed. The necessity of the passage of the University bill was now imperative.

The court waited for some time, but the jury gave no signs of coming in. Mr. Braham said it was extraordinary. The court then took a recess for a couple of hours. Upon again coming in, word was brought that the jury had not yet agreed.

But the jury had a question. The point upon which they wanted instruction was this: They wanted to know if Colonel Sellers was related to the Hawkins family. The court then adjourned till morning.

Mr. Braham, who was in something of a pet, remarked to Mr. O'Toole that they must have been deceived — that juryman with the broken nose could read !

CHAPTER XXVI.

WAITING FOR TELEGRAMS

"Wegotogwen ga-ijiwebadogwen; gonima ta-matchi-inakamigad."

THE momentous day was at hand — a day that
promised to make or mar the fortunes of the
Hawkins family for all time. Washington Hawkins
and Colonel Sellers were both up early, for neither
of them could sleep. Congress was expiring, and
was passing bill after bill as if they were gasps and
each likely to be its last. The University was on file
for its third reading this day, and to-morrow Washington would be a millionaire and Sellers no longer
impecunious; but this day, also, or at farthest the
next, the jury in Laura's case would come to a
decision of some kind or other — they would find
her guilty, Washington secretly feared, and then the
care and the trouble would all come back again and
there would be wearing months of besieging judges
for new trials; on this day, also, the re-election of
Mr. Dilworthy to the Senate would take place. So
Washington's mind was in a state of turmoil; there
were more interests at stake than it could handle

with serenity. He exulted when he thought of his millions; he was filled with dread when he thought of Laura. But Sellers was excited and happy. He said:

"Everything is going right, everything's going perfectly right. Pretty soon the telegrams will begin to rattle in, and then you'll see, my boy. Let the jury do what they please; what difference is it going to make? To-morrow we can send a million to New York and set the lawyers at work on the judges; bless your heart, they will go before judge after judge and exhort and beseech and pray and shed tears. They always do; and they always win, too. And they will win this time. They will get a writ of habeas corpus, and a stay of proceedings, and a supersedeas, and a new trial, and a nolle prosequi, and there you are! That's the routine, and it's no trick at all to a New York lawyer. That's the regular routine — everything's red tape and routine in the law, you see; it's all Greek to you, of course, but to a man who is acquainted with those things it's mere — I'll explain it to you some time. Everything's going to glide right along easy and comfortable now. You'll see, Washington, you'll see how it will be. And then, let me think. . . .Dilworthy will be elected to-day, and by day after to-morrow night he will be in New York ready to put in *his* shovel — and you haven't lived in Washington all this time not to know that the people who walk right by a Senator whose term is up without hardly seeing him will be down at the deepo to say 'Welcome back and God bless you, Senator, I'm glad to see you, sir!' when he comes along back re-elected, you know. Well, you see, his influence was naturally running low when he left here, but now he has got a new six-years start, and his suggestions will simply just weigh a couple of tons a-piece day after to-morrow. Lord bless you, he could rattle through that habeas corpus and supersedeas and all those things for Laura all by himself if he wanted to, when he gets back."

"I hadn't thought of that," said Washington, brightening, "but it is so. A newly-elected Senator *is* a power, I know that."

"Yes, indeed, he is. Why it is just human nature. Look at me. When we first came here, I was *Mr.* Sellers, and *Major* Sellers, and *Captain* Sellers, but nobody could ever get it right, somehow; but the minute our bill went through the House, I was *Colonel* Sellers every time. And nobody could do enough for me; and whatever I said was wonderful, sir, it was always wonderful; I never seemed to say any flat things at all. It was Colonel, won't you come and dine with us; and Colonel, why *don't* we ever see you at our house; and the Colonel says this; and the Colonel says that; and we know such-and-such is so-and-so, because husband heard Colonel Sellers *say* so. Don't you see? Well, the Senate adjourned and left our bill high and dry, and I'll be hanged if I warn't *Old*

Sellers from that day till our bill passed the House again last week. Now I'm the *Colonel* again; and if I were to eat all the dinners I am invited to, I reckon I'd wear my teeth down level with my gums in a couple of weeks."

"Well, I do wonder what you will be to-morrow, Colonel, after the President signs the bill?"

"*General*, sir! — General, without a doubt. Yes, sir, to-morrow it will be General, let me congratulate you, sir; General, you've done a great work, sir; — you've done a great work for the niggro; Gentlemen, allow me the honor to introduce my friend General Sellers, the humane friend of the niggro. Lord bless me, you'll see the newspapers say, General Sellers and servants arrived in the city last night and is stopping at the Fifth Avenue; and General Sellers has accepted a reception and banquet by the Cosmopolitan Club; you'll see the General's opinions quoted, too — and what the General has to say about the propriety of a new trial and a habeas corpus for the unfortunate Miss Hawkins will not be without weight in influential quarters, I can tell you."

"And I want to be the first to shake your faithful old hand and salute you with your new honors, and I want to do it *now* — General!" said Washington, suiting the action to the word, and accompanying it with all the meaning that a cordial grasp and eloquent eyes could give it.

The Colonel was touched; he was pleased and proud, too; his face answered for that.

Not very long after breakfast the telegrams began to arrive.   The first was from Braham, and ran
thus:

> "We feel certain that the verdict will be rendered to-day.   Be it
> good or bad, let it find us ready to make the next move instantly, what-
> ever it may be."

"That's the right talk," said Sellers.   "That
Braham's a wonderful man.   He was the only man
there that really understood me; he told me so
himself afterwards."

The next telegram was from Mr. Dilworthy:

> "I have not only brought over the Great Invincible, but through
> him a dozen more of the opposition.   Shall be re-elected to-day by an
> overwhelming majority."

"Good again!" said the Colonel.   "That man's
talent for organization is something marvelous.   He
wanted me to go out there and engineer that thing,
but I said, No, Dilworthy, I must be on hand here,
both on Laura's account and the bill's — but you've
no trifling genius for organization yourself, said I —
and I was right.   You go ahead, said I — you can
fix it — and so he has.   But I claim no credit for
that — if I stiffened up his backbone a little, I simply
put him in the way to make his fight — didn't make
it myself.   He has captured Noble — I consider that
a splendid piece of diplomacy — splendid, sir!"

By and by came another dispatch from New York:

> "Jury still out.   Laura calm and firm as a statue.   The report that
> the jury have brought her in guilty is false and premature."

"Premature!" gasped Washington, turning white.

" Then they all expect that sort of a verdict, when it comes."

And so did he; but he had not had courage enough to put it into words. He had been preparing himself for the worst, but after all his preparation the bare suggestion of the possibility of such a verdict struck him cold as death.

The friends grew impatient now; the telegrams did not come fast enough; even the lightning could not keep up with their anxieties. They walked the floor talking disjointedly and listening for the door bell. Telegram after telegram came. Still no result. By and by there was one which contained a single line:

"Court now coming in after brief recess to hear verdict. Jury ready."

" Oh, I wish they would finish!" said Washington. " This suspense is killing me by inches!"

Then came another telegram:

"Another hitch somewhere. Jury want a little more time and further instructions."

"Well, well, well, this *is* trying," said the Colonel. And after a pause, " No dispatch from Dilworthy for two hours, now. Even a dispatch from him would be better than nothing, just to vary this thing."

They waited twenty minutes. It seemed twenty hours.

"Come!" said Washington. "I can't wait for the telegraph boy to come all the way up here.

Let's go down to Newspaper Row — meet him on the way."

While they were passing along the avenue, they saw some one putting up a great display sheet on the bulletin board of a newspaper office, and an eager crowd of men was collecting about the place. Washington and the Colonel ran to the spot and read this:

"Tremendous sensation! Startling news from Saint's Rest! On first ballot for U. S. Senator, when voting was about to begin, Mr. Noble rose in his place and drew forth a package, walked forward and laid it on the Speaker's desk, saying, 'This contains $7,000 in bank bills and was given me by Senator Dilworthy in his bed-chamber at midnight last night to buy my vote for him — I wish the Speaker to count the money and retain it to pay the expense of prosecuting this infamous traitor for bribery.' The whole legislature was stricken speechless with dismay and astonishment. Noble further said that there were fifty members present with money in their pockets, placed there by Dilworthy to buy their votes. Amidst unparalleled excitement the ballot was now taken, and J. W. Smith elected U. S. Senator; Dilworthy receiving not one vote! *Noble promises damaging exposures concerning Dilworthy and certain measures of his now pending in Congress.*"

"Good heavens and earth!" exclaimed the Colonel.

"To the Capitol!" said Washington. "Fly!"

And they did fly. Long before they got there the newsboys were running ahead of them with extras, hot from the press, announcing the astounding news.

Arrived in the gallery of the Senate, the friends saw a curious spectacle — every Senator held an extra in his hand and looked as interested as if it contained news of the destruction of the earth. Not a single member was paying the least attention to the business of the hour.

The secretary, in a loud voice, was just beginning to read the title of a bill:

" House-Bill-No.-4,231,-An-Act-to - Found - and-Incorporate-the-Knobs-Industrial-University !-Read-first-and-second - time —considered-in-committee-of-the-whole - ordered - engrossed - and-passed-to-third-reading-and-final-passage !''

The President—" Third reading of the *bill !* ''

The two friends shook in their shoes. Senators threw down their extras and snatched a word or two with each other in whispers. Then the gavel rapped to command silence while the names were called on the ayes and nays. Washington grew paler and paler, weaker and weaker while the lagging list progressed; and when it was finished, his head fell helplessly forward on his arms. The fight was fought, the long struggle was over, and he was a pauper. Not a man had voted for the bill!

Colonel Sellers was bewildered and well nigh paralyzed, himself. But no man could long consider his own troubles in the presence of such suffering as Washington's. He got him up and supported him — almost carried him, indeed — out of the building and into a carriage. All the way home Washington lay with his face against the Colonel's shoulder and merely groaned and wept. The Colonel tried as well as he could under the dreary circumstances to hearten him a little, but it was of no

19**

use. Washington was past all hope of cheer now. He only said:

"Oh, it is all over — it is all over for good, Colonel. We must beg our bread now. We never can get up again. It was our last chance, and it is gone. They will hang Laura! My God, they will hang her! Nothing can save the poor girl now. Oh, I wish with all my soul they would hang me instead!"

Arrived at home, Washington fell into a chair and buried his face in his hands and gave full way to his misery. The Colonel did not know where to turn nor what to do. The servant maid knocked at the door and passed in a telegram, saying it had come while they were gone.

The Colonel tore it open and read with the voice of a man-of-war's broadside:

"VERDICT OF JURY, NOT GUILTY, AND LAURA IS FREE!"

CHAPTER XXVII.

THE VERDICT. LAURA ACQUITTED

分不白皂

Papel y tinta y poco justicia.

THE court room was packed on the morning on which the verdict of the jury was expected, as it had been every day of the trial, and by the same spectators, who had followed its progress with such intense interest.

There is a delicious moment of excitement which the frequenter of trials well knows, and which he would not miss for the world. It is that instant when the foreman of the jury stands up to give the verdict, and before he has opened his fateful lips.

The court assembled and waited. It was an obstinate jury. It even had another question — this intelligent jury — to ask the judge this morning.

"The question was this: "Were the doctors clear that the deceased had no disease which might soon have carried him off, if he had not been shot?" There was evidently one juryman who didn't want to waste life, and was willing to strike a general average, as the jury always does in a civil case, deciding not according to the evidence but reaching the verdict by some occult mental process.

During the delay the spectators exhibited unexampled patience, finding amusement and relief in the slightest movements of the court, the prisoner, and the lawyers. Mr. Braham divided with Laura the attention of the house. Bets were made by the sheriff's deputies on the verdict, with large odds in favor of a disagreement.

It was afternoon when it was announced that the jury was coming in. The reporters took their places and were all attention; the judge and lawyers were in their seats; the crowd swayed and pushed in eager expectancy, as the jury walked in and stood up in silence.

Judge. " Gentlemen, have you agreed upon your verdict?"

Foreman. " We have."

Judge. " What is it?"

Foreman. " NOT GUILTY."

A shout went up from the entire room and a tumult of cheering which the court in vain attempted to quell. For a few moments all order was lost. The spectators crowded within the bar and surrounded Laura who, calmer than any one else, was supporting her aged mother, who had almost fainted from excess of joy.

And now occurred one of those beautiful incidents

which no fiction-writer would dare to imagine, a
scene of touching pathos, creditable to our fallen
humanity. In the eyes of the women of the audience, Mr. Braham was the hero of the occasion; he
had saved the life of the prisoner; and besides he
was such a handsome man. The women could not
restrain their long pent-up emotions. They threw
themselves upon Mr. Braham in a transport of gratitude; they kissed him again and again, the young
as well as the advanced in years, the married as well
as the ardent single women; they improved the
opportunity with a touching self-sacrifice; in the
words of a newspaper of the day they "lavished
him with kisses." It was something sweet to do;
and it would be sweet for a woman to remember in
after years, that she had kissed Braham! Mr.
Braham himself received these fond assaults with the
gallantry of his nation, enduring the ugly, and
heartily paying back beauty in its own coin.

This beautiful scene is still known in New York as
"the kissing of Braham."

When the tumult of congratulation had a little
spent itself, and order was restored, Judge O'Shaunnessy said that it now became his duty to provide
for the proper custody and treatment of the acquitted. The verdict of the jury having left no
doubt that the woman was of an unsound mind, with
a kind of insanity dangerous to the safety of the
community, she could not be permitted to go at
large. "In accordance with the directions of the

19

law in such cases," said the judge, "and in obedience to the dictates of a wise humanity, I hereby commit Laura Hawkins to the care of the Superintendent of the State Hospital for Insane Criminals, to be held in confinement until the State Commissioners on Insanity shall order her discharge. Mr. Sheriff, you will attend at once to the execution of this decree."

Laura was overwhelmed and terror-stricken. She had expected to walk forth in freedom in a few moments. The revulsion was terrible. Her mother appeared like one shaken with an ague fit. Laura insane! And about to be locked up with madmen! She had never contemplated this. Mr. Braham said he should move at once for a writ of *habeas corpus*.

But the judge could not do less than his duty, the law must have its way. As in the stupor of a sudden calamity, and not fully comprehending it, Mrs. Hawkins saw Laura led away by the officer.

With little space for thought she was rapidly driven to the railway station, and conveyed to the Hospital for Lunatic Criminals. It was only when she was within this vast and grim abode of madness that she realized the horror of her situation. It was only when she was received by the kind physician and read pity in his eyes, and saw his look of hopeless incredulity when she attempted to tell him that she was not insane; it was only when she passed through the ward to which she was consigned and saw the horrible creatures, the victims of a double calamity, whose dreadful faces she was hereafter to see daily, and was locked into the small, bare room that was to be her home, that all her fortitude forsook her. She sank upon the bed, as soon as she was left alone — she had been searched by the matron — and tried to think. But her brain was in a whirl. She recalled Braham's speech, she recalled the testimony regarding her lunacy. She wondered if she *were* not mad; she felt that she soon should be among these loathsome creatures. Better almost to have died, than to slowly go mad in this confinement.

— We beg the reader's pardon. This is not history which has just been written. It is really what would have occurred if this were a novel. If this were a work of fiction, we should not dare to dispose of Laura otherwise. True art and any attention to dramatic proprieties required it. The novelist who would turn loose upon society an insane murderess could not escape condemnation. Besides, the safety of society, the decencies of criminal procedure, what we call our modern civilization, all would demand that Laura should be disposed of in the manner we have described. Foreigners, who read this sad story, will be unable to understand any other termination of it.

But this is history and not fiction. There is no such law or custom as that to which his Honor is supposed to have referred; Judge Shaunnessy would not probably pay any attention to it if there were. There is no Hospital for Insane Criminals; there is

8

no State Commission of Lunacy. What actually occurred when the tumult in the court room had subsided the sagacious reader will now learn.

Laura left the court room, accompanied by her mother and other friends, amid the congratulations of those assembled, and was cheered as she entered a carriage, and drove away. How sweet was the sunlight, how exhilarating the sense of freedom! Were not these following cheers the expression of popular approval and affection? Was she not the heroine of the hour?

It was with a feeling of triumph that Laura reached her hotel, a scornful feeling of victory over society with its own weapons.

Mrs. Hawkins shared not at all in this feeling; she was broken with the disgrace and the long anxiety.

"Thank God, Laura," she said, "it is over. Now we will go away from this hateful city. Let us go home at once."

"Mother," replied Laura, speaking with some tenderness, "I cannot go with you. There, don't cry, I cannot go back to that life."

Mrs. Hawkins was sobbing. This was more cruel than anything else, for she had a dim notion of what it would be to leave Laura to herself.

"No, mother, you have been everything to me. You know how dearly I love you. But I cannot go back."

A boy brought in a telegraphic dispatch. Laura took it and read:

"The bill is lost.   Dilworthy is ruined.   (Signed)
                                        WASHINGTON."

For a moment the words swam before her eyes.
The next her eyes flashed fire as she handed the
dispatch to her mother and bitterly said:

"The world is against me.   Well, let it be, let it.
I am against it."

"This is a cruel disappointment," said Mrs. Hawkins, to whom one grief more or less did not much
matter now, "to you and Washington; but we must
humbly bear it."

"Bear it," replied Laura scornfully, "I've all
my life borne it, and fate has thwarted me at every
step."

A servant came to the door to say that there was
a gentleman below who wished to speak with Miss
Hawkins. "J. Adolphe Griller" was the name
Laura read on the card. "I do not know such a
person. He probably comes from Washington.
Send him up."

Mr. Griller entered. He was a small man, slovenly
in dress, his tone confidential, his manner wholly
void of animation, all his features below the forehead
protruding — particularly the apple of his throat —
hair without a kink in it, a hand with no grip, a
meek, hang-dog countenance. He was a falsehood
done in flesh and blood; for while every visible sign
about him proclaimed him a poor, witless, useless
weakling, the truth was that he had the brains to
plan great enterprises and the pluck to carry them

through. That was his reputation, and it was a deserved one.

He softly said:

"I called to see you on business, Miss Hawkins. You have my card?"

Laura bowed.

Mr. Griller continued to purr, as softly as before:

"I will proceed to business. I am a business man. I am a lecture-agent, Miss Hawkins, and as soon as I saw that you were acquitted, it occurred to me that an early interview would be mutually beneficial."

"I don't understand you, sir," said Laura coldly.

"No? You see, Miss Hawkins, this is your opportunity. If you will enter the lecture field under good auspices, you will carry everything before you."

"But, sir, I never lectured, I haven't any lecture, I don't know anything about it."

"Ah, madam, that makes no difference — no real difference. It is not necessary to be able to lecture in order to go into the lecture field. If one's name is celebrated all over the land, especially, and if she is also beautiful, she is certain to draw large audiences."

"But what should I lecture about?" asked Laura, beginning in spite of herself to be a little interested as well as amused.

"Oh, why, woman — something about woman, I should say; the marriage relation, woman's fate, anything of that sort. Call it The Revelations of a Woman's Life; now, there's a good title. I wouldn't want any better title than that. I'm prepared to make you an offer, Miss Hawkins, a liberal offer,— twelve thousand dollars for thirty nights."

Laura thought. She hesitated. Why not? It would give her employment, money. She must do something.

"I will think of it, and let you know soon. But still, there is very little likelihood that I — however, we will not discuss it further now."

"Remember, that the sooner we get to work the better, Miss Hawkins, public curiosity is so fickle. Good day, madam."

The close of the trial released Mr. Harry Brierly and left him free to depart upon his long-talked-of Pacific coast mission. He was very mysterious about it, even to Philip.

"It's confidential, old boy," he said, "a little scheme we have hatched up. I don't mind telling you that it's a good deal bigger thing than that in Missouri, and a sure thing. I wouldn't take half a million just for my share. And it will open something for you, Phil. You will hear from me."

Philip did hear from Harry a few months afterward. Everything promised splendidly, but there was a little delay. Could Phil let him have a hundred, say for ninety days?

Philip himself hastened to Philadelphia, and, as soon as the spring opened, to the mine at Ilium, and began transforming the loan he had received from 'Squire Montague into laborers' wages. He was haunted with many anxieties; in the first place, Ruth was overtaxing her strength in her hospital labors, and Philip felt as if he must move heaven and earth to save her from such toil and suffering. His increased pecuniary obligation oppressed him. It seemed to him also that he had been one cause of the misfortune to the Bolton family, and that he was dragging into loss and ruin everybody who associated with him. He worked on day after day and week after week, with a feverish anxiety.

It would be wicked, thought Philip, and impious, to pray for luck; he felt that perhaps he ought not to ask a blessing upon the sort of labor that was only a venture; but yet in that daily petition, which this very faulty and not very consistent young Christian gentleman put up, he prayed earnestly enough for Ruth and for the Boltons and for those whom he loved and who trusted in him, and that his life might not be a misfortune to them and a failure to himself.

Since this young fellow went out into the world from his New England home, he had done some things that he would rather his mother should not know, things maybe that he would shrink from telling Ruth. At a certain green age young gentlemen are sometimes afraid of being called milksops, and Philip's associates had not always been the most select, such as these historians would have chosen for him, or whom at a later period he would have chosen for himself. It seemed inexplicable, for instance, that his life should have been thrown so much with his college acquaintance, Henry Brierly.

Yet, this was true of Philip, that in whatever company he had been he had never been ashamed to stand up for the principles he learned from his mother, and neither raillery nor looks of wonder turned him from that daily habit he learned at his mother's knees. Even flippant Harry respected this, and perhaps it was one of the reasons why Harry and all who knew Philip trusted him implicitly. And yet it must be confessed that Philip did not convey the impression to the world of a very serious young man, or of a man who might not rather easily fall into temptation. One looking for a real hero would have to go elsewhere.

The parting between Laura and her mother was exceedingly painful to both. It was as if two friends parted on a wide plain, the one to journey toward the setting and the other toward the rising sun, each comprehending that every step henceforth must separate their lives wider and wider.

CHAPTER XXVIII.

THE SENATE, JEALOUS OF ITS HONOR, REBUKES CORRUPTION

Ebok imana ebok ofut idibi.

Ὁ καρκίνος ὧδ' ἔφα
Χαλᾷ τὸν ὄφιν λαβών·
Εὐθὺν χρὴ τον ἑταῖρον, ἔμμεν,
Καὶ μὴ σκολιὰ φρονεῖν.

Mishittœnaeog noowaog
ayeuuhkone neen,
Nashpe nuskesukqunnonut
ho, ho, nunnaumunun.

WHEN Mr. Noble's bombshell fell in Senator
Dilworthy's camp, the statesman was discon-
certed for a moment. For a moment; that was all.
The next moment he was calmly up and doing.
From the center of our country to its circumference,
nothing was talked of but Mr. Noble's terrible
revelation, and the people were furious. Mind,
they were not furious because bribery was uncommon in our public life, but merely because here was
another case. Perhaps it did not occur to the nation
of good and worthy people that while they continued
to sit comfortably at home and leave the true source

(298)

of our political power (the "primaries,") in the
hands of saloon-keepers, dog-fanciers, and hod-
carriers, they could go on expecting "another"
case of this kind, and even dozens and hundreds of
them, and never be disappointed. However, they
may have thought that to sit at home and grumble
would some day right the evil.

Yes, the nation was excited, but Senator Dilworthy was calm — what was left of him after the
explosion of the shell. Calm, and up and doing.
What did he do first? What would you do first,
after you had tomahawked your mother at the
breakfast table for putting too much sugar in your
coffee? You would "ask for a suspension of public
opinion." That is what Senator Dilworthy did. It
is the custom. He got the usual amount of suspension. Far and wide he was called a thief, a briber,
a promoter of steamship subsidies, railway swindles,
robberies of the government in all possible forms and
fashions. Newspapers and everybody else called
him a pious hypocrite, a sleek, oily fraud, a reptile
who manipulated temperance movements, prayer
meetings, Sunday-schools, public charities, missionary enterprises, all for his private benefit. And as
these charges were backed up by what seemed to be
good and sufficient evidence, they were believed with
national unanimity.

Then Mr. Dilworthy made another move. He
moved instantly to Washington and "demanded an
investigation." Even this could not pass without

comment. Many papers used language to this
effect:

"Senator Dilworthy's remains have demanded an investigation.
This sounds fine and bold and innocent; but when we reflect that they
demand it at the hands of the Senate of the United States, it simply
becomes matter for derision. One might as well set the gentlemen
detained in the public prisons to trying each other. This investigation
is likely to be like all other Senatorial 'investigations'—amusing but
not useful. Query. Why does the Senate still stick to this pompous
word, 'Investigation'? One does not blindfold one's self in order to
investigate an object."

Mr. Dilworthy appeared in his place in the Senate
and offered a resolution appointing a committee to
investigate his case. It was carried, of course, and
the committee was appointed. Straightway the newspapers said:

"Under the guise of appointing a committee to investigate the late
Mr. Dilworthy, the Senate yesterday appointed a committee to *investigate his accuser*, *Mr. Noble*. This is the exact spirit and meaning of the
resolution, and the committee cannot try anybody but Mr. Noble without overstepping its authority. That Mr. Dilworthy had the effrontery
to offer such a resolution will surprise no one, and that the Senate could
entertain it without blushing and pass it without shame will surprise no
one. We are now reminded of a note which we have received from the
notorious burglar Murphy, in which he finds fault with a statement of
ours to the effect that he had served one term in the penitentiary and
also one in the U. S. Senate. He says, 'The latter statement is untrue
and does me great injustice.' After an unconscious sarcasm like that,
further comment is unnecessary."

And yet the Senate was roused by the Dilworthy
trouble. Many speeches were made. One Senator
(who was accused in the public prints of selling his
chances of re-election to his opponent for $50,000
and had not yet denied the charge) said that "the

presence in the capital of such a creature as this man Noble, to testify against a brother member of their body, was an insult to the Senate."

Another Senator said, "Let the investigation go on; and let it make an example of this man Noble; let it teach him and men like him that they could not attack the reputation of a United States Senator with impunity."

Another said he was glad the investigation was to be had, "for it was high time that the Senate should crush some cur like this man Noble, and thus show his kind that it was able and resolved to uphold its ancient dignity."

A bystander laughed at this finely-delivered peroration, and said:

"Why, this is the Senator who franked his baggage home through the mails last week — registered, at that. However, perhaps he was merely engaged in 'upholding the ancient dignity of the Senate,' then."

"No, the modern dignity of it," said another bystander. "It don't resemble its ancient dignity, but it fits its modern style like a glove."

There being no law against making offensive remarks about U. S. Senators, this conversation, and others like it, continued without let or hindrance. But our business is with the investigating committee.

Mr. Noble appeared before the committee of the Senate, and testified to the following effect:

He said that he was a member of the state legis-

20**

lature of the Happy-Land-of-Canaan; that on the —— day of —— he assembled himself together at the city of Saint's Rest, the capital of the state, along with his brother legislators; that he was known to be a political enemy of Mr. Dilworthy and bitterly opposed to his re-election; that Mr. Dilworthy came to Saint's Rest and was reported to be buying pledges of votes with money; that the said Dilworthy sent for him to come to his room in the hotel at night, and he went; was introduced to Mr. Dilworthy; called two or three times afterward at Dilworthy's request — usually after midnight; Mr. Dilworthy urged him to vote for him; Noble declined; Dilworthy argued; said he was bound to be elected, and could then ruin him (Noble) if he voted no; said he had every railway and every public office and stronghold of political power in the state under his thumb, and could set up or pull down any man he chose; gave instances showing where and how he had used this power; if Noble would vote for him he would make him a Representative in Congress; Noble still declined to vote, and said he did not believe Dilworthy was going to be elected; Dilworthy showed a list of men who would vote for him — a majority of the legislature; gave further proofs of his power by telling Noble everything the opposing party had done or said in secret caucus; claimed that his spies reported everything to him, and that——

Here a member of the committee objected that

this evidence was irrelevant and also in opposition to the spirit of the committee's instructions, because if these things reflected upon any one it was upon Mr. Dilworthy. The chairman said, let the person proceed with his statement — the committee could exclude evidence that did not bear upon the case.

Mr. Noble continued. He said that his party would cast him out if he voted for Mr. Dilworthy; Dilworthy said that that would inure to his benefit, because he would then be a recognized friend of his (Dilworthy's) and he could consistently exalt him politically and make his fortune; Noble said he was poor, and it was hard to tempt him so; Dilworthy said he would fix that; he said, "Tell me what you want, and say you will vote for me;" Noble could not say; Dilworthy said, "I will give you $5,-000 ——"

A committee man said, impatiently, that this stuff was all outside the case, and valuable time was being wasted; this was all a plain reflection upon a brother Senator. The chairman said it was the quickest way to proceed, and the evidence need have no weight.

Mr. Noble continued. He said he told Dilworthy that $5,000 was not much to pay for a man's honor, character, and everything that was worth having; Dilworthy said he was surprised; he considered $5,000 a fortune for some men; asked what Noble's figure was; Noble said he could not think $10,000 too little; Dilworthy said it was a great deal too much; he would not do it for any other man, but

he had conceived a liking for Noble, and where he
liked a man his heart yearned to help him; he was
aware that Noble was poor, and had a family to support, and that he bore an unblemished reputation
at home; for such a man and such a man's influence
he could do much, and feel that to help such a man
would be an act that would have its reward; the
struggles of the poor always touched him; he believed that Noble would make a good use of this
money and that it would cheer many a sad heart and
needy home; he would give the $10,000; all he
desired in return was that, when the balloting began,
Noble should cast his vote for him and should explain to the legislature that upon looking into the
charges against Mr. Dilworthy of bribery, corruption, and forwarding stealing measures in Congress
he had found them to be base calumnies upon a man
whose motives were pure and whose character was
stainless; he then took from his pocket $2,000 in
bank bills and handed them to Noble, and got another package containing $5,000 out of his trunk
and gave to him also. He——

A committee man jumped up and said:

"*At last*, Mr. Chairman, this shameless person has
arrived at the point. This is sufficient and conclu-
sive. By his own confession he has received a bribe
and did it deliberately. This is a grave offense, and
cannot be passed over in silence, sir. By the terms
of our instructions we can now proceed to mete out
to him such punishment as is meet for one who has

maliciously brought disrespect upon a Senator of the
United States. We have no need to hear the rest
of his evidence.''

The chairman said it would be better and more
regular to proceed with the investigation according
to the usual forms. A note would be made of Mr.
Noble's admission.

Mr. Noble continued. IIe said that it was now
far past midnight; that he took his leave and went
straight to certain legislators, told them everything,
made them count the money and also told them of
the exposure he would make in joint convention; he
made that exposure, as all the world knew. The
rest of the $10,000 was to be paid the day after
Dilworthy was elected.

Senator Dilworthy was now asked to take the
stand and tell what he knew about the man Noble.
The Senator wiped his mouth with his handkerchief,
adjusted his white cravat, and said that but for the
fact that public morality required an example, for
the warning of future Nobles, he would beg that in
Christian charity this poor misguided creature might
be forgiven and set free. He said that it was but
too evident that this person had approached him in
the hope of obtaining a bribe; he had intruded himself time and again, and always with moving stories
of his poverty. Mr. Dilworthy said that his heart
had bled for him — insomuch that he had several
times been on the point of trying to get some one to
do something for him. Some instinct had told him

20

from the beginning that this was a bad man, an evil-minded man, but his inexperience of such had blinded him to his real motives, and hence he had never dreamed that his object was to undermine the purity of a United States Senator. He regretted that it was plain now, that such was the man's object and that punishment could not with safety to the Senate's honor be withheld. He grieved to say that one of those mysterious dispensations of an inscrutable Providence which are decreed from time to time by His wisdom and for His righteous purposes, had given this conspirator's tale a color of plausibility,— but this would soon disappear under the clear light of truth which would now be thrown upon the case.

It so happened (said the Senator) that about the time in question, a poor young friend of mine, living in a distant town of my state, wished to establish a bank; he asked me to lend him the necessary money; I said I had no money just then, but would try to borrow it. The day before the election a friend said to me that my election expenses must be very large — especially my hotel bills,— and offered to lend me some money. Remembering my young friend, I said I would like a few thousands now, and a few more by and by; whereupon he gave me two packages of bills said to contain $2,000 and $5,000 respectively; I did not open the packages or count the money; I did not give any note or receipt for the same; I made no memorandum of the transaction, and neither did my friend. That night this evil man Noble came troubling me again. I could not rid myself of him, though my time was very precious. He mentioned my young friend and said he was very anxious to have $7,000 now to begin his banking operations with, and could wait a while for the rest. Noble wished to get the money and take it to him. I finally gave him the two packages of bills; I took no note or receipt from him, and made no memorandum of the matter. I no more look for duplicity and deception in another man than I would look for it in myself. I never thought of this man again until I was overwhelmed the next day by learning what a shameful use he had made of the confidence I had reposed in him and the money I had entrusted to his care. This is all, gentlemen. To the absolute truth of every detail of my statement I solemnly swear, and I call Him to witness who is the Truth and the loving Father of all whose lips abhor false speaking; I pledge my honor as a Senator, that I have spoken but the truth. May God forgive this wicked man — as I do.

Mr. Noble —'' Senator Dilworthy, your bank account shows that up to that day, and even on that very day, you conducted all your financial business through the medium of checks instead of bills, and so kept careful record of every moneyed transaction. Why did you deal in bank bills on this particular occasion?''

The Chairman —'' The gentleman will please to

T

remember that the committee is conducting this investigation.''

Mr. Noble —" Then will the committee ask the question?''

The Chairman —" The committee will — when it desires to know.''

Mr. Noble —" Which will not be during this century, perhaps.''

The Chairman —" Another remark like that, sir, will procure you the attentions of the sergeant-at-arms.''

Mr. Noble —" D——n the sergeant-at-arms, and the committee, too!''

Several Committeemen —" Mr. Chairman, this is contempt!''

Mr. Noble —" Contempt of whom?''

" Of the committee! Of the Senate of the United States!''

Mr. Noble —" Then I am become the acknowledged representative of a nation. You know as well as I do that the whole nation hold as much as three-fifths of the United States Senate in entire contempt. Three-fifths of you are Dilworthys.''

The sergeant-at-arms very soon put a quietus upon the observations of the representative of the nation, and convinced him that he was not in the over-free atmosphere of his Happy-Land-of-Canaan.

The statement of Senator Dilworthy naturally carried conviction to the minds of the committee. It was close, logical, unanswerable; it bore many internal evidences of its truth. For instance, it is customary in all countries for business men to loan large sums of money in bank bills instead of checks. It is customary for the lender to make no memorandum of the transaction. It is customary for the borrower to receive the money without making a memorandum of it, or giving a note or a receipt for it — because the borrower is not likely to die or forget about it. It is customary to lend nearly anybody money to start a bank with, especially if you have not the money to lend him and have to borrow it for the purpose. It is customary to carry large sums of money in bank bills about your person or in your trunk. It is customary to hand a large sum in bank bills to a man you have just been introduced to (if he asks you to do it) to be conveyed to a distant town and delivered to another party. It is not customary to make a memorandum of this transaction; it is not customary for the conveyor to give a note or a receipt for the money; it is not customary to require that he shall get a note or a receipt from the man he is to convey it to in the distant town. It would be at least singular in you to say to the proposed conveyor, " You might be robbed; I will deposit the money in bank and send a check for it to my friend through the mail."

Very well. It being plain that Senator Dilworthy's statement was rigidly true, and this fact being strengthened by his adding to it the support of " his honor as a Senator," the committee rendered a verdict of "Not proven that a bribe had been offered and accepted." This, in a manner, exonerated Noble and let him escape.

The committee made its report to the Senate, and that body proceeded to consider its acceptance. One Senator — indeed, several Senators — objected that the committee had failed of its duty; they had proved this man Noble guilty of nothing, they had meted out no punishment to him; if the report were accepted, he would go forth free and scathless, glorying in his crime, and it would be a tacit admission that any blackguard could insult the Senate of the United States and conspire against the sacred reputation of its members with impunity; the Senate owed it to the upholding of its ancient dignity to make an example of this man Noble — he should be crushed.

An elderly Senator got up and took another view of the case. This was a Senator of the worn-out and obsolete pattern; a man still lingering among the cobwebs of the past, and behind the spirit of the age. He said that there seemed to be a curious misunderstanding of the case. Gentlemen seemed exceedingly anxious to preserve and maintain the honor and dignity of the Senate.

Was this to be done by trying an obscure adventurer for attempting to trap a Senator into bribing him? Or would not the truer way be to find out whether the Senator was capable of *being* entrapped into so shameless an act, and then try *him*? Why, of course. *Now* the whole idea of the Senate seemed to be to shield the Senator and turn inquiry away from him. The true way to uphold the honor of the Senate was to have none but honorable men in its body. If this Senator had yielded to temptation and had offered a bribe, he was a soiled man and ought to be instantly expelled; therefore he wanted the Senator tried, and not in the usual namby-pamby way, but in good earnest. He wanted to know the truth of this matter. For himself, he believed that the guilt of Senator Dilworthy was established beyond the shadow of a doubt; and he considered that in trifling with his case and shirking it the Senate was doing a shameful and cowardly thing — a thing which suggested that in its willingness to sit longer in the company of such a man, it was acknowledging that it was itself of a kind with him and was therefore not dishonored by his presence. He desired that a rigid examination be made into Senator Dilworthy's case, and that it be continued clear into the approaching extra session if need be. There was no dodging this thing with the lame excuse of want of time.

In reply, an honorable Senator said that he thought it would be as well to drop the matter and accept the committee's report. He said with some jocularity that the more one agitated this thing, the worse it was for the agitator. He was not able to deny that he believed Senator Dilworthy to be guilty — but what then? Was it such an extraordinary case? For his part, even allowing the Senator to be guilty, he did not think his continued presence during the few remaining days of the session would contaminate the Senate to a dreadful degree. [This humorous sally was received with smiling admiration — notwithstanding it was not wholly new, having originated with the Massachusetts General in the House a day or two before, upon the occasion of the proposed expulsion of a member for selling his vote for money.]

The Senate recognized the fact that it could not be contaminated by sitting a few days longer with Senator Dilworthy, and so it accepted the committee's report and dropped the unimportant matter.

Mr. Dilworthy occupied his seat to the last hour of the session. He said that his people had reposed a trust in him, and it was not for him to desert them. He would remain at his post till he perished, if need be.

His voice was lifted up and his vote cast for the last time, in support of an ingenious measure contrived by the General from Massachusetts whereby the President's salary was proposed to be doubled and every Congressman paid several thousand dollars extra for work previously done, under an accepted contract, and already paid for once and receipted for.

Senator Dilworthy was offered a grand ovation by his friends at home, who said that their affection for him and their confidence in him were in no wise impaired by the persecutions that had pursued him, and that he was still good enough for them.*

---

* The $7,000 left by Mr. Noble with his state legislature was placed in safe keeping to await the claim of the legitimate owner. Senator Dilworthy made one little effort through his protégé, the embryo banker, to recover it, but there being no notes of hand or other memoranda to support the claim, it failed. The moral of which is, that when one loans money to start a bank with, one ought to take the party's written acknowledgment of the fact.

CHAPTER XXIX.

THE FATE OF LAURA

ભ્ગ્તાગ્ય પ્રેમ્મ જ

"Ow holan whath ythew prowte
kynthoma ogas marowe"—

FOR some days Laura had been a free woman
once more. During this time, she had experienced — first, two or three days of triumph, excitement, congratulations, a sort of sunburst of gladness,
after a long night of gloom and anxiety; then two
or three days of calming down, by degrees — a re-
ceding of tides, a quieting of the storm-wash to a
murmurous surf-beat, a diminishing of devastating
winds to a refrain that bore the spirit of a truce —
days given to solitude, rest, self-communion, and
the reasoning of herself into a realization of the fact
that she was actually done with bolts and bars,
prison horrors and impending death; then came a
day whose hours filed slowly by her, each laden with
some remnant, some remaining fragment of the
dreadful time so lately ended — a day which, closing

(314)

at last, left the past a fading shore behind her and
turned her eyes toward the broad sea of the future.
So speedily do we put the dead away and come back
to our place in the ranks to march in the pilgrimage
of life again!

And now the sun rose once more and ushered in
the first day of what Laura comprehended and accepted as a new life.

The past had sunk below the horizon, and existed
no more for her; she was done with it for all time.
She was gazing out over the trackless expanses of
the future now, with troubled eyes. Life must be
begun again — at eight and twenty years of age.
And where to begin? The page was blank, and
waiting for its first record; so this was indeed a
momentous day.

Her thoughts drifted back, stage by stage, over
her career. As far as the long highway receded
over the plain of her life, it was lined with the gilded
and pillared splendors of her ambition all crumbled
to ruin and ivy-grown; every milestone marked a
disaster; there was no green spot remaining anywhere in memory of a hope that had found its
fruition; the unresponsive earth had uttered no voice
of flowers in testimony that one who was blest had
gone that road.

Her life had been a failure. That was plain, she
said. No more of that. She would now look the
future in the face; she would mark her course upon
the chart of life, and follow it; follow it without

swerving, through rocks and shoals, through storm and calm, to a haven of rest and peace — or, shipwreck. Let the end be what it might, she would mark her course now — to-day — and follow it.

On her table lay six or seven notes. They were from lovers; from some of the prominent names in the land; men whose devotion had survived even the grisly revealments of her character which the courts had uncurtained; men who knew her now, just as she was, and yet pleaded as for their lives for the dear privilege of calling the murderess wife.

As she read these passionate, these worshiping, these supplicating missives, the woman in her nature confessed itself; a strong yearning came upon her to lay her head upon a loyal breast and find rest from the conflict of life, solace for her griefs, the healing of love for her bruised heart.

With her forehead resting upon her hand, she sat thinking, thinking, while the unheeded moments winged their flight. It was one of those mornings in early spring when nature seems just stirring to a half consciousness out of a long, exhausting lethargy; when the first faint balmy airs go wandering about, whispering the secret of the coming change; when the abused brown grass, newly relieved of snow, seems considering whether it can be worth the trouble and worry of contriving its green raiment again only to fight the inevitable fight with the implacable winter and be vanquished and buried once more; when the sun shines out and a few birds

EACH LETTER SLOWLY CONSUMED TO ASHES

venture forth and lift up a forgotten song; when a strange stillness and suspense pervade the waiting air. It is a time when one's spirit is subdued and sad, one knows not why; when the past seems a storm-swept desolation, life a vanity and a burden, and the future but a way to death. It is a time when one is filled with vague longings; when one dreams of flight to peaceful islands in the remote solitudes of the sea, or folds his hands and says, What is the use of struggling, and toiling and worrying any more? Let us give it all up.

It was into such a mood as this that Laura had drifted from the musings which the letters of her lovers had called up. Now she lifted her head and noted with surprise how the day had wasted. She thrust the letters aside, rose up and went and stood at the window. But she was soon thinking again, and was only gazing into vacancy.

By and by she turned; her countenance had cleared; the dreamy look was gone out of her face; all indecision had vanished; the poise of her head and the firm set of her lips told that her resolution was formed. She moved toward the table with all the old dignity in her carriage, and all the old pride in her mien. She took up each letter in its turn, touched a match to it and watched it slowly consume to ashes. Then she said:

"I have landed upon a foreign shore, and burned my ships behind me. These letters were the last thing that held me in sympathy with any remnant or

21**

belonging of the old life. Henceforth that life and all that appertains to it are as dead to me and as far removed from me as if I were become a denizen of another world.''

She said that love was not for her — the time that it could have satisfied her heart was gone by and could not return; the opportunity was lost, nothing could restore it. She said there could be no love without respect, and she would only despise a man who could content himself with a thing like her. Love, she said, was a woman's first necessity; love being forfeited, there was but one thing left that could give a passing zest to a wasted life, and that was fame, admiration, the applause of the multitude.

And so her resolution was taken. She would turn to that final resort of the disappointed of her sex, the lecture platform. She would array herself in fine attire, she would adorn herself with jewels, and stand in her isolated magnificence before massed audiences and enchant them with her eloquence and amaze them with her unapproachable beauty. She would move from city to city like a queen of romance, leaving marveling multitudes behind her and impatient multitudes awaiting her coming. Her life, during one hour of each day, upon the platform, would be a rapturous intoxication — and when the curtain fell, and the lights were out, and the people gone, to nestle in their homes and forget her, she would find in sleep oblivion of her homelessness, if she could, if not she would brave out the night in solitude and wait for the next day's hour of ecstasy.

So, to take up life and begin again was no great evil. She saw her way. She would be brave and strong; she would make the best of what was left for her among the possibilities.

She sent for the lecture agent, and matters were soon arranged.

Straightway all the papers were filled with her name, and all the dead walls flamed with it. The papers called down imprecations upon her head; they reviled her without stint; they wondered if all sense of decency was dead in this shameless murderess, this brazen lobbyist, this heartless seducer of the affections of weak and misguided men; they implored the people, for the sake of their pure wives, their sinless daughters, for the sake of decency, for the sake of public morals, to give this wretched creature such a rebuke as should be an all-sufficient evidence to her and to such as her that there was a limit where the flaunting of their foul acts and opinions before the world must stop; certain of them, with a higher art, and to her a finer cruelty, a sharper torture, uttered no abuse, but always spoke of her in terms of mocking eulogy and ironical admiration. Everybody talked about the new wonder, canvassed the theme of her proposed discourse, and marveled how she would handle it.

Laura's few friends wrote to her or came and talked with her, and pleaded with her to retire while

it was yet time, and not attempt to face the gather-
ing storm. But it was fruitless. She was stung to
the quick by the comments of the newspapers; her
spirit was roused, her ambition was towering, now.
She was more determined than ever. She would
show these people what a hunted and persecuted
woman could do.

The eventful night came. Laura arrived before
the great lecture hall in a close carriage within five
minutes of the time set for the lecture to begin.
When she stepped out of the vehicle her heart beat
fast and her eyes flashed with exultation; the whole
street was packed with people, and she could hardly
force her way to the hall! She reached the anteroom, threw off her wraps, and placed herself before
the dressing-glass. She turned herself this way and
that — everything was satisfactory, her attire was
perfect. She smoothed her hair, re-arranged a jewel
here and there, and all the while her heart sang within
her, and her face was radiant. She had not been so
happy for ages and ages, it seemed to her. Oh, no,
she had never been so overwhelmingly grateful and
happy in her whole life before. The lecture agent
appeared at the door. She waved him away and said:

"Do not disturb me. I want no introduction.
And do not fear for me; the moment the hands
point to eight I will step upon the platform."

He disappeared. She held her watch before her.
She was so impatient that the second hand seemed
whole tedious minutes dragging its way around the

circle.   At last the supreme moment came, and with head erect and the bearing of an empress she swept through the door and stood upon the stage.   Her eyes fell upon —

Only a vast, brilliant emptiness — there were not forty people in the house! There were only a handful of coarse men and ten or twelve still coarser women, lolling upon the benches and scattered about singly and in couples.

Her pulses stood still, her limbs quaked, the gladness went out of her face.   There was a moment of silence, and then a brutal laugh and an explosion of cat-calls and hisses saluted her from the audience. The clamor grew stronger and louder, and insulting speeches were shouted at her.   A half-intoxicated man rose up and threw something, which missed her but bespattered a chair at her side, and this evoked an outburst of laughter and boisterous admiration.   She was bewildered, her strength was forsaking her.   She reeled away from the platform, reached the anteroom, and dropped helpless upon a sofa.   The lecture agent ran in, with a hurried question upon his lips; but she put forth her hands, and with the tears raining from her eyes, said:

"Oh, do not speak! Take me away — please take me away, out of this dreadful place! Oh, this is like all my life — failure, disappointment, misery — always misery, always failure.   What have I done, to be so pursued!   Take me away, I beg of you, I implore you!"

21

Upon the pavement she was hustled by the mob, the surging masses roared her name and accompanied it with every species of insulting epithet; they thronged after the carriage, hooting, jeering, cursing, and even assailing the vehicle with missiles. A stone crushed through a blind, wounding Laura's forehead, and so stunning her that she hardly knew what further transpired during her flight.

It was long before her faculties were wholly restored, and then she found herself lying on the floor by a sofa in her own sitting-room, and alone. So she supposed she must have sat down upon the sofa and afterward fallen. She raised herself up, with difficulty, for the air was chilly and her limbs were stiff. She turned up the gas and sought the glass. She hardly knew herself, so worn and old she looked, and so marred with blood were her features. The night was far spent, and a dead stillness reigned. She sat down by her table, leaned her elbows upon it, and put her face in her hands.

Her thoughts wandered back over her old life again and her tears flowed unrestrained. Her pride was humbled, her spirit was broken. Her memory found but one resting-place; it lingered about her young girlhood with a caressing regret; it dwelt upon it as the one brief interval in her life that bore no curse. She saw herself again in the budding grace of her twelve years, decked in her dainty pride of ribbons, consorting with the bees and the butter-flies, believing in fairies, holding confidential converse with the flowers, busying herself all day long with airy trifles that were as weighty to her as the affairs that tax the brains of diplomats and emperors. She was without sin, then, and unacquainted with grief; the world was full of sunshine and her heart was full of music.   From that — to this!

"If I could only die!" she said.   "If I could only go back, and be as I was then, for one hour — and hold my father's hand in mine again, and see all the household about me, as in that old innocent time — and then die!   My God, I am humbled, my pride is all gone, my stubborn heart repents — have pity!"

When the spring morning dawned, the form still sat there, the elbows resting upon the table and the face upon the hands.   All day long the figure sat there, the sunshine enriching its costly raiment and flashing from its jewels; twilight came, and presently the stars, but still the figure remained; the moon found it there still, and framed the picture with the shadow of the window sash, and flooded it with mellow light; by and by the darkness swallowed it up, and later the gray dawn revealed it again; the new day grew toward its prime, and still the forlorn presence was undisturbed.

But now the keepers of the house had become uneasy; their periodical knockings still finding no response, they burst open the door.

The jury of inquest found that death had resulted from heart disease, and was instant and painless. That was all.   Merely heart disease.

U

CHAPTER XXX.

WASHINGTON HAWKINS TAKES A NEW START

Han ager ikke ilde som veed at vende.

Wanna unyanpi kta. Niye de kta he?

Iapi Oaye, vol. i, no. 7.

CLAY HAWKINS, years gone by, had yielded, after many a struggle, to the migratory and speculative instinct of our age and our people, and had wandered further and further westward upon trading ventures. Settling finally in Melbourne, Australia, he ceased to roam, became a steady-going, substantial merchant, and prospered greatly. His life lay beyond the theater of this tale.

His remittances had supported the Hawkins family, entirely, from the time of his father's death until latterly when Laura, by her efforts in Washington, had been able to assist in this work. Clay was away on a long absence in some of the eastward islands when Laura's troubles began, trying (and almost in vain) to arrange certain interests which had become disordered through a dishonest agent, and consequently he knew nothing of the murder till he returned and read his letters and papers. His natural impulse was to hurry to the States and save his sister, if possible, for he loved her with a deep and abiding affection.   His business was so crippled now, and so deranged, that to leave it would be ruin; therefore he sold out at a sacrifice that left him considerably reduced in worldly possessions, and began his voyage to San Francisco.   Arrived there, he perceived by the newspapers that the trial was near its close.   At Salt Lake later telegrams told him of the acquittal, and his gratitude was boundless — so boundless, indeed, that sleep was driven from his eyes by the pleasurable excitement almost as effectually as preceding weeks of anxiety had done it.   He shaped his course straight for Hawkeye, now, and his meeting with his mother and the rest of the household was joyful — albeit he had been away so long that he seemed almost a stranger in his own home.

But the greetings and congratulations were hardly finished when all the journals in the land clamored the news of Laura's miserable death.   Mrs. Hawkins was prostrated by this last blow, and it was well that Clay was at her side to stay her with comforting words and take upon himself the ordering of the household with its burden of labors and cares.

Washington Hawkins had scarcely more than entered upon that decade which carries one to the full blossom of manhood which we term the beginning of middle age, and yet a brief sojourn at the capital of the nation had made him old.   His hair was already turning gray when the late session of Congress began its sittings; it grew grayer still, and rapidly, after the memorable day that saw Laura proclaimed a murderess; it waxed grayer and still grayer during the lagging suspense that succeeded it and after the crash which ruined his last hope — the failure of his bill in the Senate and the destruction of its champion, Dilworthy. A few days later, when he stood uncovered while the last prayer was pronounced over Laura's grave, his hair was whiter and his face hardly less old than the venerable minister's whose words were sounding in his ears.

A week after this, he was sitting in a double-bedded room in a cheap boarding-house in Washington, with Colonel Sellers. The two had been living together lately, and this mutual cavern of theirs the Colonel sometimes referred to as their "premises" and sometimes as their "apartments" — more particularly when conversing with persons outside. A canvas-covered modern trunk, marked "G. W. H." stood on end by the door, strapped and ready for a journey; on it lay a small morocco satchel, also marked "G. W. H." There was another trunk close by — a worn and scarred and ancient hair relic, with "B. S." wrought in brass nails on its top; on it lay a pair of saddle-bags that probably knew more about the last century than they could tell. Washington got up and walked the floor a while in a restless sort of way, and finally was about to sit down on the hair trunk.

"Stop, don't sit down on that!" exclaimed the Colonel. "There, now — that's all right — the chair's better. I couldn't get another trunk like that — not another like it in America, I reckon."

"I am afraid not," said Washington, with a faint attempt at a smile.

"No, indeed; the man is dead that made that trunk and that saddle-bags."

"Are his great-grandchildren still living?" said Washington, with levity only in the words, not in the tone.

"Well, I don't know — I hadn't thought of that — but anyway they can't make trunks and saddle-bags like that, if they are — no man can," said the Colonel with honest simplicity. "Wife didn't like to see me going off with that trunk — she said it was nearly certain to be stolen."

"Why?"

"Why? Why, aren't trunks always being stolen?"

"Well, yes — some kinds of trunks are."

"Very well, then; this is some kind of a trunk — and an almighty rare kind, too."

"Yes, I believe it is."

"Well, then, why shouldn't a man want to steal it if he got a chance?"

"Indeed I don't know.— Why should he?"

"Washington, I never heard anybody talk like you. Suppose you were a thief, and that trunk was lying around and nobody watching — wouldn't you steal it!   Come, now, answer fair — wouldn't you steal it?"

"Well, now, since you corner me, I don't know but I would *take* it, — but I wouldn't consider it stealing."

"You wouldn't!   Well, that beats me.   Now, what would you call stealing?"

"Why, taking property is stealing."

"Property!   Now, what a way to talk that is. What do you suppose that trunk is worth?"

"Is it in good repair?"

"Perfect.   Hair rubbed off a little, but the main structure is perfectly sound."

"Does it leak anywhere?"

"Leak?   Do you want to carry water in it? What do you mean by does it leak?"

"Why — a — do the clothes fall out of it when it is — when it is stationary?"

"Confound it, Washington, you are trying to make fun of me.   I don't know what has got into you to-day; you act mighty curious.   What *is* the matter with you?"

"Well, I'll tell you, old friend.   I am almost happy.   I am, indeed.   It wasn't Clay's telegram that hurried me up so and got me ready to start with you.   It was a letter from Louise."

"Good!   What is it?   What does she say?"

"She says come home — her father has consented, at last."

"My boy, I want to congratulate you; I want to

shake you by the hand! It's a long turn that has no lane at the end of it, as the proverb says, or somehow that way. You'll be happy yet, and Beriah Sellers will be there to see, thank God!''

" I believe it. General Boswell is pretty nearly a poor man now. The railroad that was going to build up Hawkeye made short work of him, along with the rest. He isn't so opposed to a son-in-law without a fortune now.''

"Without a fortune, indeed! Why, that Tennessee Land ——"

" Never mind the Tennessee land, Colonel. I am done with that, forever and forever ——"

"Why, no! You can't mean to say ——"

" My father, away back yonder, years ago, bought it for a blessing for his children, and ——"

" Indeed he did! Si Hawkins said to me ——"

" It proved a curse to him as long as he lived, and never a curse like it was inflicted upon any man's heirs ——"

" I'm bound to say there's more or less truth ——"

" It began to curse me when I was a baby, and it has cursed every hour of my life to this day ——"

" Lord, Lord, but it's so! Time and again my wife ——"

" I depended on it all through my boyhood and never tried to do an honest stroke of work for my living ——"

" Right again — but then you ——"

"I have chased it years and years as children chase butterflies. We might all have been prosperous now; we might all have been happy, all these heart-breaking years, if we had accepted our poverty at first and gone contentedly to work and built up our own weal by our own toil and sweat——"

"It's so, it's so; bless my soul, how often I've told Si Hawkins——"

"Instead of that, we have suffered more than the damned themselves suffer! I loved my father, and I honor his memory and recognize his good intentions; but I grieve for his mistaken ideas of conferring happiness upon his children. I am going to begin my life over again, and begin it and end it with good solid work! I'll leave *my* children no Tennessee Land!"

"Spoken like a man, sir, spoken like a man! Your hand again, my boy! And always remember that when a word of advice from Beriah Sellers can help, it is at your service. I'm going to begin again, too!"

"Indeed!"

"Yes, sir. I've seen enough to show me where my mistake was. The law is what I was born for. I shall begin the study of the law. Heavens and earth, but that Braham's a wonderful man — a wonderful man, sir! Such a head! And such a way with him! But I could see that he was jealous of me. The little licks I got in in the course of my argument before the jury——"

" Your argument! Why, you were a witness."

" Oh, yes, to the popular eye, to the popular eye
— but *I* knew when I was dropping information and
when I was letting drive at the court with an insidi-
ous argument. But the court knew it, bless you,
and weakened every time! And Braham knew it.
I just reminded him of it in a quiet way, and its final
result, and he said in a whisper, ' You did it, Colonel,
you did it, sir — but keep it mum for *my* sake; and
I'll tell you what *you* do,' says he, ' you go into the
law, Colonel Sellers — go into the law, sir; that's
your native element!' And into the law the sub-
scriber is going. There's worlds of money in it! —
whole worlds of money! Practice first in Hawkeye,
then in Jefferson, then in St. Louis, then in New
York! In the metropolis of the Western world!
Climb, and climb, and climb — and wind up on the
*Su*preme bench. Beriah Sellers, Chief Justice of the
*Su*preme Court of the United States, sir! A made
man for all time and eternity! That's the way *I*
block it out, sir — and it's as clear as day — clear
as the rosy morn!"

Washington had heard little of this. The first
reference to Laura's trial had brought the old dejec-
tion to his face again, and he stood gazing out of the
window at nothing, lost in reverie.

There was a knock — the postman handed in a
letter. It was from Obedstown, East Tennessee,
and was for Washington. He opened it. There
was a note saying that enclosed he would please find

a bill for the current year's taxes on the 75,000 acres of Tennessee Land belonging to the estate of Silas Hawkins, deceased, and added that the money must be paid within sixty days or the land would be sold at public auction for the taxes, as provided by law. The bill was for $180 — something more than twice the market value of the land, perhaps.

Washington hesitated. Doubts flitted through his mind. The old instinct came upon him to cling to the land just a little longer and give it one more chance. He walked the floor feverishly, his mind tortured by indecision. Presently he stopped, took out his pocket-book and counted his money. Two hundred and thirty dollars — it was all he had in the world.

"One hundred and eighty. . . .from two hundred and thirty," he said to himself. "Fifty left. . . .It is enough to get me home. . . .Shall I do it, or shall I not?. . . .I wish I had somebody to decide for me."

The pocket-book lay open in his hand, with Louise's small letter in view. His eye fell upon that, and it decided him.

"It shall go for taxes," he said, "and never tempt me or mine any more!"

He opened the window and stood there tearing the tax bill to bits and watching the breeze waft them away, till all were gone.

"The spell is broken, the life-long curse is ended!" he said. "Let us go."

The baggage wagon had arrived; five minutes

later the two friends were mounted upon their lug-
gage in it, and rattling off toward the station, the
Colonel endeavoring to sing " Homeward Bound,"
a song whose words he knew, but whose tune, as he
rendered it, was a trial to auditors.

22^{*.*}

CHAPTER XXXI.

LUCK WILL TURN. A JOYFUL SURPRISE

Gedi kanadiben tsannawa.

—La xalog, la xamaih mi-x-ul nu qiza u quïal gih, u quïal agab?
Rabinal-Achi.

PHILIP STERLING'S circumstances were becoming straitened. The prospect was gloomy. His long siege of unproductive labor was beginning to tell upon his spirits; but what told still more upon them was the undeniable fact that the promise of ultimate success diminished every day now. That is to say, the tunnel had reached a point in the hill which was considerably beyond where the coal vein should pass (according to all his calculations) if there were a coal vein there; and so, every foot that the tunnel now progressed seemed to carry it further away from the object of the search.

Sometimes he ventured to hope that he had made a mistake in estimating the direction which the vein should naturally take after crossing the valley and entering the hill. Upon such occasions he would go into the nearest mine on the vein he was hunting

(334)

for, and once more get the bearings of the deposit and mark out its probable course; but the result was the same every time; his tunnel had manifestly pierced beyond the natural point of junction; and then his spirits fell a little lower. His men had already lost faith, and he often overheard them saying it was perfectly plain that there was no coal in the hill.

Foremen and laborers from neighboring mines, and no end of experienced loafers from the village, visited the tunnel from time to time, and their verdicts were always the same and always disheartening — "No coal in that hill." Now and then Philip would sit down and think it all over and wonder what the mystery meant; then he would go into the tunnel and ask the men if there were no signs yet. None — always "none." He would bring out a piece of rock and examine it, and say to himself, "It is limestone — it has crinoids and corals in it — the rock is right." Then he would throw it down with a sigh, and say, "But that is nothing; where coal is, limestone with these fossils in it is pretty certain to lie against its foot casing; but it does not necessarily follow that where this peculiar rock is, coal must lie above it or beyond it; this sign is not sufficient."

The thought usually followed: "There *is* one infallible sign — if I could only strike *that!*"

Three or four times in as many weeks he said to himself, "Am I a visionary? I *must* be a visionary;

everybody is in these days; everybody chases butter-
flies; everybody seeks sudden fortune and will not
lay one up by slow toil. This is not right, I will
discharge the men and go at some honest work.
There is no coal here. What a fool I have been; I
will give it up."

But he never could do it. A half hour of profound thinking always followed; and at the end of
it he was sure to get up and straighten himself and
say: "There *is* coal there; I will *not* give it up;
and coal or no coal I will drive the tunnel clear
through the hill; I will not surrender while I am
alive."

He never thought of asking Mr. Montague for
more money. He said there was now but one
chance of finding coal against nine hundred and
ninety-nine that he would not find it, and so it would
be wrong in him to make the request and foolish in
Mr. Montague to grant it.

He had been working three shifts of men.
Finally, the settling of a weekly account exhausted
his means. He could not afford to run in debt, and
therefore he gave the men their discharge. They
came into his cabin presently, where he sat with his
elbows on his knees and his chin in his hands, the picture of discouragement, and their spokesman said:

"Mr. Sterling, when Tim was down a week with
his fall you kept him on half wages, and it was a
mighty help to his family; whenever any of us was
in trouble you've done what you could to help us

out; you've acted fair and square with us every time, and I reckon we are men and know a man when we see him. We haven't got any faith in that hill, but we have a respect for a man that's got the pluck that you've showed; you've fought a good fight, with everybody agin you, and if we had grub to go on, I'm d—d if we wouldn't stand by you till the cows come home! That is what the boys say. Now we want to put in one parting blast for luck. We want to work three days more; if we don't find anything, we won't bring in no bill against you. That is what we've come to say."

Philip was touched. If he had had money enough to buy three days' " grub " he would have accepted the generous offer, but as it was, he could not consent to be less magnanimous than the men, and so he declined in a manly speech, shook hands all around, and resumed his solitary communings. The men went back to the tunnel and " put in a parting blast for luck," anyhow. They did a full day's work and then took their leave. They called at his cabin and gave him good-bye, but were not able to tell him their day's effort had given things a more promising look.

The next day Philip sold all the tools but two or three sets; he also sold one of the now deserted cabins as old lumber, together with its domestic wares, and made up his mind that he would buy provisions with the trifle of money thus gained and continue his work alone. About the middle of the afternoon he put on his roughest clothes and went to the tunnel. He lit a candle and groped his way in. Presently he heard the sound of a pick or a drill, and wondered what it meant. A spark of light now appeared in the far end of the tunnel, and when he arrived there he found the man Tim at work. Tim said:

"I'm to have a job in the Golden Brier mine by and by — in a week or ten days — and I'm going to work here till then. A man might as well be at something, and besides I consider that I owe you what you paid me when I was laid up."

Philip said, Oh, no, he didn't owe anything; but Tim persisted, and then Philip said he had a little provision now, and would share. So for several days Philip held the drill and Tim did the striking. At first Philip was impatient to see the result of every blast, and was always back and peering among the smoke the moment after the explosion. But there was never any encouraging result; and therefore he finally lost almost all interest, and hardly troubled himself to inspect results at all. He simply labored on, stubbornly and with little hope.

Tim stayed with him till the last moment, and then took up his job at the Golden Brier, apparently as depressed by the continued barrenness of their mutual labors as Philip was himself. After that, Philip fought his battle alone, day after day, and slow work it was; he could scarcely see that he made any progress.

Late one afternoon he finished drilling a hole which he had been at work at for more than two hours; he swabbed it out, and poured in the powder and inserted the fuse; then filled up the rest of the hole with dirt and small fragments of stone; tamped it down firmly, touched his candle to the fuse, and ran. By and by the dull report came, and he was about to walk back mechanically and see what was accomplished; but he halted; presently turned on his heel and thought, rather than said:

" No, this is useless, this is absurd. If I found anything it would only be one of those little aggravating seams of coal which doesn't mean anything, and ——"

By this time he was walking out of the tunnel. His thought ran on:

" I am conquered. . . .I am out of provisions, out of money. . . .I have got to give it up. . . .All this hard work lost! But I am *not* conquered! I will go and work for money, and come back and have another fight with fate. Ah, me, it may be years, it may be years."

Arrived at the mouth of the tunnel, he threw his coat upon the ground, sat down on a stone, and his eye sought the westering sun and dwelt upon the charming landscape which stretched its woody ridges, wave upon wave, to the golden horizon.

Something was taking place at his feet which did not attract his attention.

His reverie continued, and its burden grew more

v

and more gloomy. Presently he rose up and cast a look far away toward the valley, and his thoughts took a new direction:

"There it is! How good it looks! But down there is not up here. Well, I will go home and pack up — there is nothing else to do."

He moved off moodily toward his cabin. He had gone some distance before he thought of his coat; then he was about to turn back, but he smiled at the thought, and continued his journey — such a coat as that could be of little use in a civilized land. A little further on, he remembered that there were some papers of value in one of the pockets of the relic, and then with a petulant ejaculation he turned back, picked up the coat and put it on.

He made a dozen steps, and then stopped very suddenly. He stood still a moment, as one who is trying to believe something and cannot. He put a hand up over his shoulder and felt his back, and a great thrill shot through him. He grasped the skirt of the coat impulsively and another thrill followed. He snatched the coat from his back, glanced at it, threw it from him and flew back to the tunnel. He sought the spot where the coat had lain — he had to look close, for the light was waning — then, to make sure, he put his hand to the ground and a little stream of water swept against his fingers:

"Thank God, I've struck it at last!"

He lit a candle and ran into the tunnel; he picked up a piece of rubbish cast out by the last blast, and said:

"This clayey stuff is what I've longed for — I know what is behind it."

He swung his pick with hearty good will till long after the darkness had gathered upon the earth, and when he trudged home at length he knew he had a coal vein and that it was seven feet thick from wall to wall.

He found a yellow envelope lying on his rickety table, and recognized that it was of a family sacred to the transmission of telegrams:

He opened it, read it, crushed it in his hand and threw it down. It simply said:

"Ruth is very ill."

CHAPTER XXXII.

RUTH'S RECOVERY. THE FUTURE OF THE END

Alaila pomaikai kaua, ola na iwi iloko o ko kaua mau la elemakule.

Laieikawai, 9.

ܠܐܢ̈ܫܝ̈ܢ ܕܐܝܬܝܗܘܢ ܚܟ̈ܝܡܐ ܐܝܟ ܝܘܡܐ
ܐܬ : ܦ : ܐܘܢ̈ܐ

IT was evening when Philip took the cars at the Ilium station. The news of his success had preceded him, and while he waited for the train, he was the center of a group of eager questioners, who asked him a hundred things about the mine, and magnified his good fortune. There was no mistake this time.

Philip, in luck, had become suddenly a person of consideration, whose speech was freighted with meaning, whose looks were all significant. The words of the proprietor of a rich coal mine have a golden sound, and his common sayings are repeated as if they were solid wisdom.

Philip wished to be alone; his good fortune at this moment seemed an empty mockery, one of those sarcasms of fate, such as that which spreads a

(342)

dainty banquet for the man who has no appetite. He had longed for success principally for Ruth's sake; and perhaps now, at this very moment of his triumph, she was dying.

"Shust what I said, Mister Sderling," the landlord of the Ilium hotel kept repeating. "I dold Jake Schmidt he find him dere shust so sure as noting."

"You ought to have taken a share, Mr. Dusenheimer," said Philip.

"Yaas, I know. But d'old woman, she say, 'You sticks to your pisiness. So I sticks to 'em. Und I makes noting. Dat Mister Prierly, he don't never come back here no more, ain't it?"

"Why?"

"Vell, dere is so many peers, und so many oder dhrinks, I got 'em all set down, ven he coomes back."

It was a long night for Philip, and a restless one. At any other time the swing of the cars would have lulled him to sleep, and the rattle and clank of wheels and rails, the roar of the whirling iron, would have only been cheerful reminders of swift and safe travel. Now they were voices of warning and taunting; and instead of going rapidly the train seemed to crawl at a snail's pace. And it not only crawled, but it frequently stopped; and when it stopped it stood dead still, and there was an ominous silence. Was anything the matter, he wondered. Only a station, probably. Perhaps, he thought, a telegraphic station. And then he listened eagerly.

Would the conductor open the door and ask for Philip Sterling, and hand him a fatal dispatch?

How long they seemed to wait. And then slowly beginning to move, they were off again, shaking, pounding, screaming through the night. He drew his curtain from time to time and looked out. There was the lurid sky line of the wooded range along the base of which they were crawling. There was the Susquehanna, gleaming in the moonlight. There was a stretch of level valley with silent farm houses, the occupants all at rest, without trouble, without anxiety. There was a church, a graveyard, a mill, a village; and now, without pause or fear, the train had mounted a trestle work high in air and was creeping along the top of it, while a swift torrent foamed a hundred feet below.

What would the morning bring? Even while he was flying to her, her gentle spirit might have gone on another flight, whither he could not follow her. He was full of foreboding. He fell at length into a restless doze. There was a noise in his ears as of a rushing torrent when a stream is swollen by a freshet in the spring. It was like the breaking up of life; he was struggling in the consciousness of coming death; when Ruth stood by his side, clothed in white, with a face like that of an angel, radiant, smiling, pointing to the sky, and saying, " Come." He awoke with a cry — the train was roaring through a bridge, and it shot out into daylight.

When morning came the train was industriously

toiling along through the fat lands of Lancaster, with its broad farms of corn and wheat, its mean houses of stone, its vast barns and granaries, built as if for storing the riches of Heliogabalus. Then came the smiling fields of Chester, with their English green, and soon the county of Philadelphia itself, and the increasing signs of the approach to a great city. Long trains of coal cars, laden and unladen, stood upon sidings; the tracks of other roads were crossed; the smoke of other locomotives was seen on parallel lines; factories multiplied; streets appeared; the noise of a busy city began to fill the air; and with a slower and slower clank on the connecting rails and interlacing switches the train rolled into the station and stood still.

It was a hot August morning. The broad streets glowed in the sun, and the white-shuttered houses stared at the hot thoroughfares like closed bakers'-ovens set along the highway. Philip was oppressed with the heavy air; the sweltering city lay as in a swoon. Taking a street car, he rode away to the northern part of the city, the newer portion, formerly the district of Spring Garden, for in this the Boltons now lived, in a small brick house, befitting their altered fortunes.

He could scarcely restrain his impatience when he came in sight of the house. The window shutters were not '' bowed ''; thank God for that. Ruth was still living, then. He ran up the steps and rang. Mrs. Bolton met him at the door.

"Thee is very welcome, Philip."

"And Ruth?"

"She is very ill, but quieter than she has been, and the fever is a little abating. The most dangerous time will be when the fever leaves her. The doctor fears she will not have strength enough to rally from it. Yes, thee can see her."

Mrs. Bolton led the way to the little chamber where Ruth lay. "Oh," said her mother, "if she were only in her cool and spacious room in our old home. She says that seems like heaven."

Mr. Bolton sat by Ruth's bedside, and he rose and silently pressed Philip's hand. The room had but one window; that was wide open to admit the air, but the air that came in was hot and lifeless. Upon the table stood a vase of flowers. Ruth's eyes were closed; her cheeks were flushed with fever, and she moved her head restlessly as if in pain.

"Ruth," said her mother, bending over her, "Philip is here."

Ruth's eyes unclosed, there was a gleam of recognition in them, there was an attempt at a smile upon her face, and she tried to raise her thin hand, as Philip touched her forehead with his lips; and he heard her murmur:

"Dear Phil."

There was nothing to be done but to watch and wait for the cruel fever to burn itself out. Dr. Longstreet told Philip that the fever had undoubt-

edly been contracted in the hospital, but it was not
malignant, and would be little dangerous if Ruth
were not so worn down with work, or if she had a
less delicate constitution.

"It is only her indomitable will that has kept her
up for weeks. And if that should leave her now,
there will be no hope. You can do more for her
now, sir, than I can."

"How?" asked Philip eagerly.

"Your presence, more than anything else, will
inspire her with the desire to live."

When the fever turned Ruth was in a very criti-
cal condition. For two days her life was like the
fluttering of a lighted candle in the wind. Philip
was constantly by her side, and she seemed to be
conscious of his presence, and to cling to him, as
one borne away by a swift stream clings to a
stretched-out hand from the shore. If he was absent a moment her restless eyes sought something
they were disappointed not to find.

Philip so yearned to bring her back to life, he
willed it so strongly and passionately, that his will
appeared to affect hers and she seemed slowly to
draw life from his.

After two days of this struggle with the grasping
enemy, it was evident to Dr. Longstreet that Ruth's
will was beginning to issue its orders to her body
with some force, and that strength was slowly
coming back. In another day there was a decided
improvement. As Philip sat holding her weak hand

and watching the least sign of resolution in her face, Ruth was able to whisper:

"I so want to live, for you, Phil!"

"You will, darling, you must," said Philip, in a tone of faith and courage that carried a thrill of determination — of command — along all her nerves.

Slowly Philip drew her back to life. Slowly she came back, as one willing but well nigh helpless. It was new for Ruth to feel this dependence on another's nature, to consciously draw strength of will from the will of another. It was a new but a dear joy, to be lifted up and carried back into the happy world, which was now all aglow with the light of love; to be lifted and carried by the one she loved more than her own life.

"Sweetheart," she said to Philip, "I would not have cared to come back but for thy love."

"Not for thy profession?"

"Oh, thee may be glad enough of that some day, when thy coal bed is dug out and thee and father are in the air again."

When Ruth was able to ride she was taken into the country, for the pure air was necessary to her speedy recovery. The family went with her. Philip could not be spared from her side, and Mr. Bolton had gone up to Ilium to look into that wonderful coal mine and to make arrangements for developing it, and bringing its wealth to market. Philip had insisted on re-conveying the Ilium property to Mr. Bolton, retaining only the share originally contemplated for himself, and Mr. Bolton, therefore, once more found himself engaged in business and a person of some consequence in Third street. The mine turned out even better than was at first hoped, and would, if judiciously managed, be a fortune to them all. This also seemed to be the opinion of Mr. Bigler, who heard of it as soon as anybody, and, with the impudence of his class, called upon Mr. Bolton for a little aid in a patent car-wheel he had bought an interest in. That rascal, Small, he said, had swindled him out of all he had.

Mr. Bolton told him he was very sorry, and recommended him to sue Small.

Mr. Small also came with a similar story about Mr. Bigler; and Mr. Bolton had the grace to give him like advice. And he added, " If you and Bigler will procure the indictment of each other, you may have the satisfaction of putting each other in the penitentiary for the forgery of my acceptances."

Bigler and Small did not quarrel, however. They both attacked Mr. Bolton behind his back as a swindler, and circulated the story that he had made a fortune by failing.

In the pure air of the highlands, amid the golden glories of ripening September, Ruth rapidly came back to health. How beautiful the world is to an invalid, whose senses are all clarified, who has been so near the world of spirits that she is sensitive to the finest influences, and whose frame responds with a thrill to the subtlest ministrations of soothing

23**

nature.   Mere life is a luxury, and the color of the
grass, of the flowers, of the sky, the wind in the
trees, the outlines of the horizon, the forms of
clouds, all give a pleasure as exquisite as the sweetest music to the ear famishing for it.   The world
was all new and fresh to Ruth, as if it had just been
created for her, and love filled it, till her heart was
overflowing with happiness.

It was golden September also at Fallkill.   And
Alice sat by the open window in her room at home,
looking out upon the meadows where the laborers
were cutting the second crop of clover.   The
fragrance of it floated to her nostrils.   Perhaps she
did not mind it.   She was thinking.   She had just
been writing to Ruth, and on the table before her
was a yellow piece of paper with a faded four-leaved
clover pinned on it — only a memory now.   In her
letter to Ruth she had poured out her heartiest
blessings upon them both, with her dear love forever
and forever.

" Thank God," she said, " they will never know."

They never would know.   And the world never
knows how many women there are like Alice, whose
sweet but lonely lives of self-sacrifice, gentle, faithful, loving souls, bless it continually.

" She is a dear girl," said Philip, when Ruth
showed him the letter.

" Yes, Phil, and we can spare a great deal of love
for her, our own lives are so full."

טוב אחרית דבר מראשיתו

APPENDIX

Nothing gives such weight and
dignity to a book as an Appendix.

Herodotus

APPENDIX.

Perhaps some apology to the reader is necessary in view of our failure to find Laura's father. We supposed, from the ease with which lost persons are found in novels, that it would not be difficult. But it was; indeed, it was impossible; and therefore the portions of the narrative containing the record of the search have been stricken out. Not because they were not interesting — for they were; but inasmuch as the man was not found, after all, it did not seem wise to harass and excite the reader to no purpose.　　　　　THE AUTHORS.

TRANSLATIONS

OF CHAPTER-HEAD MOTTOES

BY

J. HAMMOND TRUMBULL, LL.D., L.H.D.

CHAPTER II, page 14.

Sioux (Dakota) translation of the *Pilgrim's Progress*. By-Ends names his distinguished friends, in the City of Fair-Speech:

— "My Lord Turn-about, my Lord Time-server, my Lord Fair-speech, from whose ancestors the town first took its name; also Mr. Smooth-man, Mr. Facing-both-ways, Mr. Anything," etc.

Semi-Saxon:

"The richest women all — that were in the land,
And the higher men's daughters —
There was many a rich garment — on the fair folk,
There was mickle envy — from [all parts of the country],
For each weened to be — better than others."

CHAPTER III, page 38.

Danish proverb: One hair of a maiden's head pulls stronger than ten yoke of oxen.

CHAPTER IV, page 46.

Quiché (Guatemalan), from a native drama, published by Brasseur des Bourbourg:

"I have snared and caught him, I have taken and bound him, with my brilliant snares, with my white noose, with my bracelets of chiseled gold, with my rings, and with my enchantments."

Old French proverb: Every one has the palms of his hands turned *toward himself.*

(355)

CHAPTER V, page 56.

    Tamul: "Books."

    Chippeway: "My books are many and they are all good."
"Although his books are good, he does not much look into them."

CHAPTER VI, page 64.

    Assyrian (from Smith's Assurbanipal): "Ni-ni-id [dag]-ga ra a-ha-mis, "We will (help) each other."

    [Note. The fourth group varies in different copies of the cuneiform record. Mr. Smith puts *dag*, marking it as a variant, and translates by "help." Others may prefer to read *gul*, "to cheat." As philological criticism would have been out of place in the "Gilded Age," and as the passage is a familiar one, it seemed best to *omit* the questionable group — leaving it to the reader to fill the blank as in his better judgment he might determine.]

    Italian, from the *Jerusalem Delivered,* c. iv., st. 78:

        "All arts the enchantress practised to beguile
          Some new admirer in her well-spread snare;
        Nor used with all, nor always, the same wile,
          But shaped to every taste her grace and air."

CHAPTER VIII, page 80.

    Provençal: Dear friend, return, for pity's sake, to me, at once.

    Basque (*Souletin* dialect); from a popular song, published by Vallaberry: "You gave me your word — not once only, twice — that you would be mine. I am the same as in other times; I have not changed, for I took it to my heart, and I loved you." — *Chants populaires du pays Basque,* pp. 6, 7.

CHAPTER X, page 97.

    Arabic:

    "And her denying increased his devotion in love:

        For lovely, as a thing, to man, is that which is denied him."

    From an Arabic poet quoted in the *Tâj el-'Aroos* (of the Seyyid Murtada) which, as everybody knows, is a commentary on the *Kâmoos* — the Arabic "Webster's Unabridged."

    Basque. From the *Poésies Basques* of Bernard d'Echeparre (Bordeaux, 1545), edited by G. Brunet, 1847:

    "Was there ever any one so unfortunate as I am?

        She whom I adore does not love me at all, and yet I cannot
        renounce her."

CHAPTER XI, page 108.

Efik (or *Old Calabar*) proverb: "The rat enters the trap, the trap catches him; if he did not go into the trap, the trap would not do so." From R. F. Burton's *Wit and Wisdom of West Africa*, p. 367.

CHAPTER XII, page 130.

Arrawak version of Acts xix. 23: "And the same time there arose no small stir (Gr. τάραχος οὐκ ὀλίγος) about that way."

CHAPTER XIII, page 137.

Latin (Seneca): "In an evil career a reckless downward course is inevitably taken."

Latin (Cicero): "For men are subject to their own impulses as soon as they have once parted company with reason; and their very weakness gives way to itself, incautiously sails into deep water and finds no place of anchorage."

CHAPTER XIV, page 147.

Quiché (Guatemalan), from the *Popol Vuh*, or Sacred Book, edited by Brasseur de Bourbourg, p. 222:

—"'What will you give us, then, if we will take pity on you?' they said. 'Ah, well we will give you silver,' responded the associate [petitioners]."

CHAPTER XV, page 162.

Italian proverb: "Strong is the vinegar of sweet wine."

Anglo-Saxon : "Such is no feminine usage
for a woman to practise,
although she be beautiful,—
that a peace-weaver
machinate to deprive of life,
after burning anger,
a man beloved."

—*Thorpe's translation*, 3885–91.

CHAPTER XVI, page 173.

Quiché (from a native drama): "My bravery and my power have availed me nothing! Alas, let heaven and earth hear me! Is it true that I must die, that I must die here, between earth and sky."

CHAPTER XVII, page 183.

"A poison-toothed serpent (*moonihoawa*) is debt."

CHAPTER XVIII, page 194.

Russian: "The sun began to shine, but not for a long time; it shone for a moment and disappeared."

Yoruba proverb: "I *almost* killed the bird." "Nobody can make a stew of *almost*" (or "*Almost* never made a stew").— *Crowther's* Yoruba Proverbs, in Grammar, p. 229.

CHAPTER XIX, page 205.

Icelandic, from a modern poem:

> "When anguish wars in thy heavy breast,
> and adverse scourges lash thy cheeks,
> and the world turns her back on thee,
> and pleasure mocketh at thy pain:
> Think *all is round* and easily turns;
> he weeps to-morrow who laughs to-day;
> Time makes all good."

CHAPTER XX, page 218.

Wolof (*Senegambian*) proverb: "If you go to the sparrows' ball, take with you some ears of corn for them." R. F. Burton, from Dard's *Grammaire Wolofe*.

Hungarian, from 2 Kings, viii. 13:

—"Is thy servant a dog, that he should do this great thing?"

CHAPTER XXI, page 228.

French of Molière:

> "Nothing in the world is more noble and more beautiful
> Than the holy fervor of true zeal." — *Molière*.

French: [The Fox] "assumed a benign and tender expression,
He bade them good day with a *Laudate Deum*,
And invited the whole world to share his brotherly love."

CHAPTER XXII, page 232.

French of Molière: Tartuffe, the hypocrite, is speaking:

> "According to differing emergencies, there is a science
> Of stretching the limitations of our conscience,
> And of compensating the evil of our acts
> By the purity of our motives."

CHAPTER XXIII, page 242.

Sanskrit : "The distinctions of obscurity are eightfold, as are also those of illusion; extreme illusion is tenfold; gloom is eighteen-fold, and so is utter darkness."

[This description of a New York jury is from Memorial Verses on the Sankya philosophy, translated by Colebrooke.]

Old Welsh : "Nobody is a judge through learning; although a person may always learn he will not be a judge unless there be wisdom in his heart; however wise a person may be, he will not be a judge unless there be learning with the wisdom." — *Ancient Laws of Wales*, ii. 207.

CHAPTER XXIV, page 253.

Danish proverb : "Virtue in the middle," said the Devil, when he sat down between two lawyers.

Breton : "This is a great pleader! Have you heard him plead?" — *Legonidec's Descrip. de Braham.*

CHAPTER XXV, page 265.

Old French : "'Yea, but,' asked Trinquamelle, 'how do you proceed, my friend, in criminal causes, the culpable and guilty party being taken and seized upon *flagrante crimine?*' 'Even as your other worships use to do,' answered (Judge) Bridlegoose."

—*Rabelais, Pantagruel*, b. ii., ch. 137.

Breton : "Have you anything to say for her justification?"— *Legonidec.*

CHAPTER XXVI, page 278.

Chippeway : "I don't know what may have happened; per-haps we shall hear bad news!" — *Baraga.*

CHAPTER XXVII, page 287.

Chinese (Canton dialect, *Tsow pak păt fun*): "Black and white not distinguished," i. e., Right and wrong not perceived.

Spanish proverb (of a court of law): Paper and ink and little justice.

CHAPTER XXVIII, page 298.

    Efik (Old Calabar) proverb: "One monkey does not like to see another get his belly full." — *Burton's W. African Proverbs.*

    Grecian. From the *Greek Anthology :* "When the Crab caught with his claw the Snake, he reproved him for his indirect course." [An old version of what the Pot said to the Kettle.]

    Massachusetts Indian, from Eliot's translation of Psalm xxxv., 21: "Yea, they opened their mouth wide against me, and said, Aha, aha, our eye hath seen it!"

CHAPTER XXIX, page 314.

    Javanese : "Alas!"

    Cornish : "My heart yet is proud
             Though I am nearly dead." — *The Creation.*

CHAPTER XXX, page 324.

    Danish proverb : "He is a good driver who knows how *to turn.*"

    Sioux (Dakota): "Let us go now. Will you go?" [The *Iapi Oaye* is a Dakota newspaper published monthly in the Dakota language.]

CHAPTER XXXI, page 334.

    Kanuri (Borneo): "At the bottom of patience there is heaven." — R. F. Burton's West African Proverbs.

    Quiché : "Is it in vain, is it without profit, that I am come here to lose so many days, so many nights?"

CHAPTER XXXII, page 342.

    Hawaiian : "Then we two shall be happy, our offspring shall live in the days of our old age."

    Syriac (from the Old Testament; the blessing on Naomi transferred to Ruth): "And he shall be unto thee a restorer of thy life [*consolator animæ*, as Walton translates from the Syriac version,] and a nourisher of thine old age." Ruth iv., 15.

TAIL-PIECE, page 350.

    Hebrew : "The end of a thing is better than the beginning." Eccles. vii. 8.